DIVE INTO ME

A GRUMPY SUNSHINE BILLIONAIRE ROMANCE

B-SCHOOL BILLIONAIRES

ALINA PARKER

COPYRIGHT

Copyright © 2024 by Alina Parker

All rights reserved.

No part of this book may be reproduced in any form or by any electronic or mechanical means, including information storage and retrieval systems, without written permission from the author, except for the use of brief quotations in a book review.

CONTENTS

1. Jamie — 1
2. Charlotte — 9
3. Jamie — 15
4. Charlotte — 21
5. Jamie — 29
6. Charlotte — 36
7. Charlotte — 43
8. Jamie — 50
9. Charlotte — 58
10. Jamie — 66
11. Charlotte — 75
12. Jamie — 82
13. Jamie — 88
14. Charlotte — 96
15. Jamie — 102
16. Charlotte — 108
17. Jamie — 115
18. Jamie — 122
19. Charlotte — 129
20. Jamie — 136
21. Charlotte — 143
22. Jamie — 150
23. Charlotte — 156
24. Jamie — 166
25. Charlotte — 175
26. Jamie — 182
27. Charlotte — 190
28. Jamie — 196
29. Charlotte — 203
30. Charlotte — 211
31. Jamie — 217
32. Charlotte — 222
33. Charlotte — 232
34. Jamie — 239

35. Jamie	249
36. Charlotte	257
Also by Alina Parker	263

1

JAMIE

It was almost that time again, and I dreaded it. I wondered if anyone else had such an intense disdain for their birthday... Probably not. Not normal people, anyway. The approaching date always casted a shadow over my mood. I'd grown accustomed to the weight of sadness that accompanied the day I was born but my friends hadn't. They all arrived like they did every year to ensure that I had fun leading up to the big day.

I watched from my penthouse apartment as a sleek black limousine stopped in front of the portico and the liveried chauffeur stepped out. I stood far enough away from the window. Despite my choice of a top-floor apartment, I was afraid of heights. My feet on steady ground usually quelled that fear though.

I took a sip from the glass of Stroh I'd been nursing—the third one since I decided not to go into the office this morning. As my friends came out one by one with travel bags, I snorted my amusement. I bet the limo was Alex's doing. He was extra like that.

From this far up, they looked like ants, but I could imagine the smiles they each wore... Well, except for Michael, who brooded more than he smiled. We had that in common. I already felt the comfort that being around my four closest friends brought. My cell vibrated, and I pulled it out of my pocket. As I squinted, I saw Lincoln craning his neck to look up at the building as if he knew I was watching, so I knew it was him calling.

"Hey," I answered.

"Hey, man. We're here. You're staring out the window brooding and drinking something strong, aren't you?"

"That's exactly what he's doing," I heard Spencer say.

My friends knew me well. Still, I lied. "No."

Lincoln's snort rang with skepticism. "Uh-huh. We're on our way up."

They moved up the sidewalk and disappeared inside. Security already knew to lead them to the private elevator that led to my apartment, so I just waited. Minutes later, the swish of the elevator doors opening announced my visitors. The tiniest smile lifted my lips as I put my glass on the nearest table and headed toward the lobby. Lincoln Ford, former NFL superstar, now sports agent to some of the biggest athletes, rounded the corner first. His green eyes sparkled with excitement when he saw me.

Behind him was Spencer Beaumont, a.k.a the prince... really. His family came from a royal bloodline across the pond, but he went to great lengths to hide it. We started calling him the prince because of the British accent. He dropped his luggage, raked his fingers through his chestnut brown hair, and blew out a breath. "It's hot enough out there to boil a cuppa on the pavement!"

I guess July in Seattle didn't get as hot as in Manhattan.

"A *what*? We've been friends for over a decade, and I still don't know what you're saying half the time." Alexander Knight smirked as he addressed Spencer. He was the youngest of us five and such a genius that he started Harvard at seventeen years old. That's where we all met.

"He means a *cup of tea*," Michael Hayes translated. He was richer than Croesus and a professional scowler… as Alex liked to say. Michael dropped his bag next to Spencer's. When he spotted me, his typical stoney expression softened a little. "Hey, man."

My smile grew a tad as I stepped forward to engage in a series of "heys" and manly, affectionate pats on the shoulders. "You guys are early," I said.

"We figured we shouldn't give you too much time to plunge into brooding," Alex replied, aiming for the living room.

"That and for once, Mr. Can't-Keep-It-In-His-Pants over there…" Lincoln pointed to Alex, "wasn't late picking us up at the airport because he was shacked up with his flavor of the month."

Chuckling, I grabbed my glass and flopped down onto a sofa. Having company in my otherwise quiet and lonely apartment was already cheering me up. Alex lived in Boston. Since he was the closest to me, he usually reached New York first and picked up the others who flew in from Seattle and Los Angeles.

"Is the football star jealous that a non-athlete has more game with the ladies than he does?" Alex gave Lincoln his signature grin as he got behind the bar and got busy. He was a tech genius *and* our mixologist.

Lincoln gave him a dirty look but took a seat at the bar to await whatever concoction Alex had learned to make this year. Michael did the same while Spencer moved to the windows to look out. He was the creative type, so he was probably working up a poem or song lyrics in his head about the picturesque view or something. He then turned to us. "So, what are we doing this year?"

"Yeah, we haven't discussed it," Michael said. "Maybe Alex can decide. He's probably familiar with every club and tittie bar on the east coast."

"I probably am," Alex drawled as he slid Lincoln a glass filled with golden brown liquid.

"He has no shame," Spencer remarked.

I stayed quiet and listened as the guys planned a week of keep-Jamie-from-spiraling-into-despair. I was accustomed to having things planned for me. My entire life was mapped out before I was born. James Winchester would fall in line to follow a path that would lead him to take over the family business and one day take a suitable bride to continue the Winchester legacy.

However, my friends planning fun activities wasn't the same as my father demanding I give in to social expectations. My entire life was about conforming to social expectations, and it got tiring. While a part of me wanted to stay locked in my apartment to suffer in silence, I needed a break from my life. My friends helped me get that reprieve every year.

"Forget getting wasted at clubs," Lincoln said. "This year, for Jamie's birthday, we're going to Hawaii."

I glanced at him. That was different. "What's in Hawaii?"

"Other than the sun and gorgeous beaches? Pacific Paradise Resort."

We all stared at him blankly, waiting for more.

He huffed. "Jesus, you're all such rigid workaholics. You don't even get excited at the mention of a tropical vacation."

I snorted. He had a point. Plenty of people would squeal with delight at the sound of *Hawaii* and a *resort*.

"I only have one week," Michael said. "I have to get back to work and my kid."

Lincoln put his drink down. "Relax. If we leave tomorrow, we'll have the entire seven days we had planned at the resort. You'll be back on time."

That had Michael convinced. He shrugged. "Fine. Hawaii... I'm in."

"But why a resort?" Alex asked. His furrowed eyebrows said he didn't think a resort would be as much fun as clubs and naked dancing ladies.

Spencer sighed. "I'm sure they have plenty of breast bars in Hawaii, Alex, and I like the idea of somewhere tropical."

"*Tittie* bars," Alex corrected with a scoff. He then threw his hands up. "If that's what everyone wants. Jamie...?" Alex eyed me with hope in his eyes.

I hated that I was about to burst his bubble and choose a resort over falling out of clubs shitfaced. A tropical vacation sounded nice. When was the last time I flew to an exotic location to unwind? "I like Linc's idea."

Lincoln fist-pumped the air. "Awesome. I already have a private jet lined up. I knew you guys would agree. We can use this evening to get anything we didn't bring for a beach getaway."

"Fine. I guess we can all do with *that* sort of vacation," Alex grumbled as he poured himself another drink.

"Full disclosure. I have an ulterior motive for Hawaii," Lincoln announced.

All eyes landed on him again.

"Jamie, I know it's supposed to be your birthday trip, but I *need* to go to Pacific Paradise Resort."

"It had better not be for work," Spencer warned. "If you're chasing some spoiled athlete all the way to—"

"It's not work." Lincoln rubbed his nape. "It's about a woman."

"Well, now Hawaii has the potential to be interesting," Alex said.

"Spill," I demanded, watching Lincoln through narrowed eyes. He wasn't one to chase women. Back in college, he'd been laser-focused on his studies and after that, his football career. While his teammates entertained groupies, he never did.

Lincoln threw back the rest of his drink and then swiveled his barstool around to face us. His sheepish expression made me raise my eyebrows. "Do you guys remember me mentioning someone named Charlotte back in the day?"

I nodded. "Yeah, a couple of years into your football career." We'd never met the mysterious Charlotte though, and it seemed his relationship with her didn't last that long.

"Well, I've been thinking…" Lincoln stared into his empty glass. "What if she's the one?"

My jaw practically touched the oriental run I had in front of the sofa. I'd never heard Lincoln sound like that. I'd never heard *any* of the guys sound like that… and certainly not me.

Alex's laughter boomed and circulated the room. When he saw that Lincoln didn't share in his amusement, the sound faded and so did his smile. "Shit, you're serious."

"I am." Lincoln crossed his arms over his chest as if he felt the need to defend himself. "I'm not getting any younger. A few weeks ago, I thought of Charlotte and how easy being with her was. We never got the chance to fully explore things between us. Then she popped up on my social media and I reached out to her." He shrugged. "She said she works at Pacific Paradise Resort. I figured I could…"

I, along with the others, gawked at Lincoln. Was that a tinge of pink I saw in his cheeks? Perhaps I wasn't the only one going through something emotional.

"Rekindle your romance?" Spencer finished. He already had a light of interest in his eyes. He was all about exploring relationships and love, and he explored plenty... too damn much. I didn't know what it was about women and musicians. They flocked to him in droves.

"I don't see why not..." Lincoln shrugged, still seemingly embarrassed.

Alex let out a loud snort. "Cute story, but there is no such thing as *the one*."

"I agree with Casanova there," Michael said. "The whole idea of there being one person made for you is just..." He sighed heavily. "True love and all that is a myth, man."

Lincoln's eyebrows drew together as he considered this. Spencer and I exchanged looks. Sure, I agreed with Micheal and Alex. *The one* didn't exist, and I was skeptical about falling in love and trusting someone with my whole heart... It was *insane*. However, there was no way I'd let Lincoln's bubble of hope be destroyed.

I'd never seen him like this, so I'd wholeheartedly support his mission to win his woman back, just as he was always supportive of the rest of us.

"Alright, everyone. Pipe down," I declared. "This is *my* birthday trip. If Lincoln wants to go to Hawaii to reconnect with..." I glanced at him.

"Charlotte."

"Right, Charlotte. Then that's what the fuck we're going to do so get your sunscreen and speedos ready."

Spencer chuckled when Alex groaned.

Micheal shrugged as if he didn't care one way or the other

what we did for the week. Lincoln gave me an appreciative look, and I nodded. Just because I was miserable, it didn't mean one of my best friends shouldn't pursue his happiness.

As the guys launched into chatter about our impromptu tropical getaway, I couldn't help contemplating the whole love and romance thing further. I'd never experienced it, and since my father badgered me every other day about hooking up with some socialite who he thought was *suitable* for a Winchester, I probably never would.

After a while, I shrugged off the thought. I'd end up doing what Dad wanted and enter a relationship of convenience. After the way I ruined his life when I was born, I owed it to the old man.

2

CHARLOTTE

I stepped out of the confines of the employee quarters and blinked against the brilliant morning sun. As I strolled barefoot to the beach, I wiggled my toes to appreciate the feeling of the sand filtering through them.

I glanced at the colossal structure of the hotel on the other side of the wall. The contrast between our humble quarters and the opulent space for the guests made me smile. I preferred simplicity. Plus, the employees got the best perk… the beach was our backyard. When I reached the water's edge, the warm breeze carried the scent of saltwater and tropical blooms. I inhaled to absorb it all.

"You gotta love it right, Char?" asked Kaia, a fellow staff member, as she walked past me with her surfboard. She was a native of Hawaii, and I envied her for having grown up in this paradise. By *it*, I knew she meant *everything*.

"Absolutely," I said, smiling from ear to ear.

My dad would have loved waking up to this every morning, I thought as I gazed out at the blue expanse of the ocean. He was one reason I chose a job in Kohala, a long way from my hometown in Oregon. After he passed last year, I decided that I'd not only live for me but for him too in a way. He loved the outdoors, and so did I.

That's why I liked working at Pacific Paradise as an adventure sports instructor. It was one of the best jobs I'd ever had. Well... Hawaii had stiff competition. Before I ended up here, I was in the Maldives, leading water sports excursions for another luxury resort. That job was pretty damn awesome. A wave of sadness hit me as I remembered why I left the job. Dad had gotten pretty sick, and I didn't want to be too far away when he...

Taking another deep breath, I pulled my phone out of my pocket to check on Mom. She seemed to be doing well after Dad, but with her, one could never tell if she was truly okay or merely putting up a brave front.

The phone rang twice before a sharp, "Charlotte..." greeted me.

Mom was pissed.

"Goodness, sweetie. I've been worried sick."

"Hi, Mom." I looked skyward. "You know that being a worry wart ages you faster, right?"

Her irritated huff made me smile as I stuck my toes into the water.

"I've been trying to reach you for days." Her voice was tinged with exasperation.

I winced as guilt pricked me in the chest. "Yeah... I'm sorry about that. I was on a two-day hike with guests. You know how it is sometimes."

"That's how it is *all* the time," she harrumphed. "That's how it was when you were in college and then when you got it into your head to explore the Amazon. And don't even get me started on your time in the Sahara Desert! I swear, Charlotte, you caused most of my gray hairs."

I chuckled, knowing how melodramatic Mom got sometimes. "You don't have to worry. I'm being careful."

Wait, what was I saying? There was no telling Faye Brooks not to worry. Worry was what she specialized in.

"Honey, I know you're every bit like your father... God rest his soul. That's a great thing because he was an extraordinary man."

I smiled. He sure was. Dad was so full of life and never afraid to dive into something new.

"But you just turned twenty-eight..." Mom added.

My smile tumbled from my face. "What's your point?"

Her sigh sounded as if she was gathering her patience. "Charlotte, my sweet, sweet baby girl..."

I braced myself because I knew what came after the saccharine endearments. She was about to low-key insult me. However, I knew she never *meant* to be offensive.

"You're not getting any younger. It's time you stopped taking off to unknown parts of the world to seek thrills."

And here we go... This topic wasn't anything new. Mom lectured me about my lifestyle at least once a month. "I'm not just *seeking thrills*, I'm working."

"Okay, but... Hawaii? A sports instructor? You have a masters in education, Charlotte. I think it's time for you to consider coming home and getting a normal job. You should settle down, get married, and start a family like your sister. Victoria is six months along with her second child, you know."

I rolled my eyes so hard that I was surprised they didn't pop out of their sockets and float away into the sea. There it was. The real issue that Mom had. I wasn't married with two-point-five kids and a dog while living the domestic dream behind a white picket fence. She was so old-fashioned and assumed that every woman should be in a certain domestic setup by the time they reached twenty-five.

"Of course, I know how far along Vicky is," I said. I talked to my sister more than I did with Mom because Vicky didn't give me shit about what I chose to do with my life. "Have you ever considered that getting married and having kids isn't the source of every woman's happiness?"

Silence ensued, and I let out a soft sigh. Knowing Mom, at any moment, she could burst into tears and rant about me throwing my life away. In order to prevent the dramatics, I mentioned something I knew she'd love to hear.

"You need to relax and not worry so much about the trajectory of my life, Mom. I have great news."

"Oh?"

"Guess who reached out to me a few weeks ago?"

"Please don't tell me it's some longtime friend who has another adventurous job opportunity." Mom heaved a sigh.

I understood the mix of skepticism and frustration in her tone. That was how I'd landed most of my jobs, like this one in Hawaii.

"It's a longtime friend but nothing about another job. It was Lincoln."

Her choked gasp resonated with excitement. I didn't even have to mention a last name for her to remember who I spoke of. Lincoln Ford, my ex-boyfriend. We broke up about six years ago, and it shattered Mom's heart more than it did mine or Lincoln's. She adored him. I always thought her weird mom crush on him was insane.

"Lincoln! That's wonderful, Charlotte. Does this mean you two are…? You know…"

Getting back together and getting married within the next

six months to start popping out babies by next year... I knew my mother. That was exactly what was going through her overly romantic and *crazy* mind. I considered bursting her fantasy bubble. It wasn't likely that was the reason for my ex reaching out. He probably just stumbled upon my name on his social media and wanted to say hi. I told him about Pacific Paradise, and he mentioned coming to check it out this week. We also chatted over the phone a few times and the conversations were always light and friendly. There was nothing more to Lincoln reaching out to me.

Sure, we'd been good together. Lincoln and I had just clicked. Hell, we felt more like besties than romantic partners, in my opinion. However, why disappoint Mom so soon? The longer she thought I was getting back with my ex, the longer she'd stay off my ass about my job and settling down. *Sweet reprieve for at least a few weeks...*

"You never know..." I replied vaguely.

Mom squealed with sheer delight. "Tell Lincoln that this old girl would love to see him again."

"Sure thing, Mom." I felt bad about giving her false hope, but honestly, she was driving me nuts with her constant lectures about what I did with my life. "I have to get to work soon."

"Right. It was good to hear from you. Please don't let me wait too long for a call, Charlotte. You know I worry about you."

My heart softened and the indignation I felt about her wanting me to follow a path *she* thought was better lessened. When she gave me a hard time, it was coming from a good place. "I know. I love you, Mom."

"I love you too."

I hung up before she either started crying or before she launched into another lecture. Staring at my phone screen, I shook my head and let out a laugh. One thing was for sure: Mom could lecture me all she wanted. Ultimately, I did whatever the hell I wanted. Dad always said I was stubborn.

As I slid my phone into my pocket and lifted my face to the sky to take in a little more of the tropical morning before heading inside, a thought struck me. If Lincoln was interested in getting back together, would that be something I'd want?

My eyes popped open as I considered this. I wasn't hit with any spark of interest or enthusiasm about the possibility so that must mean it wasn't something I'd want. Right…? My nose wrinkled. Why was I even thinking about it? That was *not* why Lincoln was visiting the resort. The man probably just thought it sounded like a nice place to unwind. He could afford the luxurious vacation spot, after all. Since we parted on amicable terms, I was happy to see him again. As I walked back to the tiny apartments, I forgot all about getting back together with my ex-boyfriend.

3

JAMIE

The Hawaiian island of Kohala was beautiful… from what I glimpsed in my periphery, anyway. Since I was afraid of heights, admiring the surroundings from a helicopter wasn't ideal. The aircraft's door was open for fuck's sake, and I might just hurl up the lunch I had on the jet.

We could have driven up to Kohala Coast, but Lincoln, Mr. Adventure, thought it would be *awesome* to get to the resort via helicopter. The others seemed excited about it and I didn't want to be the killjoy of the group, so I gathered my balls and got into the godforsaken tiny tin can.

Sweat beaded on my forehead when I chanced a look outside. I got a glimpse of pristine blue water bordered by white sand and lush vegetation before a wave of nausea hit me. I immediately took my eyes off the ground and proceeded to distract myself with thoughts of business projections and analytics… boring CEO stuff.

Although I was glad to get away from work, thoughts of it would no doubt pop up from time to time. My friends didn't call me a workaholic for nothing... as if they weren't all the same way. They were busy staring below, admiring the view, so no one noticed that I was on the verge of passing out.

However, when Spencer glanced my way, his smile melted. "Hey. Are you alright, Jamie?"

I gulped and spoke into the microphone attached to my earphones. "I'm great. Taking in the beauty of the place."

Spencer's raised eyebrows screamed *skeptical*. "You've barely looked down."

Our conversation got everyone else's attention. Lincoln did a double take at my face. "Oh, fuck. I totally forgot."

"Forgot what?" Alex asked.

"He's afraid of heights."

"Oh, right," Alex hummed.

My jaw tightened. They would have remembered my fear had I *wanted* them to. "I'm fine," I growled into the microphone. "And I'm not *that* afraid of heights." *Yeah, right.* I was a second away from *swooning*. Still, I kept up a brave facade.

"Is that right?" Michael regarded me with amusement. "Is that why you're so green?"

I guess my courageous front wasn't so effective... I gave Michael a dirty look. "How about you all just shut the hell up?" I grumbled. I wasn't sure if they heard me with all the noise, but no one else said a word.

Finally, *thankfully*, we landed on the helipad on top of a rugged cliff that overlooked the coastline. The rotors wound down as we disembarked. When my feet hit solid ground, relief flooded me, and the bout of nausea that assailed me dissipated. Since I was no longer hovering in the air, I could comfortably admire the panoramic picture spread out before me with awe.

Below, the cerulean blue of the Pacific Ocean stretched out to the horizon. The helipad was surrounded by swaying palm trees and flowers. It was beautiful. Perhaps it was the change of environment that brought on a sense of peace. I closed my eyes when the salty breeze brushed my skin and ruffled my hair.

The sound of waves crashing in the distance was a serene melody. I never felt this relaxed back home. I'd been caught up in an emotional turmoil for so long, and barely five minutes into this getaway, I already felt better. I was in a tropical paradise, a world away from my real life.

Someone clapped me on the shoulder, and I opened my eyes. It was Alex. He gazed at me with understanding as he smiled. I was surprised that he perceived how I felt at that moment because he didn't want to take the trip, and he rarely took anything seriously.

"You good, bro?" he asked.

The others watched me, waiting for my answer.

"Sure," I replied.

And for once, I wasn't lying. While I never had an enthusiasm about vacations or life in general like my friends, I always found solace in their company. They were genuine guys—a trait you didn't find in most nowadays. That's why we'd held on to our friendship for so long. I looked forward to hanging out with them for a few days.

"Let's get this party started, shall we?"

A few eyebrows went up because that was usually Alex's line, not mine.

"Let's go. Our things should be at the hotel already," Lincoln announced. "I already love this place. They think of everything."

"Please, you only love it because your girlfriend is here," Michael grumbled.

"She's not my girlfriend." Lincoln smirked. "Yet."

As we set off on our short walk down to the hotel, I caught up with Lincoln. Curiosity about this Charlotte had me in a chokehold. I mean, the woman must be a fairy sprinkling love dust to have Lincoln behaving like this. One thing we all had in common—even the romantic Spencer—was our aversion to commitment. We never stuck with a relationship for too long before getting antsy.

"Hey, Linc. Thanks for this, even though you suggested the trip with an ulterior motive."

His lips twisted into a wry grin. "Don't worry. We're going to have plenty of just-us-guys-time."

"I wasn't worried. I may not understand your sudden need to pursue your ex, but I'm in full support."

I glanced back to see the others immersed in conversation. Michael looked annoyed, so that meant Alex was probably saying something ridiculous.

Lowering my voice, I asked, "You care to share what's up with you?"

Lincoln rubbed his jaw and laughed. "Why does something have to be up for me to reach out to a woman I know? An amazing woman, by the way."

"Huh, so there's no more to it other than Charlotte being amazing? I see." I side-eyed him. "So you're not going through a version of a midlife crisis or anything…?"

His booming laughter echoed, and we received amused glances from our friends and the uniformed staff escorting us. He gazed at me for a moment, but he didn't answer. My suspicion mounted. Something was definitely going on with Lincoln, something deeper than just one day deciding that he wanted to catch up with Charlotte.

However, I knew how annoying it could get when someone pressed about an issue you didn't want to discuss, so I didn't pressure him for more. "So, tell me about your Charlotte."

"*My* Charlotte..." He chuckled. "If she heard you refer to her as mine, she'd likely knee you in the balls."

"Ah, she's feisty, huh?"

"A real pistol. That's one of the things that attracted me to her back in the day." Lincoln stared ahead as if reliving the time he and Charlotte met. "She didn't fawn over me or my teammates because we were professional athletes, you know?"

I nodded. It irritated the hell out of me when women discovered the weight of my last name and started acting differently. Some of them got downright conniving and predatory, wanting to sink their claws in and hold on to a certain lifestyle. Correction, it wasn't just women. It was everybody.

"Charlotte gave me shit about my arrogance," Lincoln continued with a smile. "Kept me grounded while we dated. And she was always compassionate, supportive, and *fun*. I always had a great time with Charlotte Brooks." He shrugged. "I guess I want to recapture a bit of those good times."

"Hmmm." Out of nowhere, a pang of longing struck me in the chest. I realized that I'd never felt a genuine connection with a woman I've dated—if you wanted to call those brief encounters dating.

My father had been pushing me to enter an arranged marriage because he was such a stickler for legacy and tradition. Listening to Lincoln gush about Charlotte made me wonder if I could have more in a relationship than merely fulfilling familial and social expectations... or maybe I was thinking crazy. Still, I couldn't shake the feeling of emptiness that gnawed at me.

I didn't dwell on it much longer because I was distracted by a low whistle. Alex had come up beside me and was staring ahead. "Now *this* is more like it. This vacation might turn out to be better than I thought."

I followed his gaze to the entrance of the hotel where a couple of women waited. They wore traditional hula dancer outfits. I shook my head at Alex, who practically salivated over the women.

As one greeter draped a flower necklace around me and welcomed me to the Kohala and Pacific Paradise Resort, I thought about Lincoln's mysterious woman. For the first time in my life, I wondered if there was possibly a Charlotte out there for me too… probably not. Surely, I would have found her already…

4

CHARLOTTE

I felt eyes boring into my back and slowly turned around. Two pairs of dark browns filled with curiosity were fixed on me.

"What?" I asked.

Vera and Kaia, my co-workers, exchanged glances. Vera was the one to speak. "You said you're meeting up with your ex after what...? Six years?"

"Uh-huh." I eyed her with confusion.

Vera and I stuck together because we arrived at the resort at the same time. She was from a small town in California and was feeling overwhelmed and homesick, so my presence was comforting to her. We had become good friends.

She wrinkled her nose as she gave me a once-over. "Then you most definitely *cannot* go out there in *that*."

I paused in the middle of throwing my hair up into a haphazard ponytail to look down at myself. What was wrong with my yoga pants and white T-shirt? My top had a sizable coffee stain from lunch, but... so what?

"What's wrong with what I'm wearing? Should I head into the lobby to mingle with the wealthy guests naked?" I snickered at my joke.

Vera's sigh echoed with the dwindling patience of someone who had been trying with me for months. Trying to get me into something other than yoga pants and T-shirts, that is.

Kaia got up from my bed and came toward me. "No offense, Char, but you should put a little more effort into your appearance to meet a guy you once dated."

I glowered at Kaia. She was just eighteen, working at the resort as a housekeeper to gather money for college tuition.

"What are you still doing here?" I asked.

She didn't live far, so she didn't stay at the employee housing, yet she was here before the sun rose and long after it went down every day.

She grinned. "I didn't want you and Vera to miss me too much, so I stuck around. I might even spend the night with you, Char. I know you'll love that."

I rolled my eyes, but it was with pure affection. Kaia was like an annoying little sister whom I adored. I suspected she was trying to avoid her home, but she wouldn't tell me why. So, I usually let her spend the night without question.

"Sure... and what do you guys suggest I wear?"

The two exchanged glances again. Their conspiring smiles made me a tad nervous. I squinted my eyes with suspicion as they approached much like predators with juicy prey in their sights...

Thirty minutes later, I stared at myself in the full-length mirror. My friends had gotten me to put on a floral dress that had been burning a hole in the back of my closet. It was white with an array of colorful blooms all over it.

The waist was cinched by a belt and the skirt reached only

mid-thigh, showing off my legs. My hair had been brushed and hung in waves around my shoulders. I had on light eyeshadow and my lips were painted red. I lifted an eyebrow at the reflection of my stylists standing proudly behind me.

"Lipstick, you guys? Really? I'm just going to the lobby for five minutes to say howdy to the guy."

"Doesn't matter," Vera says. "He's your ex-boyfriend. Never let your ex see you looking less than glamorous. You should always show them what they've been missing."

"Who the hell makes these rules?" I threw my arms up.

"Who cares?" Kaia rested her hands on my shoulders and smiled. "You look great. He's going to want you back for sure."

"Oh, my god," I groaned. "Girls, you misunderstood. Lincoln is a *buddy* now."

"He called to tell you that he was here," Vera reasoned. "That must mean something."

"Yeah, he's happy to see an old friend, as am I."

Vera and Kaia didn't look happy.

"I'm not getting back with my ex, guys. I doubt Lincoln has even considered it. Sorry to burst your bubble." I chuckled because their disappointed pouts reminded me of my mother. Everyone was trying to marry me off, and it was comical.

"You've been here for seven months, and I've never seen you go on a date," Kaia said.

"And it isn't like you lack male attention," Vera added. "Staff *and* guests have flirted with you, but you never seem to notice. Josh has been shamelessly throwing himself at you for months."

Josh was another instructor in my department. Vera was right. He wasn't subtle with his flirting.

"Oh, I notice," I told her as I smoothed my dress. I resigned myself to taking a stroll to the lobby in the ridiculously dressy outfit. "I'm just not interested."

"Why not?" Kaia asked.

I took no offense to her asking that like I would if Mom had asked. Kaia looked at me with genuine curiosity, not with outrage and disbelief.

"Well, Kaia, I'm not sure if you'll understand at your age, but I like my freedom. I feel like getting seriously involved with anyone will be cumbersome in a way. Not that being with someone you like or love isn't great." I shrugged. "I just like to be able to move where and when I want without having to worry about how my partner feels about it." That was a major reason Lincoln and I didn't work out.

Kaia's eyeballs did a full rotation as she considered what I said. "I get it. You like being a free spirit."

I smiled.

Vera watched me closely. She then said with confidence, "You just haven't met the right guy yet, that's all."

I shrugged. I had nothing against love and romance, so I didn't disagree. I wasn't looking for Mr. Right, but I sure as hell wouldn't turn him away if he showed up. I glanced at the clock hanging above my door.

"I should get to the lobby. Lincoln said he'd likely be at the hotel around five."

Vera beamed. "We'll be here waiting for you to tell us all about it."

Snorting, I grabbed my phone off the dresser. "I know you will. Later."

* * *

The hotel's lobby was abuzz with the arrival of guests. Pacific Paradise hadn't been around all that long, but it was growing in popularity. The resort was supposedly for everyone, but let's be real... not everyone could afford the visit. I'd never in a million years be able to afford the place had I not worked there.

Lincoln could afford to live here year-round if he wanted. When I met him, he was a rising NFL star, signing million-dollar contracts. The few times we spoke since we reconnected, I'd learned that he was now an agent to the richest athletes. He was still raking in the big bucks, I was sure.

It had always been surreal, knowing that a small-town girl like me had dated someone famous back in the day. However, Lincoln had been so down to earth during our relationship that sometimes I forgot what he did for a living. I wondered if he was still that humble guy who snuck away from A-list parties to hang out with me at hole-in-the-wall burger joints.

My thoughts about my ex vanished like vapor in the wind when I spotted a man enter the lobby. My next breath got stuck in my throat. The man was tall and had such a commanding presence that I couldn't look away. I could tell from his confidence—bordering on arrogance—that he was somebody important, and he was in charge of *something*.

His somber expression piqued my curiosity. Arriving guests usually looked more excited. However, his serious air took nothing away from his looks. He was masculinely beautiful with chiseled angular features. His rich espresso hair was neatly trimmed in a classic style—short at the sides and back with a slightly longer top. Sometimes, you could tell a lot from a haircut. His style told me that he was probably reserved and sophisticated.

He looked my way, and I gasped. Heat infused my cheeks because I was caught staring. The longer his gaze lingered on me, the hotter my skin got. I couldn't see the color of his eyes from across the room, but I bet they were just as gorgeous as he was.

I blew out a breath of disbelief as my gaze skated away from the hot guy. I'd never had such a profound interest in a man at first sight before. It was like a spark of attraction hitting me square in the chest… and in my nether region. *God.*

When I chanced a look at the man again, because I couldn't resist, I sucked in a breath. He still stared at me with his head tilted. Dare I say he studied me with interest and attraction too? I realized that I'd stopped walking and just stood there, looking at the stranger. Suddenly, I felt ridiculous.

Just as I shook myself out of the haze I'd fallen into, a familiar face came into view. Lincoln. He clapped the man I was checking out on the shoulder and said something. My pounding heart came to a screeching halt. *Oh, no.* I was drooling over my ex's friend. Talk about awkward. *Hot Guy's* gaze finally drifted away from me, and I exhaled loudly. That staring contest was intense.

Lincoln searched the room, and I knew he was looking for me, so I waved. His grin blossomed when he spotted me and he immediately barreled in my direction. My feet stayed glued to the floor because I felt guilty about checking out his friend. Behind Lincoln, a group of guys—Hot Guy included—approached me too.

"I'll be damned," Lincoln rumbled. "Charlotte Brooks in the flesh."

I smiled. "Lincoln Ford."

I was swept up into a bear hug. I wasn't too surprised by the warm greeting because, despite our romantic relationship ending years ago, he had sounded super excited to see me over the phone. However, I didn't read much into it. Lincoln probably had a girlfriend or wife by now.

"It's good to see you," I said through my giggles as he swung me around like a rag doll.

He put me back on my feet but kept his palms on my shoulders. He beamed, jade eyes sparkling. "It's good to see you, too. Damn, you look good."

I was sure that my face was bright red as I looked down at my feet. Vera and Kaia would be happy to hear that. "Here he goes with the flattery."

"I'm serious," he said.

There was something in his tone and the way he gazed at me that made me pause. However, before I could process it, he glanced behind him.

"These are my friends."

One by one, he introduced them. I shook hands with Spencer, Michael, and Alex. I noticed the one I'd had the staredown with had fallen back. Lincoln introduced him as James but added that all his friends called him Jamie.

I was taken aback when James hesitated to offer his hand. His expression was hard as stone as he unfolded his arms and tentatively extended one in my direction. My eyebrows bunched together as I placed my hand in his. What was his problem?

I raised an eyebrow when he gave me a gruff, "Hi." There was no smile or "nice to meet you" like I'd gotten from the others, so I guess he didn't care about the introduction.

"Pleasure to meet you, Jamie," I bit out, fighting the urge to throw out an insult because I was embarrassed.

"James," he corrected.

I blinked when I realized that he low-key put it out there that we weren't friends, so I had no right to call him Jamie. Sure, we just met, but he didn't have to be so cold.

I glanced at Lincoln with disbelief. He and the others were staring at James with slack jaws, so I guess this wasn't his normal behavior. Interesting. Was I the problem? Maybe he was one of those rich guys—it was obvious that he was well off—who didn't like peasants below his tax bracket.

I wasn't surprised. Working at this resort, I'd encountered quite a few pompous snobs. However, I was disappointed. I'd just wasted precious seconds being utterly attracted to an ass. *Damn.* Still, I gave Jamie… *James* another appreciative glance. The gorgeous jerk.

5

JAMIE

Shoot me, mount me, stuff me, and toss me into the most fiery part of hell. I deserved that for drooling over Lincoln's ex-girlfriend who he was here to win back. In my defense, I had no idea that the delectable woman I'd spotted across the room was Lincoln's Charlotte.

When he approached her and wrapped her in his arms, my jaw nearly hit the white tiles in the lobby. That was Charlotte? Holy fuck. His descriptions didn't do her justice. The moment I stepped inside, she'd had my attention.

My gaze had landed on a goddess with sun-kissed skin, flowing hair that looked like golden sunshine, and the longest, leanest legs I'd ever seen. The way her white floral print dress hugged her curves made my mouth water... Then my lascivious thoughts came to an abrupt halt when I realized that she was the Charlotte whom my friend spoke so fondly of.

Fuck me. The one time a woman commanded my attention, had me completely intrigued, and made me feel a spark of... *something*, she turned out to be a woman I couldn't have. I'd gone through a series of emotions watching Charlotte and Lincoln's warm embrace—shock, dismay, jealousy, and guilt.

And how did I handle the rapid fire of emotions that assaulted me? I was a jerk to Charlotte, that's how. Lincoln now stared at me as if he planned to murder me later for being a prick to his lady. I didn't blame him. I wanted to kick myself in the ass for my behavior. I mean, I was hesitant to shake Charlotte's hand as if I was a toddler afraid of touching a girl with *cooties*. It was the guilt after practically undressing her in my head… I was afraid to touch her, fearing that Lincoln would somehow see that I was into her.

Now, as Charlotte wrinkled her cute little nose at me and my friends watched me with disbelief, I was embarrassed. Clearing my throat, I grumbled, "So are we going to check in or what?"

Since my friends still stared at me as if I'd sprouted another head, things got awkward. Charlotte jumped in to quell it. "Welcome to Pacific Paradise, guys. You're going to enjoy your time here, I promise."

God… her voice. It had a velvety cadence, smooth and cool, each word dripping with contagious enthusiasm. The sound danced in the air, and it was utterly captivating. And that smile… it was carefree, stretching her full lips and lighting up her entire face. Even Michael, the professional scowler, smiled back at her. It was as I'd thought. She really was a fairy sprinkling love *and* happy dust.

"I'm holding you to that, Char," Lincoln said. "You'll be a major player in ensuring that we do, right?"

She laughed. "Definitely. If you want fun and adventure, I've got you covered."

"Great." Lincoln rubbed his nape. "So, can I see you later or will you be busy?"

She beckoned us with a wave and moved toward the receptionist counter as she replied, "I'm free for the rest of the evening."

"What do you say about dinner to catch up?" Lincoln gave her a hopeful glance.

"I'd like that." Her response was easy with no hesitation. She must have entertained thoughts about rekindling their romance too.

Bile rose in my throat and my jaw tightened at hearing how familiar Lincoln was with her. I shook my head to get my shit together and to stop gawking at Charlotte. I didn't *want* to be attracted to my friend's ex-girlfriend. As Charlotte chatted with the receptionist and told her to take care of her friends, I kept sneaking peeks at her.

She was so exuberant and sweet. She turned to Lincoln with her incredible smile. "While you guys settle in, I'll head back to my room and prepare for our dinner, okay? Give me a buzz when you're ready."

My gaze followed the hand she placed affectionately on Lincoln's arm. That feeling of longing for an intimate connection with someone that hit me earlier reappeared. *No, no, no. Not with her. Never with her.* What the hell was wrong with me? I never desired... *romance* before. All of this had to stem from all the emotional unrest caused by my upcoming birthday. Yeah, that had to be it. I wasn't *really* attracted to Charlotte... right?

"Of course," Lincoln said. "I'll see you in a bit."

Charlotte walked away, her very gait radiating energy. When she was out of sight, Lincoln turned to us with a boyish grin. "What did I tell you? She's great, right?"

"That she is, mate," Spencer said.

"I like her," Michael said.

That said a lot. He didn't take to many so easily.

"Dude, your ex is *hot*," Alex remarked, still staring at where Charlotte had disappeared to.

Lincoln's eyes narrowed to slits in warning.

"*Jeez-us*, Alex," I growled. "Keep it in your pants." My words were a tad too vehement because I didn't want him to have the same thoughts I'd had of the intriguing Charlotte.

"You're one to talk," Lincoln hissed when the others stepped up to the counter and were paying us no mind. "What the hell was that back there?"

"What are you talking about?" I asked, feigning ignorance.

"You were so rude to Charlotte."

"Was I?"

"For the love of God, Jamie. Do not go into grump mode and behave like an asshole to her again. Do not ruin this for me."

My mouth opened and closed but I had nothing, because goddamn it, a tiny jealous part of me wanted to ruin things for him. When did I become the poster child for the worst friend in history? I needed to stop this *thing* with Charlotte before it matured.

"Look, man, I'm sorry if I was abrupt. My mind was… elsewhere."

His expression softened with understanding and I felt ten times the guilt for lying and playing on his sympathy. "Hey, I get it, but Charlotte doesn't know you're going through a rough time. Keep the grumpster away from her, got it?"

I snorted. "Sure."

I wasn't a prayerful person, but I launched into a mental petition to whichever higher being was listening. *Please let me forget the filthy things that entered my mind when I saw Charlotte. And please, for the love of my sanity, and friendship with Lincoln, erase everything I felt when I met her…*

* * *

Apparently, my prayer fell on deaf ears. As soon as I saw Charlotte this morning, the idea of ignoring my attraction to her fled my mind. Only a mixture of desire and confusion remained. I couldn't fathom why I was so drawn to her.

She was an attractive woman. That thought had my gaze dropping to her long, tanned legs, displayed by a pair of shorts that hugged her ass to perfection. However, it wasn't just her appearance.

The warmth she exuded drew me in like a moth to a flame. It was crazy because I barely knew her enough to be certain that she was a good person. I suppose I could just tell that she was…

"An adventure sports instructor, huh?" Alex said in response to Charlotte explaining her position at the resort. "I wouldn't have guessed when I met you yesterday."

I wouldn't have guessed either. When Lincoln said she worked here, I imagined she was employed as an entertainer or something along that line. She certainly had the look to be in a skin-tight red dress, crooning sultrily into a microphone, and seducing men with her earthy deep brown eyes and natural allure. Instead, I discovered that she was the exact opposite of what I'd envisioned, which made me like her even more.

When Lincoln announced that we'd kick start the week with a little adventure, I had pictured a massage on the beach or something similar. I was wrong. We were going on a hike and Charlotte was our guide. So much for avoiding her…

Charlotte chuckled as she adjusted the straps of her backpack. The soft sound wrapped around me even though she had directed her attention at Alex. "I get that a lot. If you don't like me as your guide, you can always go with Josh over there."

She hiked her thumb over her shoulder toward a guy with shaggy blond hair. He looked like the stereotypical *surfer dude*. Charlotte watched us expectantly and with a bit of wariness. It was like she was accustomed to men questioning her expertise because she was female and that pissed me off. Misogynistic types irked me.

"Hell, no. We don't want Josh," Alex said. "We don't want anyone but you, Char."

Five minutes in our company and she was already close enough to be *Char*. The guys really liked her, and I could tell that pleased Lincoln. He grinned approvingly from ear to ear.

"Damn straight." Spencer winked. "Besides, you're much prettier to look at."

Charlotte rolled her eyes but her cheeks lit up a pretty pink. She was adorable yet sexy when she blushed. *Incredible.*

Stop it, Winchester, I reminded myself.

"Hey," Lincoln warned. "Let's not make Charlotte uncomfortable."

"It's okay, Lincoln. I'm used to it."

Of their own accord, my eyes traveled over her perfectly sculpted face, toned torso in a tight tank top, and the delicious flare of her hip. I bet she was accustomed to getting hit on.

She flashed Spencer a cheeky smile. "A girl doesn't mind a little compliment now and then."

Spencer laughed. "I like you, Charlotte." He clapped Lincoln on the shoulder and winked as if to tell him *we know she's yours*. "Relax, will you?"

Michael, who was taking in the interaction quietly, smirked when Lincoln's cheeks flushed the most subtle shade of red. He then glanced at me, probably to share his amusement, but he frowned because I wasn't smiling. I imagined my scowl rivaled his typical one. Realizing that he watched me with curiosity, I wiped away the sour expression that had formed at the thought of Charlotte being *Lincoln's*.

How had their dinner gone last night? Were they already back together? The sliver of resentment I felt for my friend, who was like a brother, had me wallowing in shame.

Michael lifted an eyebrow in askance, but I ignored him. I lifted my backpack and hoisted it onto my shoulders.

Charlotte turned to us, eyes sparkling with anticipation. "Alright, guys. Ready for some fun?"

I wasn't the outdoors type but her enthusiasm rubbed off on me. After a chorus of affirmative responses, she grinned and led us outside.

6

CHARLOTTE

I guided my group along the winding trail. Foliage enveloped us, and the air was thick with the heady scent of tropical bloom. I loved it out here. It was so peaceful and relaxing. The further you walked, the lighter your mind got. I hoped the hike had the same effect on everyone as it did on me.

Each time Lincoln made his way to the front of the line to chat, I had to fall back after a while. It wasn't that I didn't want to talk with him. Catching up over dinner last night was fun, and I wouldn't mind doing it again. However, considering that I had an entire group with me, I didn't want anyone to think I was paying Lincoln more attention because I knew him. I had to share my time with everyone.

When Lincoln specifically requested me as a guide for his group, I'd been a little nervous. Working with a group of men like this usually had uncomfortable moments because plenty of them assumed that because I didn't have a dick between my legs, I was less qualified to instruct them on anything about sports or the outdoors.

These guys were different though. I liked Lincoln's friends. Even when Alex and Spencer flirted with me, I knew they meant no harm. It was clear that they did it just to mess with Lincoln. It was cute but unnecessary. It wasn't like Lincoln and I were a thing anymore.

I glanced at Spencer, who seemed immersed in the environment. He gazed at everything with a gleam of appreciation in his eyes that most didn't have. I learned that he was a songwriter, so I got it. Alex and Michael were walking side by side, murmuring amongst themselves. They stopped to listen each time I pointed out native flora and interesting landmarks or shared a snippet about the island's history.

As we trekked deeper, the trail grew steeper and more challenging, so I knew we had to turn back soon. I wouldn't push them too much on the first day, even though they all looked fit. Seriously, I felt like I was leading a group of models to their tropical photo shoot. Lincoln's friends were all swoon-worthy, but there was something about Jamie that kept pulling my attention back to him.

I looked around and noticed he had fallen back. "Alright, guys. It's time to turn around."

"Already?" Spencer asked.

"Yeah, we're enjoying the trek," Alex said.

Lincoln snorted. "Really? There are no scantily dressed women along the trail and *you're* enjoying it?"

"Shut up," Alex grumbled, which had me fighting back a smile.

Between Lincoln telling me about his friends and spending the morning with them, I had their personalities figured out. Alex was the reckless playboy of the five friends for sure.

Lincoln was the humorous one which I already knew. Again, my mind kept wandering back to Jamie.

As I tried to shove him out of my head once more, I said, "I'm glad you guys are enjoying the hike and I'm sorry it has to end. However, we're not prepared to go any further. Things get stickier further up. Maybe we can take the challenge another day when we're more prepared."

I didn't imagine they'd have such a great time. I was guilty of misjudging the group, assuming that a bunch of rich guys who made millions behind their desks wouldn't appreciate a nature walk. Shame on me.

As we turned back, I couldn't fight the urge to speak with Jamie anymore. I noticed that he'd avoided me like I was contagious all morning, and I wasn't going to let him get away with it.

Since we were heading in the opposite direction, he was the one ahead of the group, so I hurried my steps to fall into stride with him.

"Hello, *James*."

I saw him frown at me from my periphery and folded my lips to keep my grin suppressed.

"Why do you say my name like that?" he asked.

My grin emerged because he took my bait. "You mean in that snooty tone?"

I glanced at him and found him staring at me with furrowed eyebrows. "Yes." His eyes then narrowed.

Despite my playful mood, my breath hitched. This close to him, I could finally look into his eyes. They were like pools of shimmering liquid silver fanned by thick black lashes. When they landed on you, they were magnetic. You couldn't look away. I swallowed hard, noting the haunting intensity of their depth. They said the eyes were the windows to the soul, so what haunted Jamie?

I blinked to shake off the snare he'd caught me in with his gaze. "Well, you seem the arrogant type. Plus, your surname is Winchester. I imagine that when one says your full name it should sound snobbish." I squared my shoulders, lifted my nose into the air like plenty of the self-important rich folks I encountered at the resort, and said in a deep, haughty tone, *"James Winchester."*

He stared at me for a moment and then there was a suspicious twitch at one corner of his mouth. *Aha!* I almost got a smile out of him.

"First, how do you know my surname? Second, what's with the British accent?" he asked, a trace of amusement lining his words.

He had a nice voice... deep, yet smooth and velvety. It was made for whispering sweet words into a woman's ear. Goodness, I was into James Winchester after convincing myself that I didn't like him.

I laughed. "Lincoln told me all about you guys last night."

So I knew that Jamie was more out of my league than I thought. He was a billionaire CEO who ran EcoEnergy Solutions, a renewable energy conglomerate. I liked that he cared about the environment.

"And I don't know... James Winchester just sounds like it should be delivered with an accent."

He made a grunting noise that resonated with amusement. "My middle name is *Wilfred*." His shoulders relaxed a bit. When I first approached, they'd practically hiked to his ears. He was so tense that his poor shoulders must be sore every night.

It took me a moment to realize that Mr. Surly was engaging in a bit of comedy. I gasped dramatically. *"No."*

"Yup. After my grandfather."

I winced. "Yikes. When you use your full name, you sound like a stuffy old man."

He flashed me the tiniest smile, and I almost clutched my chest. When his flinty features softened, he was doubly handsome. "Hence, I prefer Jamie."

"But only your friends can call you that, and I'm not your friend. You were very clear about that yesterday."

He looked down at the path as we walked and said nothing for a few seconds. "You can call me Jamie."

I smiled. "Are we friends now?"

As Jamie held my gaze, my smile almost melted away. He took so long to answer that I thought he'd be rude and embarrass me again. I was a little perplexed when he glanced back at Lincoln, who wasn't too far behind. He then swallowed and nodded. "Sure."

The gleam of worry in his eyes caught me off guard, so it took me a moment to gather my thoughts to form a response. "Sounds good. So, now that we're besties…"

A tiny smile lifted his lips.

"Care to tell me what that was yesterday?"

He glanced at me. "What are you talking about?"

"The tortured look on your face when we met. I assumed you hated me on sight or something."

His eyes widened slightly. "God, no… Charlotte… that wasn't… I was just…"

My eyebrows popped up as Jamie stuttered.

He then blew out a long breath. "I'm sorry about that. I was a little off yesterday, that's all."

"Why's that?"

Jamie stared ahead. As I studied his profile, the tightness of his jaw told me that he was debating sharing with me or not. I hoped he decided to because after learning that he wasn't really the snooty, rich prick I'd pegged him to be, my interest in him grew.

"Well, it wasn't just yesterday. I suppose I haven't been myself for a few days. My—"

"Hey, what are you two whispering about?" Lincoln interrupted, coming up behind us.

I'd been so engrossed in Jamie and in what he was about to say that Lincoln's voice was like a thunderclap. I even jumped and almost clutched my chest. Jamie moved away from me—it was subtle, but I noticed it—as if we were caught doing something naughty.

"Nothing important," Jamie muttered.

I watched with disappointment as he withdrew, his expression shifting into serious mode once again. Goodness, it was like Jamie fled the scene and *James* was back. Maybe it was my imagination, but the warmth that had been building between Jamie and me cooled in an instant... as if the connection we were about to make severed.

I couldn't help but feel irritated by the interruption. However, I forced a smile for Lincoln. "Yeah, nothing important," I said, as I swallowed my disappointment.

Perhaps it was for the best that I didn't learn more about Jamie Winchester because I'd probably get to like him too much and that was a bad idea. For one, he was my ex's close friend and what was the point of getting to know him better? He'd vanish from my life in an instant. Plus, I wasn't looking for anything serious with a guy right now... Yet, I couldn't help stealing glances at Jamie as Lincoln fell into step beside me and threw his arm around my shoulders.

I knew he didn't mean to make me uncomfortable—I wouldn't be in a typical scenario—but with Jamie on my other side, it was *awkward*. Jamie didn't even glance back in my direction for the duration of our journey back to the resort, and I thought that maybe he had the right idea. We should stay away from each other because something was brewing between us that spelled *complicated*. The smart thing for me to do would be to avoid him.

7

CHARLOTTE

*I*gnoring Jamie and the undeniable spark between us was easier said than done. As much as I tried to focus on everyone else and the good time they seemed to be having, my attention kept straying back to him.

Letting out a deep gusty breath, I tried to shake off my consuming thoughts about Jamie.

"Alright, guys. Who's ready to hit the waves?" I called out as I led the group down the shoreline. The enthusiasm in my voice wasn't forced because I was excited about our windsurfing session. I loved the water and the way the wind caressed my skin as I glided on the waves.

Lincoln grinned. "Lead the way, Char. We're ready for some action."

Of course Lincoln was eager. The major thing that we had in common was our love for sports and the outdoors.

Michael gazed out at the water as we stopped beside the colorful sails and sleek boards that were lined out. The waves were a tad rougher today, creating a rhythmic crash against the shore. "I've never done this before…"

"Not to worry, Mike. Under Charlotte's expert guidance, we'll be fine." Alex hit me with his charming smile.

I resisted the urge to roll my eyes while Lincoln gave him a seething look. Alex was a shameless flirt, but I appreciated the vote of confidence. Lincoln and his friends were helping me out a lot.

My supervisor took notice of the fact that I was requested as their outdoor guide again. He gave me a pat on the shoulder and said, "The guests seem to enjoy themselves with you, Charlotte. Good job."

I didn't bother mentioning that this particular group chose me because of my history with Lincoln. After just seven months of working here, I was still the rookie trying to make a name for myself. I noticed that Josh, my coworker, was a little sour over the extra attention I'd gotten… and the hefty tips.

"Alex is right," I said to Michael. "Don't worry, we'll start with the basics."

I began with selecting a board and sail for each of them and then I adjusted the rigging to suit each one.

As we waded into shallow water, I asked, "You're sure you're all strong swimmers?"

"We are, Charlotte. You don't have to worry about us," Spencer said.

Still, I'd keep a close eye. Jamie had yet to speak… of course. I'd gathered that he wasn't much of a talker. Yet, yesterday, he was about to tell me something he didn't share with many others. I just knew it.

"Hey, Charlotte. It's pretty early," Lincoln said. "What do you suggest we do after this?"

I considered it. It seemed they were hellbent on staying

outside and engaging in sports and other activities for as long as they were here. These were the types of guests I loved. The other type spent all day inside, luxuriating in room service and spa treatments... *boring*.

"How do you guys feel about zip lining or bungee jumping? I could take you—"

"Hell, no," Jamie said.

Ah. He speaks. And each time he did, my attention zeroed in on him and everyone else faded. I really needed to get a grip.

"I mean something that *all* of us can do," Lincoln added.

My gaze flickered between Jamie and Lincoln as I wondered what Jamie had against zip lining. "Okay..." I smirked. "Maybe you guys should head back to the hotel and hit the spa. That sounds more like Jamie's speed."

The dig earned me a glare from him while his friends all visibly struggled to hold back laughter.

There was a suspicious twitch to Jamie's lips when he grumbled, "Hilarious, Charlotte," that told me he didn't mind all that much that I teased him. He'd been amused when I gave him shit about his name yesterday. I wondered what other nuances there were to Jamie's personality because I was learning that he wasn't serious *all* the time.

I grinned at him and the smile he tried to hold back threatened to emerge. Lincoln's gaze swiveled between us, and he cleared his throat. That was when I realized that Jamie and I were still staring at each other. Our eyes skated away from each other fast.

"We'll stick to land or water activities, Charlotte," Lincoln said.

Jamie, who had no trace of his earlier amusement on his face, shook his head. "No, if you guys want to zip line or risk your necks dangling in the air from a rope, that's fine. I'll just sit those activities out. Don't let me ruin your fun."

"But this trip is for you," Spencer pointed out.

"Yeah, we're not doing anything without you," Michael interjected.

I listened to the guys with growing interest as I got my board ready to give them a demonstration. The trip was *for* Jamie? What did that mean? Maybe he was the one who planned it and not Lincoln as I'd thought…?

"Look, I don't mind, you guys," Jamie said. "I don't do heights, but I'm sure I'll be plenty entertained watching you guys do crazy shit."

So he was afraid of heights… I glanced at the man who often seemed so somber and reserved. One would never guess that he had any fears. The discovery was interesting. There was something else that I'd discovered about him too. Something weighed heavily on his mind.

Jamie engaged with his friends, but I saw him zone out plenty of times, becoming detached from everything going on around him. For a moment, I got caught up in watching him move in the water as I wondered what troubled him. His muscles rippled under his skin as he guided his board on the water's surface. He wasn't excessively muscular. He was… just right. Tall and lean from hours in a gym, I assumed.

Amid conversation with his friends, he glanced my way as if he felt me watching him. Our gazes collided for the briefest moment before mine skated away. I was embarrassed that he caught me checking him out. And did I really see what I thought I saw in his eyes? It was something intense and smoldering that rivaled the tropical sun. It sent a jolt of electricity through me that reached deep and turned into a hot desire, which curled in my core.

I gulped, not even wanting to know what the hell that was. A little breathless, I announced, "Okay, guys. Let me show you how to do this."

*　*　*

"Are you sure it's okay if I tag along?" Kaia asked, running a hand over the dress I'd loaned her.

"Of course."

Lincoln invited me to dinner earlier. He said that the guys liked me and wouldn't mind if I joined them.

"Yeah, we don't want to impose," Vera said.

"You're not. I told Lincoln that I wouldn't ditch you guys this evening, and he said I was more than welcome to bring friends."

"He knows I'm eighteen, right?"

"Uh-huh. And his exact words were: *Of course, you can bring the kid, Char. We're just having dinner on the beach.*"

"Kid?" Kaia wrinkled her nose.

"You are a kid... *kid*," Vera teased as she ruffled Kaia's hair.

The younger woman batted at her hand and grumbled about being an adult.

I smiled as we strolled around the area of the beach that was set up for dining. The resort was so massive that it took us almost ten minutes to walk from our side to the guests' area.

Alex spotted me first and his face lit up. He was so much fun in a silly brother kind of way. The others saw us and waved, except Jamie. He stared at me for a moment then frowned and looked away. His reaction gave me pause. What did that mean? Did he not want me here? *Why?*

Vera interrupted my runaway thoughts. "Jeez, Char," she

murmured as we neared the guys. "Are your boyfriend's friends all models or something?"

"Seriously." Kaia put her fingers together to create a frame. She peered through her fingers. "Look at them sitting under that tiki hut… It's like a freaking GQ cover."

I chuckled. The guys were good-looking alright. "Lincoln is my *ex*," I reminded Vera.

"Who knows?" Kaia gave me a mischievous grin. "Maybe by the end of dinner tonight, he'll be your *current* boyfriend."

I huffed. "Not another word about me and Lincoln from the two of you."

"Okay, okay," she said, holding up her palms.

"How many of Lincoln's friends are single?" Vera asked. "I'm on the prowl tonight."

I rolled my eyes. "I have no clue. You'll have to find that out on your own."

She glanced at me. "And you said they're all super rich?"

"Yup."

"Goodness…" Vera patted her voluminous afro as she eyed the men as if they were dishes set out on an open buffet.

We ended the conversation about Lincoln's crew when he was within earshot. "Char, I'm glad you made it." He swept me into an embrace that caught me off guard. Was it my imagination or was Lincoln becoming increasingly affectionate?

"Thanks for the invite." I turned to my friends. "This is Vera, and this is Kaia. Ladies, meet Lincoln."

"Pleasure, ladies." He shook their hands, but his attention came right back to me. "You look amazing."

My cheeks heated, and I shot my friends a warning glare because they were wearing shit-eating grins.

Alex came to greet us too. "Ladies, ladies. Looking lovely.

Char..." He gave me exaggerated air kisses that made me chuckle. I then introduced him to my companions.

"So, which one of you is the eighteen-year-old?" he asked.

Kaia held up a finger.

"Ah." He took her hand and gave it a friendly pat. "Nice to meet you, kiddo."

Kaia pouted at that, and I had to stifle my amused snort.

He turned to Vera. "And you are...?"

"Twenty-six," Vera announced proudly. She batted her eyelashes with such force they could have kicked up a stiff wind.

"Hello," Alex purred, kissing the back of her hand, which elicited the girliest giggle I'd ever heard from Vera.

Kaia and I exchanged amused glances while Lincoln shook his head and looked skyward. He said he and all the guys had been friends since college so that meant he'd been putting up with Alex's antics for over a decade. That also meant he knew a lot about Jamie...

Damn. Why couldn't my mind just stay away from him? I'd refrained from asking Lincoln too much about Jamie because it might be weird to badger my ex for information about one of his friends whom I was interested in.

As Lincoln escorted us to their tiki hut, I saw Jamie scowling... at *me*? It was disheartening and annoying because our interactions leading up to tonight had been warmer than when we first met. So what was the problem now?

8

JAMIE

I wasn't surprised when Charlotte showed up for dinner because Lincoln had asked us if it would be okay. The others had accepted with gusto. The guys loved Charlotte, which said a lot about her because my friends were typically guarded around people they just met.

I didn't blame them for loving Charlotte already. She was as amazing as Lincoln had said. So sweet, funny, authentic, and full of energy. She was witty too... the complete and perfect package.

However, I would have preferred if she wasn't invited to dinner, but I couldn't voice that when everyone else got so excited about the idea. They would have demanded to know why, and I couldn't tell them that I was uncomfortable watching Lincoln try to win her back because I had the hots for her.

Looking around the table, it was clear that the guys loved having Vera and Kaia around too. Animated conversations circulated, but I didn't take part. My emotions were out of whack. It was caused by a mixture of my disturbing feelings for Charlotte and my upcoming birthday. I'd be thirty-one in two days. Thirty-one years of carrying the heavy burden of guilt…

"We need to do something awesome for your birthday, Jamie," Lincoln said.

"When is his birthday?" Charlotte asked. She looked from me to Lincoln with the usual curious glint in her eyes.

My jaw was locked tighter than a vise grip. "In a couple of days," I grumbled.

"That's why we took this trip," Lincoln shared. "Every year—"

"I'm sure Charlotte isn't interested in what we do every year, Lincoln," I growled.

Silence ensued as everyone gawked at me. Charlotte's expression crumbled, and my heart dropped. She misinterpreted, and it was my fault because my tone was gruffer than I intended. It wasn't that I minded her knowing more about me. I didn't want *Lincoln* to tell her. *I* wanted to be the one to share things with her… to have her to myself for a little while without Lincoln getting in the way. I felt terrible about what I wanted because I shouldn't want it.

"So… Vera, Kaia, you both work here too?" Spencer jumped in to save my ass. "What is it that you do?"

The others dove into the new topic… to quell the tension, I guess. However, Lincoln stared at me, his expression stony and his eyes blazing with fury. Yeah, I knew that I came off like a huge dick.

"Excuse me, I…" I was about to say that I was going to get some air, but we were already outside. "I'll be back."

I stepped out of our rustic beach hut and trekked through the sand to the bar, passing other chatting and laughing diners. Lanterns lit the way, creating a glowing, peaceful ambiance.

The waves lapping against the shore were like music of nature made to calm the soul, but it didn't work on me. I stayed wallowing in my emotional turmoil and regret about hurting Charlotte's feelings. The look on her face would be another thing to haunt me.

When I reached the bar and signaled to the bartender, I wasn't surprised to see Lincoln appear beside me. When I had the bartender's attention, I ordered. "A shot of the strongest whiskey you have. Neat."

"Make that two," Lincoln said. He then proceeded to frown thunderously at me.

I gave him a sheepish look. "I know... You want to deck me in the face. Any chance I can avoid the blow because it's almost my birthday?" My lame attempt at a joke did nothing to calm him down.

"What the fuck is wrong with you, man?" He scoffed. "You didn't have to snap like that."

I sighed. "I *didn't*... It wasn't intentional."

His derisive snort resonated with disbelief. "What, do you not like Charlotte?"

Jesus Christ. I gawked at him. *Not* like Charlotte? I spent every other minute thinking about how much I *did* like her... and why I *shouldn't*. I spent every five minutes wondering if she was going to rekindle her romance with my best friend and what the hell I'd do if they became a thing again*. What a mess.* I tucked my chin into my chest and said, "I'll apologize to her."

He nodded. "The others love her, and I want you to feel the same."

Lincoln wanted me to *love* Charlotte. The irony. If he knew that my feelings toward her were far from the platonic affection like the others, he'd gut me like a fish.

"So we can be one big, happy family?" I asked. There was a

hint of bitterness lacing my words. Hopefully, Lincoln didn't hear it.

He shrugged. "It'll be better if my future girlfriend has great relationships with the men I consider my brothers."

My molars snapped together as I fought off a wave of jealousy. My drink arrived, and I snatched it up to gulp down the entire thing. Wincing against the burn of it going down my throat, I nodded. "Yeah. I'll make things right with her."

Lincoln took his shot and then slapped me on the shoulder. "Are you coming back to the party or what?"

"In a few."

"Okay." After a concerned look, he walked away.

I scowled into my empty glass. Sometimes, I hated the way my friends looked at me when it got to this time of year. I didn't want anybody's pity, for fuck's sake.

"Hey, there, Grumpy Gus."

I glance to my left to see Kaia resting her arms on the bar. She inspected the rows of bottles on the shelves.

"Did you just call me—?"

"Yup. You were scowling at your glass just now. I thought it would burst into flames."

I grunted. "Can I help you?"

"Nope. I took a walk over here because you seemed lonely."

That softened me quickly. She wasn't wrong. I often felt lonely in a crowd.

"I'll have what he's having," she told the bartender.

I raised my eyebrows at the teenager. "Like hell, you will."

"*Aw*, come on, Grumpy Gus. Eighteen isn't that far off from twenty-one."

"Uh-huh. She'll have a soda," I told the bartender.

Kaia sucked her teeth but accepted the decision. She hopped

on a bar stool beside me. "So, what's your deal? Aren't you supposed to be happy or whatnot on your birthday trip?"

I gazed at the young woman with mild amusement. She had a lot in common with Charlotte. They just steamrolled right in and started conversations…. personal ones. "It's complicated."

"That's what old folks always say. *It's complicated.*" She shook her head, obviously disgusted.

I chuckled and the sound surprised me. This kid was something else. "You make it sound like I'm eighty."

She gave me a lopsided grin. "Compared to eighteen, you might as well be."

My laughter echoed again, and I looked at Kaia with appreciation. I needed something to laugh about. She grinned broadly and took up the glass of soda that slid her way.

"So you're buying, right?" she asked.

"Sure."

"In that case, bartender, keep the sodas coming."

Jesus. Kaia was the most entertaining teen I'd ever encountered. I studied her for a moment. She had an indigenous look, but I didn't want to assume.

"Where are you from, Kaia?"

"Here," she confirmed.

"But you live with Charlotte and Vera at the resort?"

"Not exactly. I don't live far from work, but I prefer to stay with Charlotte most nights. I've sort of latched on to her, and she hasn't kicked me out of her space yet." She shrugged. "She's cool like that, you know?"

I took a sip from my refilled glass. "I bet."

"I hate going home," she sighed.

"Why is that?"

She glanced at me with a little pout. "My dad hates me."

I stared at her, a little shocked. That wasn't what I

expected to hear. The thing is, I had no experience with teens. I was an only child, and I had trouble connecting even with my peers… What on earth was I supposed to say in response to that?

"I'm sure that's not true…" That was all I had.

Kaia snorted. "He does because I don't want to be a doctor like him."

The burden of parental expectation… I could relate. "I see. What do you want to do?"

"I want to be like Charlotte," she revealed. Every ounce of despair vanished from her eyes, replaced by utter excitement. "She is so awesome. Do you know she's been to a gazillion countries? Her last job was in South Asia. She's been on safari in Africa. Two years ago, she climbed Mount Kilimanjaro, but she said she didn't get all the way to the top. She's been to Australia…"

I listened with wide eyes as Kaia listed Charlotte's adventures. Hell, like Kaia, *I* wanted to be like Charlotte too. She sounded like she knew how to live. I never really had…

"Wow, that's… seeing the world sounds great."

"Right? But Dad doesn't understand. He won't pay for college or fund any of my trips if I don't do what he wants, so I got a job here to save up some money."

I found the eighteen-year-old pretty damn admirable. She'd barely reached anywhere in life, but she knew what she wanted. She was brave and determined enough to fight for it.

"What do you want to study?"

Her eyeballs rolled around as she considered, and I smiled. "I'm thinking along the lines of anthropology and sociology. I should learn about different people and cultures and how to interact with them if I'm going to travel the world, right?"

I gulped down more whiskey. "Good point."

"You don't think I'm crazy for ignoring a lucrative career in medicine to see the world?"

I glanced at her. She was so full of life and enthusiastic about her future. My zest for life wilted away a long time ago and despite the thirteen years I had on her… it was pretty sad that this young woman had more drive than I did.

I didn't want her to end up like me, dangerously scaling the line of depression at thirty-one. I had money, power, and the world at my fingertips yet, I hadn't truly lived.

"Do what makes you happy, Kaia. Just be smart about it, not that it isn't okay to make mistakes. You're young, so you've got time to figure out life."

She smiled. "Jeez, I wish Dad would sound like you."

My lips lifted upward at the corners. "Don't count your dad out. I don't think he hates you. He just loves you so much that he wants what's best for you, and he's convinced that it's becoming a doctor. Maybe try talking to him again. He might surprise you and understand where you're coming from."

She pulled in a deep breath and nodded. "Okay. You know… You're alright, Grumpy Gus."

My shoulders shook with barely contained amusement. "You are too, kid." I fished my wallet out of my pocket and took out a business card. "If you ever need help while you're seeing the world, give me a call." I meant it. She was pretty much a stranger, but I felt this urge to help at least *one* person achieve something I never had… *Happiness.*

Kaia stared at the business card wide-eyed and then she looked at me. "Like *seriously*? No bullshit?"

I snorted. I liked her. "No bullshit."

"Awesome. Thanks."

I nodded and held up my glass. She tapped hers on it and

then we drank in silence. After a while, I glanced back at our hut. Everyone was there except Charlotte.

"Hey, Kaia. Charlotte hasn't left, has she?"

"No, she said she was taking a walk over to the quieter side of the beach." She pointed in the distance where the lantern lights barely reached.

"Okay. Let me walk you back to the others."

I had to find Charlotte and apologize.

9

CHARLOTTE

"Bye, Vicky. Love you."

I ended the call with my sister. I'd found a comfy, private spot a good distance away from the lively dining area. I sat in one of the cabanas scattered on the beach and stared out at the water. Dad had come up during Victoria's and my conversation, and I was feeling a little sentimental.

He would have loved this view. The moonlight glistened on the ocean's dark surface, and millions of stars lit up the sky. I leaned against the plush cushions of the cabana and got lost in the rhythmic lullaby of the waves. Dad appreciated the beauty of nature and I understood why. Sitting there, surrounded by pure tropical beauty, the cares of the world melted away.

"Charlotte?"

I gasped and jumped at the sound of the timbre disrupting my peace. "Oh, it's you." I scowled at Jamie who stood at the cabana's opening with his hands in his pockets.

His lips twisted into a wry grin. "Yes, it's me... I'm sorry to disturb you."

"Look, if Lincoln twisted your arm to come and apologize, let's just skip it and say you did."

He cleared his throat lightly and rocked back on his heels. "He didn't exactly twist my arm..."

I rolled my eyes. "I don't care for insincere apologies."

"This isn't one. I want... I *need* to apologize. I'm sorry about earlier. I didn't mean to sound..."

The remorse flitting across his features was enough to tell me that he really was sorry.

I sighed. "It's okay. It's none of my business what you do with your time or what you do on your birthday. *You* are none of my business."

I tried desperately to ignore how good he looked framed by the glow of the moon and the backdrop of the stars and ocean. The warm breeze fluttered his hair and the T-shirt he wore. He looked like a hot hero on the cover of a romance novel. *Ugh*. Why did my mind go there?

He pulled his hands from his pockets and shoved one through his hair. "Would it be weird if I said I like that you're interested in me?"

I sat taller and my eyes darted from side to side. While I tried not to read too much into his question, my silly heart shimmied with hope. "Why would it be weird?"

Jamie tucked his chin into his chest and blew out a puff of air. "You know what? Never mind that."

He advanced into the cabana and sat beside me. I almost scooted away from him because his proximity wreaked havoc on my body. My heart thundered and my breath hitched. God, he smelled good... like rich musk and spicy cinnamon. Some super expensive cologne, I bet.

"Whether you want to hear my apology or not, I'm sorry about the way I sounded," he said. "I'm not an asshole, I swear."

I laughed. "Yeah, I figured you aren't, not after what you did for Kaia."

He turned to me with a frown and my face heated up several degrees.

"I didn't mean to eavesdrop. After I told her I was taking a walk, I saw her head to the bar. I followed her to make sure she didn't pull a stunt to get her hands on alcohol… *Teenagers.*"

He laughed, and the sound practically wrapped around me. I tried not to gawk at his softened features.

"Anyway, I heard how you encouraged her. I was stunned that she opened up to you. I've spent six months trying to figure out why she found every excuse to stay here with me in my tiny apartment instead of going home. She wouldn't tell me why."

Jamie shrugged. "Maybe she sensed that I'd understand her."

I turned to stare at him then, not caring if it was weird. Was he saying that he didn't get along with his parents? No matter how much I tried to get over my interest in all things Jamie, I kept getting reeled back in.

"It was sweet of you to engage her and listen like that. You made that girl's night, Jamie… or should I go back to calling you *James Wilfred Winchester*?" I even added the haughty tone and accent he teased me about using the last time.

His lips kicked up at the corners. "Why would you do that?"

I shrugged. "I'm a little confused about our friendship status. It was hard not to notice that you weren't happy about me joining you guys for dinner. I mean, you *scowled* at the sight of me."

He grunted and shook his head. "I keep messing up with you, don't I? Look, Charlotte, it wasn't like that. When I saw you..." He stopped and deep furrows formed in his forehead as if he contemplated finishing his statement or not.

Once again, he struggled to tell me what he was thinking, and I wondered why. In the end, I guess he decided not to tell me what was on his mind because he said, "We're friends. Jamie will do."

My lips twisted into a half-smile because I was disappointed that he kept holding back something from me. "Alrighty, Jamie Wilfred."

"I'm starting to regret telling you my middle name."

"You should. I've got plenty of material for jokes now."

He laughed as he rubbed his chin. "I see why Lincoln likes you."

My eyebrows furrowed. Did Lincoln say that? And what *kind* of like? Surely, as a friend. I shoved the thought aside because Jamie and I were having another one of our moments, and I didn't want to ruin it.

"So, are you okay?" Jamie asked.

"Sure. Why?"

"You seemed a little sad when I arrived." He glanced at the phone I'd placed on the bench beside me. "Did it have anything to do with your phone call?"

Our gazes locked, and I felt that familiar kick in my chest and the flutter in my stomach. I was shocked that he noticed. I was pleased too because maybe his level of interest in me matched my interest in him... Dare I ask him if I was right?

I decided against it and replied, "I was thinking about my dad and about how he'd love to be here on the beach. He died last year."

"I'm sorry."

I nodded and then we sat in silence. It was a comfortable

silence though. After a while, I felt him looking at me and I turned to him.

"What?" I asked with a little nervous laugh. "You're staring."

His throat bobbed up and down as he gulped and then he looked away. "It's nothing. I was just thinking…"

"About?"

"It doesn't matter."

My breath escaped with a little laugh. "You're doing it again."

His eyebrows went up in askance.

"You're holding something back." It was beyond frustrating because I couldn't gauge how he felt about me. I wanted to know so I could avoid making a fool of myself by telling him that I was into him… as more than Lincoln's friend who had become my friend, too.

"Maybe I am, but why does that bother you so much, Charlotte?" he asked.

I held his gaze. You know what? To hell with it. *Carpe diem.* If there was indeed something sizzling between us, I had to seize the moment because we only had days left together.

"Because I like you, Jamie. You know… *like* you…" My face felt as if it would melt off. I probably blushed from the root of my hair to my toes.

He swallowed hard. "I like you too," he said, his voice low and husky. However, he stared at me with a frown, which had me floored.

"And you're not happy about it…?" I asked, cautiously and utterly confused.

"Fuck, no," he said. The words almost sounded like a groan of agony.

My heart dropped into my stomach. "You know what? Let's just forget this whole thing, Jamie." I shot up and took a step to dash out of the cabana before I wilted away from the heat of my embarrassment.

"Dammit!" he hissed as he snagged my wrist. He stood up and tugged me back so I was forced to turn around and face him. "Charlotte, wait... I'm sorry that I keep... I didn't mean... It's more complicated than you think..."

"What are you going on about?" I tried to break free of his hold, but it was futile.

Before I could take my next breath, I found myself pressed against his chest. His breathing was almost as labored as mine as he peered down at me. I swore that when I looked into his eyes, I saw him fighting something. He then stopped battling with whatever it was and pressed his lips to mine.

Instantly, I melted and let out a soft sigh as I wound my arms around his shoulders. His movements were tentative at first but not for long. Soon, his kiss became demanding as his tongue slid between my lips to explore. I tipped on my toes, desperate to press my body closer to his.

I felt that tingling sensation again, the one I felt when I first saw him watching me from across the hotel lobby. The prickling sensation danced across my skin, hiking up my body temperature. The phenomenon was crazy and unlike anything I'd ever felt. I inched my hands up to thread my fingers through his hair. The strands were just as silky as I'd imagined.

A low, rumbling moan vibrated in Jamie's chest, the sound echoing with need. It made my heart race because I was glad to know that he also felt whatever had been sizzling between us since day one.

His hand tightened around my waist as the other cupped my face. He touched me with a desperation that I felt too. It seemed like our kiss went on forever, yet it ended too soon. When he pulled away, an involuntary sound of protest escaped me.

Jamie rested his forehead against mine as we caught our breath. His hold on me gradually loosened until he no longer held me. He took a step back and scrubbed a hand over his face. *"Fuck..."*

His eyes were cloudy with passion and... *regret?*

What? I could practically read the remorse on his face. But he was so into our kiss. He initiated it. I didn't understand.

"Jamie, what's wrong? That was—"

"That was a mistake, Charlotte. It can't happen again."

Fighting through the haze of my arousal and then shock, I scoffed. "Excuse me? A mistake? You didn't kiss me like you didn't mean it, Jamie." Hurt pierced me in the chest. I barely knew this man, and I'd allowed him to hurt my feelings so many times in just two days. What had gotten into me?

His jaw tightened and a muscle ticked on one side. "It doesn't matter."

He kept saying that about every damn thing. "Does *anything* matter to you?" I scoffed.

"Lincoln wants you back," he hissed. "That's why he came here so we shouldn't be kissing, Charlotte."

"Say what now?" My jaw hung on its hinges as I stared at Jamie.

His eyes widened. "He hasn't told you yet. I just kissed his girl *and* ruined the big conversation... *double fuck.*"

I threw my arms out. "If I was Lincoln's girl, I wouldn't be here sucking faces with you, Jamie."

Lincoln wants me back?! This was bad because that was the last thing I wanted.

"Just forget this happened," Jamie said. *"Please.* We can't hurt him."

"But, I—"

Jamie dashed out of the cabana and took off across the beach as if the hounds of hell were on his heels.

"Jamie, wait…"

He didn't turn back. I stood there staring after him, reeling from his revelation and his kiss. I pressed my fingers to my lips because I could still taste him…

10

JAMIE

I'm the worst friend in the world.

As I stared into the ocean from my room's balcony, I rubbed a finger across my lips as if I could somehow erase the feeling of Charlotte's lips against mine. I wish I could, yet I didn't really want to. That kiss was *everything* with *all* the feelings that I'd never experienced in all my years of kissing.

Clutching the banister, I bent over and let out a long, agonizing groan. I felt like I was shoving the knife deeper into Lincoln's back by thinking about how much I enjoyed locking lips with Charlotte.

"Why are you groaning? Are you in pain?" Lincoln's voice boomed behind me.

I nearly jumped out of my skin. Spinning around, I gawked at him as if he caught me red-handed. "No… Jesus, Linc, you scared the shit out of me."

"Sorry." He squinted at me. "Why are you so jumpy? You have been this way since we got back from dinner."

"What...? No... I haven't..." God, I couldn't even look him in the eye.

The suspicion in his eyes remained. "I'm getting the feeling that it isn't just about your upcoming birthday. What else is going on with you?"

My stomach did a sickening flip because I never lied to him—to any of my friends—and I was about to commit the sin now.

"It's nothing more, I promise." I shrugged. "I guess my emotions are more intense this year. Maybe it's because I'm getting older. I don't know, man..."

He nodded, folded his arms over his chest, and leaned against the door frame. As he peered into the night, he said, "Okay. Knowing you, you probably don't want to discuss it further."

I only lifted a shoulder in response because I was too busy wallowing in guilt to think of anything to say.

"So, you spoke to Charlotte..."

Every muscle in my body went taut. "I did."

"She said you apologized."

I watched him closely. He hadn't punched me or tried to shove me off the balcony, so she didn't tell him what else I did.

"Yes."

"Thanks."

"No thanks necessary. I owed it to her."

The problem was that I did way more than apologize... and now I owed it to Lincoln to stay the hell away from Charlotte. I would. I'd avoid her like my life depended on it.

Long after Lincoln left, I lay in bed, staring at the star-studded sky visible through the glass doors. Was Charlotte in bed too? Did she feel as guilty as I did? Would she walk right into Lincoln's arms when he told her he wanted to get back together? The questions swirled in my mind like an overflowing cauldron. I almost went insane.

My brain then shifted gears in a direction that I wished it didn't, but I couldn't help it. I imagined Charlotte lying in bed, staring at the same bejeweled sky, thinking about me as I thought about her. Finally, my eyelids drooped and then closed. My visions were of her. That was the only way I could have her. In my dreams…

We were back on the beach. It was dark as it had been when we kissed for the first time. She wore the floral dress she had on when we met. The one that showed off her long, tanned legs and hugged her breasts. She had nice breasts—not too small or too big. They were perfect handfuls.

She gazed up at me with a smile that although was warm and sweet, also held a hint of mischief. "Were you waiting for me, Jamie?" she asked, her tone thick with sensual suggestion.

"I've been waiting a long time for you, Charlotte." A hell of a long time because in my entire adult life, I'd never felt this magnetism to anyone, and I never expected to feel it with anyone in my lifetime.

Her smile widened. "You're sweet when you're not trying to be detached."

I smiled back because she got me, which was why I was so drawn to her. She saw through the cool, serious facade I kept in place. I was happy that she was here with me. In her company, I relaxed because I could be myself.

"Why did you come tonight?" I asked her.

She reached up to circle my shoulders, pressing her soft breast against my chest. I almost groaned out loud at the wonderful feeling.

"I missed you, and I wanted to kiss you again." Her gaze lingered on my mouth and I ducked my head, inching closer to her.

"What about Lincoln?" I asked.

"You're the one I want…"

My lips touched hers and I felt the same electric spark I did when we first kissed. *I'm the one she wants.*

I felt bad about my friend getting hurt, but I wanted Charlotte to want me and only me. For once, I was selfish and took what I wanted. I did what *I* wanted, not what someone else said was best for me. I kissed the hell out of Charlotte. My fingers were tangled in her luxurious golden mane so I could hold her in place and explore her mouth as thoroughly as possible.

The way she melted against me and moaned made my arousal skyrocket. I had to have more of her.

When we came up for air, she whispered, "What now, Jamie?"

I'd make her completely mine. That's what would come next. Without a word, I hooked my fingers into the straps of her dress and tugged them off her shoulders. Her eyes gleamed with anticipation, telling me to continue. I gave the dress one more tug, and it fell to the sand and pooled around her feet.

She wore nothing under the dress, so she stood before me naked… perfectly naked with her sun-kissed skin, perky tits, and neatly trimmed mound. My mouth watered. She was even lovelier than I'd imagined.

Charlotte grinned and dropped to her knees, taking me by surprise. "Ever had a blow job on the beach, Jamie?"

I gulped. "No."

"I thought so. You seem way too uptight, like you never do anything fun." Her gorgeous brown eyes sparkled with laughter, a look I'd become familiar with in the short time I'd known her. "Good thing you have me now, to show you how to enjoy life a little."

I traced a finger along her jaw and over her plump bottom lip. "A very good thing."

She unbuttoned my pants and unzipped the fly, pulling my pants down just far enough to expose my stiff as a board cock. It pulsed, aching for her touch. When she wrapped her fingers around me, I groaned and arched my back. The sensation of her hot yet gentle touch sent tingles down my spine. Charlotte was perfect in every way.

I watched her through heavy-lidded eyes as she leaned closer, her warm breath caressing my skin. Charlotte's lips trailed along my length, teasingly, sending a wave of desire coursing through me.

"Take me in, Charlotte," I demanded, my voice thick with need. My hands were already bunched in her hair, urging her closer.

"You like being in control, don't you?" she asked with a little smirk.

"I do. It's one of my flaws."

"Hmmm," she hummed, tightening her hold on my shaft. "I'll see what I can do about getting you to loosen up."

Finally, she took me into her mouth, and I almost jumped out of my skin and shuttled to heaven. Each suckle, each flick of her tongue, drove me to the brink of ecstasy.

My hips involuntarily thrust forward, begging her to take me deeper. "Charlotte, you're incredible. I knew you were from the moment I laid eyes on you."

She murmured something and the vibration on my sensitive cock heightened my pleasure.

"You're a goddess…"

A muffled sound of amusement gave me pause. Was she *laughing* at me? I popped one eye open. The sensation of her tongue gliding along my length became less intense until it stopped. I no longer felt the strands of her hair between my fingers. When I looked down, disappointment pierced me between the ribs. My sensual goddess was gone, leaving me to stare at the sand. The laughter intensified, but it didn't sound airy and feminine at all. It was familiar though. It sounded like... *Alex...?*

My eyes flew open and immediately I realized I'd been dreaming. Alex was relaxing on the chaise lounge on the balcony, staring at me through the open doors.

"Alex? What the hell are you doing here?" I growled.

He roared and slapped his knee. "Do you always hump your pillow in your sleep?"

With an irritated huff, I grabbed one of the pillows and sailed it at his head. Laughing, he swatted it away. I picked up the pillow I had been *humping* and covered my semi with it.

Christ. Charlotte giving me a blow job... What a dream. I wish I had stayed in my vision longer to see what else we'd do.

I glowered at a chuckling Alex as I sat up and combed my fingers through my hair. The morning breeze coming off the sea cooled my hot skin.

"How did you get in?"

We all had separate rooms and no one had the other's keycard, and I didn't leave my door unlocked before heading to bed.

Alex raised one eyebrow. "Seriously?"

I snorted. *Right.* He was a genius. He probably hacked the system with his pinky finger or something. Thank God he wasn't an *evil* genius or the entire world would be in trouble.

"What happened to boundaries, man?" I asked. I was only

slightly vexed. Alex was everyone's annoying but lovable younger brother.

"I only came in because we pounded on your door for a good five minutes this morning and you didn't answer."

"What time is it?" I grabbed my phone off the nightstand. My eyes bulged. "Fuck, it's almost noon."

"Exactly." Alex sipped from a mug. "The others went on another adventure with Charlotte. I stayed back to make sure you hadn't died in here. I was seriously worried. You never sleep late."

I sighed. Well, then, I guess I could forgive him for breaking and entering. He was right. Sleeping in wasn't my thing.

"You alright?" He watched me through narrowed eyes.

"Yeah. Took me a while to get to sleep last night." Because of my guilt about betraying Lincoln and my non-stop thoughts about Charlotte. "I was tired."

"I heard you murmuring about her." Alex smirked.

I went absolutely still as my eyes locked on his face. *Fucking hell*. Did I say Charlotte's name? I was so busted. "Who?"

"Your *goddess*." He chuckled. "Who is she and why haven't I met her yet?"

Thank God. "Nobody. Men have wet dreams about random women all the time."

"Based on the amount of sickeningly sweet praises and words of adoration you murmured about your *goddess*, I'm calling bullshit. Come on, you can share. Your secret will be safe with me."

As my gaze locked onto him, my heart pounded. What if I told him the truth? Would he think less of me, that I was deliberately trying to swipe Charlotte away from Lincoln? Which I *wasn't*. I'd been fighting tooth and nail to not feel what I felt for her. But that would be what everyone might think. That would be what Lincoln would assume, and he'd hate me... *No one can know.*

Alex tilted his head as he studied me. "Is it that woman your father wants you to marry?"

Before, at the mention of my father's ridiculous demand to marry a "suitable woman of equal status", I never felt anything. No disdain, no reluctance... nothing, because I didn't give a shit. I thought I'd never find a woman who could capture my interest enough for me to care about a real relationship so an arranged marriage was just another criterion of being a Winchester. After meeting Charlotte, fuck Dad's idea about tying myself to some generic socialite who probably has a dull personality and no mind of her own. I wanted more because I'd seen the possibility of getting it.

"No. I've never even met her."

"Huh." Alex lifted an eyebrow. "Then who were you fantasizing about?"

"I'm not discussing my sex dream with you, Alex. *Boundaries.*"

He let out a dramatic sigh and stood up. "Fine. Now that I've seen for myself that you're not dead, let's go. I told everyone that as soon as you were up, we'd join them."

The thought of seeing Charlotte after last night, after my hot dream... *fuck no.* I couldn't parade around with her and Lincoln, pretending that everything was a-okay.

"I can't today." Rubbing the bridge of my nose, I said, "I'm feeling a little under the weather. Must be the change in climate. You go ahead."

"Are you sure? I can hang out here."

"No, I know you want to have fun with the others."

"*And* Charlotte. She's so hot."

That she is and more. "I hadn't noticed," I lied.

Alex snorted. "Lincoln is a lucky bastard."

I gritted my teeth but kept my expression carefully guarded.

11

CHARLOTTE

"Hey, Char. Wait up."

I glanced over my shoulder to see Lincoln hurrying up the hill toward me. *Shit.* I'd gone out of my way to avoid him all morning. That was a little easier to accomplish because my group was bigger today. Two instructors called out so the rest of us picked up the slack. The larger group had worked out in my favor until now.

Slowing my steps, I forced a smile. "Hey, Lincoln." Relaxing around him after what Jamie revealed last night was impossible.

He fell into step beside me and I immediately felt a wave of unease. I didn't know how to act around him anymore. Every word and gesture would feel like I was walking on eggshells because I was afraid of doing or saying the wrong thing. I didn't want to risk unintentionally giving him any idea that I was interested in rekindling our romance.

"What's up with you today?" he asks.

When I glanced at him, his penetrating stare was fixed on me, so I faced forward. "What do you mean?"

"Is it me or have you been avoiding me all morning?"

Busted. "What? Of course not. It's just that I have a bigger group today and I don't want the newcomers to think I'm giving you and your friends special attention." Not wanting him to be too suspicious, I forced myself to be the easy-going woman he knew. Lowering my voice, I added, "Your group is my favorite, but let's keep that between us." My conspiratorial wink made him laugh.

"Your secret is safe with me." After a beat of silence, he said "Still, you were so jumpy this morning."

Dammit. I stifled a groan, wishing he'd drop it.

Watching me closely, he began, "Jamie didn't…"

My heart stopped and then stuttered back to life to race like a frightened rabbit fleeing a predator. *Oh, God. He knows. Did he see us? Is he pissed? Hurt?*

"He didn't offend you again last night, did he? You said he apologized but maybe he said something you didn't like…?"

Relief flooded me and my poor heart slowed to a normal pace. It wasn't that I was afraid to be honest with Lincoln about my feelings for his friend. What I was afraid of was hurting him. When I glanced at him, a heavy feeling settled on my chest. I'd have to disappoint him sooner or later. Maybe tell him about Jamie…

Or maybe it wasn't worth ruining our friendship over something that wouldn't last. I mean, Jamie and I were from completely different worlds. He would leave the island in a few days, and I'd likely never see him again. I'd never been so confused about anything in my life. For once, I wasn't confident in my ability to make the right choice.

"Absolutely not," I replied. "Jamie was a perfect gentleman." *And then he kissed me with enough passion to light the entire island on fire.* "I didn't get much sleep last night, and I had a shit ton of coffee this morning."

"That's right. I remember how jumpy you get when you have too much caffeine."

"Yeah…"

"I know you pretty well, don't I, Char?" Lincoln smiled at me. "I wonder if there's a lot more that I haven't learned yet."

Crap on toast! Was this the moment? Was he going to announce that he wanted us to be a thing again? *What should I do?* My gaze swiveled around the forest, desperately searching for a way out of the conversation. Fortunately, the zip line platform came into view.

"We're here!" I point ahead. "Are you ready to soar, Linc?"

"Of course. First, there's something—"

"Hey, hold that thought. I have to get started on a safety briefing."

Lincoln blew out a breath. The slightest tinge of color highlighted his cheekbones. "Right. Go ahead and do your thing. We'll talk later."

Swallowing hard, I scurried to the platform to mount the first few steps so everyone had a view of me. "Ladies and gentlemen, I hope you're ready for our ziplining adventure."

A chorus of *"yeah"* and whistles filled the air.

"Before we get started, I'm going to go through the safety protocols…" I glanced at Lincoln once more. He gave me a thumbs-up. I felt so stupid ducking and dodging to avoid a conversation… as if I wasn't a mature adult.

As I led the group up the spiral staircase to the launch platform, I couldn't help thinking about Jamie. He was absent, and I wondered if it was because he didn't do heights or because he was avoiding me. If he was… I wasn't even sure how I felt about it. Perhaps it was for the best.

* * *

"Vera, let's go out tonight," I announced as I waltzed into her room.

She lowered the magazine that she'd been engrossed in to raise her eyebrows at me. "To…?"

"I don't know… a club…" *Anywhere but here.*

Her gaze narrowed on me. "What about Kaia? If we hit the club tonight, she can't tag along. She'll feel left out."

"She went home this evening."

"Huh." Vera swung her feet off the bed. "That's new."

"She took Jamie's advice. I think she's trying with her dad again."

"That's great. So…" Vera studied me with curiosity. "Are we going out with the gang?"

By the gang, she meant Lincoln's group of friends. "No, just us girls."

"Hmmm." After a moment's consideration, she shrugged. "Okay, let's do it. We haven't left this place in a while."

Relief flooded me. Now, I had a valid reason to dodge Lincoln. He'd hinted at us having dinner tonight but he didn't get to deliver an official invitation on account of me giving him the slip all day. I was sure that he'd call to invite me to dinner and when he did, I could tell him I was hanging out with Vera tonight.

"Awesome. I'm going to find something to wear. We'll leave in an hour."

As I walked out of her room, she called, "If I see you in yoga pants and a T-shirt, I'll lose my shit. Wear something slutty!"

I rolled my eyes but chuckled. "Something slutty," I muttered. I didn't think I owned anything in that category but I'd try my best.

A little over an hour later, I was dressed... in something *semi*-slutty. The slinky pink dress clung to my body like a second skin but the neckline covered my chest entirely. The back, however... I spun around to check it out in the mirror. There was *no* back so I had to go without a bra and the tiniest pair of panties that I owned. While the dress wasn't too short, the daring slits at the sides revealed a great portion of thighs with each step. I decided that the dress was slutty enough to please Vera.

As I grabbed my purse and threw a few essentials into it, I realized that I'd left my phone in Vera's room. I recalled putting it on her dresser when I went to demand that we go out for the night.

Locking up, I scurried out of my apartment and headed to Vera's. "All I have to do is avoid being alone with Lincoln for a few more days," I muttered to myself. And I definitely had to avoid Jamie too. Once they both disappeared from my life, things would go back to normal.

Vera stepped out before I reached her door. After an assessment, she gasped. "You look hot. Where have you been hiding that dress?"

I snorted. "In the darkest recesses of my closet. I didn't think it would ever see the light of day."

"That's because you spend every waking moment doing crazy outdoor stuff that doesn't require sexy dresses."

She handed me my phone and I gave her a pout as I grabbed it. She sounded like Mom. I refused to apologize for not being a *girly girl* as Mom would say. When I aimed for the back exit of the employee quarters, Vera pointed in the opposite direction.

"We're going to the hotel lobby," she announced.

"Why?"

"Because we have to go meet our escorts for the night."

"Huh?"

"Okay, so you're going to love me for this." She grinned broadly. "You left your cell in my room and Lincoln called. I only answered to tell him you didn't have your phone, and he mentioned wanting to invite you to dinner. I told him we were going out and then I had a brilliant idea."

Oh, no. I gazed at her with horror as we walked, praying that she didn't say it.

"I invited Lincoln and his friends to party with us. He loved the idea and said they were all in."

Dammit, she said it. *All* his friends? My heart sank into my stomach.

"Isn't that great?" She clapped her hands with glee. "You're welcome, by the way."

I snorted inwardly. She had no idea what she'd done. "For…?"

"The goal is to spend as much time with Lincoln as possible, right? I figured you wouldn't mind if I invited him."

Swallowing hard, I said, "Not at all."

I couldn't be mad at Vera. She thought she was helping. I'd just have to resign myself to stewing in awkwardness as I hung out with Jamie and Lincoln, pretending that everything was cool.

How hard could it be? Besides, Jamie had skipped out on the activities with his friends today—I was pretty sure he was avoiding me—so maybe he wouldn't come out with us.

Of course, my hopes were dashed when we rounded the corner into the posh lobby and I saw him standing at the exit with his hands in his pockets. His shoulders were so rigid, I was sure that they ached. I guess he was just as reluctant about our impromptu group date as I was.

"There they are." Vera pointed to the guys. "Tonight is going to be so much fun."

"So much fun," I repeated with little enthusiasm. It was going to be downright torture.

"I have another surprise."

"You do?" I was so nervous that I was terrified about what she'd say.

"Lincoln said he'd get a limo so we could all travel together. When was the last time you luxuriated in a limo?"

I blew out a long breath. The last time I was in one, Lincoln and I broke up. Now I'd be forced to sit in one with my ex who wanted me back and his friend who *I* wanted. Yup, it was going to be sheer torture. Still, I slapped on a smile and waved to the guys.

1 2

JAMIE

You have got to be fucking kidding me. I went out of my way to avoid Charlotte only to end up sitting beside her at the back of a damn limo. As we'd all scrambled inside, somehow we ended up together. Lincoln sat on her other side.

When we had settled in, I saw the moment Charlotte realized that she was sandwiched between us. Her eyes widened and flashed with disbelief as her gaze swiveled between us. She had then schooled her expression.

Yeah, I saw the irony of the situation too. If I wasn't so disturbed by it, I would have laughed.

"Thanks for inviting us." Alex smiled at Vera and then Charlotte. "It's nice to get away from the resort. I'm enjoying it, but I'm glad we get to see a bit more of the island."

From my periphery, I saw Charlotte smile, but it wasn't as bright as usual. I got the impression that our group outing wasn't her idea. As everyone chatted, I subtly admired Charlotte. She looked amazing… good enough to eat. Images of her on her knees with my cock in her mouth surfaced in my mind. It was the worst moment for me to conjure pictures from that dream. I shifted uncomfortably and then eyed the minibar.

"Hey, Alex. I'm in the mood for something strong. Why don't you work your magic?" I nodded to the bar.

He grinned and pointed at me. "Start the party early... My man! You know, Jamie, this is more like it. You're finally getting into birthday mode."

"Uh-huh." All I wanted was a few stiff drinks to hopefully quench my thirst for the goddess sitting beside me and to dampen my jealousy about the way she chatted and smiled with Lincoln. "Make sure it's *very* strong," I said.

"You got it." Alex switched seats with Michael for better access to the drinks and went to work.

"So, are you an expert at mixing or something, Alex?" Charlotte asked.

"I worked as a bartender in high school."

"What?" Charlotte gawked at him and he chuckled.

"By then, I was an expert at making infallible fake IDs." He shrugged. "I needed the job and the tips for college tuition."

His self-congratulatory smirk made Charlotte shake her head. "Wow..."

"He had the potential to become a criminal mastermind," Spencer said.

"Yeah. Luckily, he met us," Michael added.

Charlotte studied each of them quietly for a moment. When she turned to look at me, my heart skipped a beat. "You're an interesting group," she said.

"I'm glad you think so." Lincoln smirked at her. He then slung an arm around her shoulders and whispered something in her ear.

The jealous beast inside me that had apparently been in

hibernation until I met Charlotte lifted its head. Jealousy surged through me with such intensity that it shocked me to the core. Before now, I'd never had an envious bone in my body, especially toward my friends. It took one woman for me to resent Lincoln at the moment and I wasn't sure what to do with the feeling.

Swallowing hard, I turned away from them to stare out the window. I focused on the swaying palm trees lining the sides of the road instead.

* * *

The vibrant lights of the nightclub were like beacons, welcoming us before our limo pulled up to the curb. The guys climbed out first. Spencer, ever the gentleman, assisted Vera out of the vehicle. Without thinking, I turned to offer Charlotte a hand only to realize that Lincoln beat me to it.

Of course, he did. He had more right to help her than I did. My jaw tightened as I watched Lincoln's hand wrap around Charlotte's smaller one. A clap on the shoulder forced my attention away from the duo.

"What are you frowning about?" Alex asked. "Careful, you might outdo the professional scowler over there."

He pointed to Micheal who was frowning at the crowded entrance of the club. Like me, this was probably the last place he wanted to be, but he'd endure the night because everyone else wanted to do this. Maybe I'd stick with Micheal tonight. We could find a corner and keep socialization to a minimum.

"Oh, my gosh. Look at that line." Vera gawked at the crowd at the entrance. "We'll never get in."

"Let me see what I can do," Lincoln said.

"Work your magic, Mr. Hollywood," Alex drawled.

Lincoln approached the two security guards who were checking IDs. It didn't take long before their no-nonsense masks turned into smiles of recognition. Despite retiring from the NFL, he was still a legend. I'd always watched the way people gushed over him because of his celebrity status with amusement. Tonight, however, it didn't make me laugh. Instead, I gazed at Charlotte with a frown. Was she impressed by Lincoln's celebrity status?

Lincoln grinned at us as he waved us over. The people in line watched with curiosity and resentment as we skipped over them and walked through the red rope barriers. Music assaulted my ears as we stepped inside.

Michael eyed the crowd with disdain. "There are less crowded VIP sections here, right?"

"But we can't afford the VIP sections," Charlotte said.

Michael's eyebrows popped up as he gazed at her with amusement and Spencer chuckled. I liked that she forgot who she was partying with. It said a lot about how down-to-earth my group of friends was, and I'd always liked them for that.

As if reading Michael's expression, she blushed and giggled. "Billionaires... right. In that case, lead the way to the VIP section."

Minutes later, we were ushered to a part of the club where the atmosphere shifted from chaotic to much calmer.

"This is more like it," Michael said as he aimed for a table. He then pulled out his phone and started tapping away.

We all settled in and the drinks soon started flowing. I was quiet for the most part because I was busy watching Lincoln and Charlotte's interactions.

Did they have the talk yet? Was she officially his girlfriend again? The way he'd been touching her with familiarity all night said she might be. The touches were innocent enough but still...

Charlotte didn't seem the type to let just any man invade her personal space. Not knowing what was going on between them was driving me crazy.

Vera approached with a glass in hand. She smiled at me. "Hey, Jamie. You don't seem to be enjoying yourself."

How could I? My best friend was all over the woman I wanted and there wasn't a damn thing I could do about it.

"Clubs aren't my scene." I gulped the liquor in my glass.

Vera perched on the leather bench beside me. "It doesn't seem to be Michael's either. He hasn't looked up from his phone since he got here."

"Don't mind him, he's probably chatting with his nanny."

"Oh, he has kids?"

"A daughter."

"I see…"

I swallowed a smile because Vera sounded disappointed. She showed interest in Alex the other night, but she probably realized that he was a playboy. I guess she saw that Spencer wasn't much better. Lincoln was all about Charlotte. I must have been taken out of the lineup because all she'd ever seen me do was brood, so Michael had likely been her last hope. She probably assumed he was married after my revelation. He was single, but it wasn't my place to tell her that.

After a heavy sigh, she got up. "I'd ask you to dance but I'm sure you'd decline, so I'm gonna head to the dance floor solo."

My lips twisted into a ghost of a smile. "Sorry."

"It's fine."

She took a step away then stopped. Turning back, she studied me with an intensity that made me frown. She then looked away and I followed her gaze to where Charlotte and Lincoln were in deep conversation.

When Vera turned back to me, she hit me with a shocking

suggestion. "You know, Jamie, if you like her, just tell her. I know it might be complicated, but the heart wants what it wants, right?"

My eyes bulged and my jaw slackened. Had Charlotte told Vera about our kiss or had she figured it out because of my longing looks at her friend? I'd tried to be subtle but surely *someone* would catch on to me watching Charlotte like a creepy stalker. I didn't think the guys realized, especially Lincoln, but... I blew out a breath as I held Vera's gaze. Women were probably more intuitive about that kind of thing.

"I have no idea what you're talking about, Vera," I replied.

There was no way I'd act on what I felt for Charlotte. For the sake of my friendship with Lincoln, I *couldn't*.

Her mouth curved into a faint ironic twist. "Right... Later, Jamie. Try to have some fun."

After Vera took off, I sat there staring into space and practically drowning my anxiety over the Charlotte situation in alcohol. However, my mind kept going back to her. Her smile, the way her eyes twinkled when she laughed, her humor, and her energy. It was so easy to relax and talk to her when we had our brief private moments. The kiss we shared replayed in my mind because I simply couldn't stop it. Every good thing I felt that night rose to hit me in the chest. I wanted to feel them again.

However, loyalty to Lincoln and the *bro code* flashed in my mind like a warning sign. I couldn't possibly do what Vera suggested.

"Jesus," I whispered, pressing my fingers against my tightly shut eyes.

I couldn't take the mental torture anymore, so I got up and walked to the metal rails to search for Vera.

13

JAMIE

*V*era was easy to spot in the crowd because she had the biggest hair and the ends were dyed blonde. I headed to the stairs to get to the dance floor. Vera saw me barreling toward her and grinned. She twirled and beckoned to me with her finger.

"Jamie, you decided to take my advice and have fun."

I dodged a couple gyrating dangerously close to me. "Not really. I don't know the first thing about having fun." I had to shout above the music. "I've been uptight my entire life… so I've been told."

Vera threw her head back and laughed. "So what are you doing on the dance floor?"

I snorted. "Certainly not dancing. I don't know how."

Standing there while everyone moved in rhythm made me feel so out of place.

Vera shook her head and gave me a look that I was sure meant: *Aww, you poor thing.* She placed her hands on my shoulders. "Relax, Jamie. Just let loose and move to the music."

"Uh-huh..." I awkwardly placed my hands on her waist and did what had to be the most rhythmless two-step in history.

Vera didn't laugh hysterically at my attempt to dance—she was too sweet.

"I wanted to ask you something," I shouted.

"Ah, the real reason why he braved the dance floor. She must mean a lot to you."

Once again, she caught me off guard. I stared at her for a moment, taking in the amusement that lit up her eyes. Was she fucking psychic? "How do you—?"

"I'm not stupid, Jamie. The way you look at Charlotte says it all." She must have read the dismay on my face because she smiled and said, "Don't worry, I doubt anyone else has noticed... yet."

I blew out a breath. I'd better keep my eyes off Charlotte in the company of others from now on.

"So, what's your question?" Vera asked.

I leaned closer to her so she could hear my every word. "If I were to do what you suggested earlier..."

Her eyebrows elevated in silent encouragement for me to continue.

"Don't you think that would make me the biggest asshole and the worst friend in the world?"

The anticipation that I felt as I waited for her answer bordered on ridiculous. A grown man seeking validation like this... so sad.

Vera took her time with her answer, but finally, she exhaled. "Well, Jamie, I barely know you, but I'm very observant."

Obviously. She had been in the same space with Charlotte and me all of two times and she caught on to my secret feelings.

"The thing is..." Her eyebrows puckered. "You don't strike

me as a bad friend or an asshole—a bit broody on occasion—but not at all assholish."

I snorted. "Thanks…"

"So I doubt that you *deliberately* developed the hots for the woman your friend wants to win back."

I shook my head emphatically. As a matter of fact, I wished I could magically stop liking Charlotte. "I feel awful. Not about being into her but about what it will do to Lincoln."

Vera grimaced. "You're in a tough spot, Jamie."

That was an understatement. A couple bumped into us and I shuffled away, taking Vera with me. I wouldn't stop making a fool of myself on the dance floor until she confirmed that I wasn't a monster for wanting a woman I shouldn't.

"So… Do you have any other suggestions…?" I watched her hopefully.

This was so out of character for me. I was usually the one people asked what to do, and I never failed to have sure solutions. This thing with Charlotte and Lincoln had me seriously messed up in the head… and the heart.

Vera smiled sympathetically. "I can't tell you what to do, and you know that, but I can tell you that I don't think you're awful for being attracted to someone. I can also tell you that…" She glanced up and so did I.

Charlotte was on the second floor, still in the VIP section, dancing with Lincoln. Yet, she stared down at us. When our eyes met, she looked away.

"Your interest in a certain someone is obviously reciprocated."

I looked up at Charlotte again to find her stealing glances at Vera and me as Lincoln said something to her. He then leaned closer to her—so close that his lips touched her ear. He whispered something because she pulled her gaze away from me, smiled, and nodded at him.

I saw red... green, rather, as if the intensity of my jealousy mounted each time I saw those two together. Surely, I'd explode soon.

"Are you okay, Jamie?"

Returning my attention to Vera, I stopped dancing—*shuffling, really*—and let her go. "I don't know yet..."

She frowned.

"Thanks, Vera. I'm going to go get some air. Can I escort you back upstairs first?"

"I'm going to enjoy the dance floor a little while longer. I'll see you later."

After a curt nod, I weaved my way through the crowd, feeling ashamed about my illogical jealousy and angry as fuck that Charlotte might have just said yes to Lincoln's *let's reconnect* proposal. They looked pretty cozy...

I headed to a set of open doors on the other side of the room. It turned out to be a terrace that overlooked the ocean. I liked that just about anywhere you were in Kohala, you could see the water.

The area was fairly empty. There were just a few people scattered about. The music was still audible from out here, but not as blaring. I found the darkest corner and disappeared into it. I figured the fresh air would calm me down and help me get my shit together.

"Damn..." I sighed as I raked my fingers through my hair.

A moment later, I heard a familiar voice that ignited warmth in my chest. It was always so melodious and soothing. "Jamie?"

I stifled a groan. "What are you doing out here, Charlotte?"

She peered into the shadows and I stepped forward a little

so she could see me. "I saw you slip out and followed to make sure you're okay."

"I'm fine."

She stepped in my corner, and I had to suppress another groan. She was clueless about the havoc she wrecked with her proximity. We proceeded to watch each other, no one saying a word.

In order to break the awkward staring contest, I asked, "Did you follow me out here to *glare* at me, Charlotte, or is there something on your mind?"

She was indeed throwing daggers at me with her eyes, and I couldn't fathom what she had to be upset about.

"You and Vera looked pretty cozy," she said.

My eyes snapped to her face. Vera was right. Charlotte was as into me as I was into her. Of course, I had suspected. Each time we interacted, I felt the connection and she had made it pretty clear that she was interested in something other than friendship, *but...*

"So did you and Lincoln." The words came out as a low growl and I hadn't intended to take that tone. Clearing my throat, I asked, "Has he asked you yet?"

Charlotte sighed and stepped closer to lean against the terrace's guard rails. The position placed her directly in front of me. We stood so close that I could see the hint of pink in her cheeks even in the dim lighting.

Instead of answering, she asked, "Do you like Vera?"

My eyes narrowed on her. If she insisted on playing... fine. "She's nice."

"You know what I mean."

"Why does it matter to you if I do?" A flash of irritation lit up her orbs and my lips twitched. Admittedly, I just wanted to see the fierceness in her eyes and the way her cheeks burned crimson. I chuckled. "I'm not into your friend, Charlotte. We were just talking."

"Oh…" She looked down and I studied the top of her head.

"It's your turn to answer my question," I said.

Her eyes met mine again. "No, he hasn't asked yet."

"Hmm. If he had, what would your answer have been?"

"Seriously?" She scoffed.

I lifted my eyebrows and she rolled her eyes.

"Maybe I would have told him that my interest lies elsewhere… in someone else."

She lifted her chin defiantly as if daring me to ask if it was me. It had better be me… even though we couldn't do anything about it. That thought reminded me why we shouldn't be alone in a dark corner with our mouths practically touching. I hadn't even noticed that I'd inched closer to her and lowered my head.

Catching up on myself, I drew back. "You should get back inside. Lincoln will miss you."

"He went to find a quiet place to take a phone call. Something about a client."

I shook my head. No doubt it was one of his athletes badgering him about something crazy like how to operate an oven… Seriously. Some of his adult clients acted like spoiled, rich, children who saw him as their parent.

"Still, you should go back inside. We don't want him finding us—"

"Doing what, Jamie? *Talking?* What's the big deal?"

"The big deal is the other night," I practically growled. I didn't mean to be harsh with her but my frustration—with myself—had me on edge. Of all the women to be interested in, it had to be my friend's ex. If I could kick myself in the ass, I would. If I could stop wanting Charlotte… I would.

She folded her arms and glared at me. "We kissed. So what?

Why do we keep doing this, Jamie? Why keep skirting around the obvious? We're into each other. You act as if that's the worst thing—"

"It *is*," I bit out.

"Why because I dated Lincoln eons ago? Look, Jamie, I know—"

"No, you don't know, Charlotte." I took another step away from her. "We need to end this now. No further discussion. And that kiss was a mistake."

"You're so full of shit," she snapped. Her eyes sparked with annoyance. The orbs rivaled the tiny fireballs scattered in the night sky.

I glowered at her. "You know, in my world, no one talks to me like that. They don't dare."

"Well, Jamie, I don't care what you're the CEO of and how many people you get to boss around. Here, your severe scowl and arrogance have no effect. I won't stop talking about something because *you* say so. Welcome to *my* world."

I shoved my hands into my pockets as I studied her features, alive with emotions. She was so hot, especially with that sexy pout. The things I wanted to do to that mouth... My gaze dipped to travel over her curves in the tight dress. The things I wanted to do to that body.

Somehow, I managed to hold back my amusement at her response. Charlotte had the kind of attitude that a man like me, who was always in control of every situation, couldn't help but find intriguing. Her sass and defiance stimulated my mind *and* body.

However, I couldn't do this with her. Yeah, I considered Vera's advice and had been leaning toward it, but then I saw Lincoln and Charlotte together and remembered why I shouldn't complicate matters. I raked my fingers through my hair, my hand shaking with agitation.

"Just go back inside, Charlotte. We're *done*."

"But—"

"We have nothing to talk about."

She huffed. "You're such a coward."

Fury, frustration, confusion… *everything* came to a boil. Why did she insist on making this so hard for me? I wasn't able to reign in my temper.

"I could be or maybe I'm a loyal friend who refuses to hurt a man I consider my brother over some woman I just met!"

The air crackled with uneasy silence and then she took a step back, her face flushed. Charlotte searched my face as if she didn't believe me. I kept my expression hard, hoping to convince her that I wasn't lying through my teeth—about her being *some woman*, anyway. She was so much more than that.

Finally, she believed what I wanted her to. Without another word, she turned and walked away.

I stared at her retreating form. As I took in her hunched shoulders, I felt like scum. I deserved a bullet in the foot for that, but it had to be done.

14

CHARLOTTE

"Where are your boyfriends this morning, Char?" My co-worker, Josh, smirked at me.

I bit the inside of my cheeks hard to keep my temper in check. After last night, I was not in the mood for anybody's shit. *"Boyfriends?"*

Josh took up a harness used for indoor rock climbing to assess it. "You know, the bunch of guys who stroll in here every morning, demanding you as their guide."

I rolled my eyes. He was such a hater. "I'm never salty when guests come in here and request you, am I, Josh?"

He glared. "All I'm saying is, you girls have the upper hand around here. All you have to do is flash a little cleavage and the guys flock to you."

Kendra, another outdoor guide, overheard. She scoffed as she glowered at Josh and then glanced at me with an *is-he-for-real* look.

I shook my head. "You know what I think, Josh? You're just pissed that I've turned you down multiple times when you asked me out. Man up, stop being a sassy woman about it, and don't disrespect me again."

Kendra guffawed, slapped a hand over her mouth, and scurried toward the station that housed a row of mountain bikes.

Josh's jaw almost hit the floor. His eyes narrowed to slits and I straightened from where I leaned against the wall to give him a seething glare. A muscle ticked in his jaw and he turned to walk away.

"That's what I thought, you punk," I grumbled, scowling at his back.

I'd met plenty of Joshes in my line of work and I knew how to handle them. Plus, Dad always said that my tongue was as sharp as a hornet's sting… unexpected, painful, and left my victim reeling with disbelief. He never made me feel bad about having a smart mouth, unlike Mom who hated that I wasn't a *proper lady*.

I hadn't been my usual tough and sassy self last night though. Jamie stuck it to me real good and I ran away like a sissy on the verge of tears. I hadn't even retaliated to hurt his feelings the way he'd hurt mine. It was scary how much control someone I barely knew had over my emotions. How did I let that happen?

When I spotted the guys walking in, I wiped away whatever sadness might be present on my face. They all looked so eager about what adventure I'd surprise them with today, and I felt bad about disappointing them. I glanced out the window as they neared. The sky was darker than it had been five minutes ago and the rain had already started.

I forced aside my sour mood and smiled at the guys. "Good morning, gentlemen."

"Morning, Charlotte," they chorus.

I received grins from everyone except Lincoln and guilt

pricked me in the chest. Last night, after we got back from the club, he expressed frustration about me seemingly evading every opportunity to talk for the last couple of days. Of course, I proved his suspicion by quickly making my escape with a lame excuse of being exhausted.

In my defense, I couldn't stand in the hotel's lobby and listen to Lincoln tell me he wanted me back only to disappoint him by telling him that I wasn't interested. Not when I was still languishing in hurt and humiliation over the way Jamie shut me down.

Michael, Spencer, and Alex eyed us with curiosity as if they noticed the shift of energy between Lincoln and me. However, no one said a word.

"Where's the fifth member of your boy band?" I joked.

Jamie was missing… and maybe it was for the best because I wasn't enthusiastic about facing him.

Spencer chuckled. "We have no idea. He was MIA this morning."

"Oh…" Not wanting to show too much interest in Jamie, I announced, "I hate to do this, guys, but no outdoor fun for today."

Alex glanced outside. "We figured we wouldn't be able to do anything crazy like hang gliding today, but what about something a little less adventurous like a nice walk in the forest? We can get raincoats."

My eyebrows shot up. "You guys are probably the most eager for outdoor activity of any guest I've ever met."

"Of course, we are," Michael said. "We sit behind desks day in, day out. This week is the most exercise we'll get all year."

"Ah, I get it now. Still, I can't take you guys out. It isn't safe out there. The paths winding through the forest will be flooded soon if they aren't already."

"Well, then we have a problem," Lincoln said, staring at his phone. "I haven't checked my messages all morning."

He held up the device and we all squinted at it. There was a text from Jamie.

Linc... left early for a solo walk. Really needed to be alone today.

"If he was strolling on the beach, surely he would have been back once the rain started," Spencer reasoned.

Lincoln sighed. "I'm pretty sure he went further than the beach."

"What makes you so sure?" I asked as I gazed at the ever-darkening clouds that let out a deluge of water.

"Today is his birthday," everyone chorused solemnly.

My gaze moved over every concerned face. "Right..."

I was missing something major, but it was none of my business what the deal was about Jamie's birthday. He'd been crystal clear last night. There was nothing between us.

Still, he was a guest who was in danger out there alone. I was just as worried as his friends were. Jamie was an asshole to me, but I didn't want anything bad to happen to him.

"I have to go get him," I said. "It will be near impossible for a guest to navigate the terrain in this downpour but... where exactly did he go?"

"He headed in the direction of our first hike," Spencer said.

"What makes you so sure?" I asked.

"We discussed the scenery and the serenity after the hike. Jamie mentioned wanting to trek the same path again and go further."

I let out a long exhale. "Crap." That particular path was already washed out. I was certain of it. Jamie must have been spinning in circles as we spoke. "Okay, no problem. I'll go get him." I was already heading over to where I stashed my backpack earlier. There were raincoats and water boots in the storeroom.

"*We'll* go get him," Lincoln said, coming up behind me.

The others followed, nodding their agreement.

I scoffed as I turned to face them. *Five* guests in danger instead of one? If anything happened, I bet I'd be the one to catch all the shit.

"Absolutely not. You guys are going to go back to your rooms where you'll stay nice and dry and *safe* because I'm sure the resort isn't looking for a lawsuit."

Lincoln huffed. "He's our friend, Char. We're not leaving him out there in possible danger. Alright, what do you say just you and I make the trip? The others can stay here if that will make you feel better."

My eyebrows furrowed as I considered. Lincoln was probably more athletic than the others. He could handle the walk but not the unfamiliar and hazardous terrain. "No."

"Charlotte." He had that edge to his voice. The one where easy-going Lincoln took a back seat and he got all stubborn and incredibly bossy. "You are not going out there alone."

"Why? Because I'm a girl?" I was kidding, but I still watched him closely to see if that was really it.

His eyebrows snapped together into irritated lines. "Because you said it's dangerous."

"Yeah, for someone who isn't familiar with the place. I can hike those woods with my eyes closed, rain or shine. I'll move faster alone, and you know it. We're wasting time standing here arguing about it."

Lincoln ran his fingers through his hair as he warily looked outside. It wasn't a hurricane, just a surprise tropical storm but it looked like all hell had broken loose out there.

"Fine, just be careful."

I gave him a grateful smile. No matter what, I'd always care about Lincoln and he'd always care about me.

"I will. I promise."

I quickly gathered my gear and went on my *rescue Jamie* mission.

15

JAMIE

I was so fucked... from all angles. I did a three-sixty, blinking rapidly as water assaulted my face, obscuring my vision. Which direction did I come from again? The path that I had followed was gone, wiped away by the heavy rain, and the wind was strong enough to move a damn house. I was completely lost.

One minute, I was enjoying my time alone in the tranquil forest, which did wonders for my peace of mind. The next minute, I was soaked and shivering. The rain came down without much warning and it worsened pretty fast. I'd taken a handful of steps when I realized that I had no idea which direction the resort was in. At that point, I wasn't sure if I'd ventured closer to or further away from the hotel.

This was a nasty storm. However, it had only been mildly overcast this morning when I left the hotel. I assumed the weather would stay fair for a hike. It was like the universe was sticking it to me for hurting Charlotte's feelings last night.

Heaving a sigh, I walked aimlessly, thinking that it was better than standing in one place. However, I learned that walking had become highly dangerous. My foot slipped in mud and I almost lost my balance. I eyed the ravine to my left warily and felt that familiar nausea that overwhelmed me when I was high up without a barrier protecting me. If I took a tumble, I'd probably be done for.

"It would be just my luck to die on my birthday," I said as I carefully navigated my steps. Maybe I'd deserve it... I shook my head.

Push away the negative thoughts. Find your happy place. That was what my therapist, the one Dad forced me to go to as a teen, told me to do. Dr. Anya was alright, a pleasant lady. However, I started ditching my sessions with her shortly after I started. I didn't need a damn therapist. What I needed was for my father to stop being a frigid asshole. If he'd been a decent parent, I wouldn't have been such a sad kid.

Now wasn't the time to think about my miserable, lonely childhood. I had to stay focused on how epically screwed I was presently. I groaned and stopped walking to look around in defeat, then, like an angel to my rescue, I saw Charlotte waving to me. She was covered by a huge raincoat, but I was certain it was her.

"Thank God." I took off toward her and she held up both hands and shook her head.

She said something but I didn't hear it over the gusty wind. However, I assumed her gesture meant to stay put. I stopped and waited. Her steps were more confident than mine and even though she seemed to be navigating fine, she skidded and stumbled a couple of times.

When she was in earshot, she shouted, "Jamie, thank God I found you in one piece!" Her words were whipped away by the wind. I felt like it would lift us and hurl us into the ravine at any moment.

"It's damn good to see you," I said, although I didn't think she heard me.

"We can't go back in that direction," she shouted, hiking her thumb over her shoulder. "I barely made it up, and I'm sure that the area is impassable by now—completely flooded.

Well... Shit. Was there another way to the resort? "What do we do?"

She grabbed my hand and led me uphill. Despite our situation, I felt a jolt shoot up my arm and I gazed at our point of contact, a little dazed. I was surprised that she was the one who came to my rescue after what happened between us last night. Charlotte hadn't even looked my way for the rest of the night after we parted ways on the club's terrace. We walked in silence for a while—it would have been hard to hear each other anyway.

Finally, my curiosity got the better of me. Based on the direction that Charlotte came in, we seemed to be heading much further away from the resort. "Where are we going?"

She let go of my hand as she glanced back, and I immediately missed the contact. "What?"

I shouted the question louder.

"There are a bunch of abandoned cabins up here," she replied. "The safest thing to do now is to seek shelter in one of them."

I nodded and asked nothing further because I trusted her judgment. The things I saw her do and heard of her doing—like climbing mountains and roaming the desert—I had no doubt she knew how to survive in a forest during a storm.

It was hard to tell how much time passed until a rustic cabin came into view. It was at the top of the hill, a long way to go when wading through mud and water, but it was a lovely sight.

Finally...

Charlotte looked back. "How are you holding up back there, city boy?"

I snorted. "I'm managing."

She smiled and I couldn't help returning it. By the time I blinked, she was upright and then she wasn't. Her shriek was carried on by the wind as she tumbled out of my sight... toward the ravine.

My heart damn near leaped out of my chest. "Charlotte!" I took off running but her head popped up into view and relief almost had me weak in the knees. "Jesus Christ." For a moment, I had feared the worst.

"No, Jamie, don't come any closer," she ordered, looking over her shoulder into the ditch.

I stopped, torn between listening to her instruction and disregarding it to help her up. She was hanging on a vine for fuck's sake, and I was terrified that she'd lose her hold.

However, I watched in amazement as she climbed back up with impressive strength.

When she seemed to be in a safer spot, I hurried to her. The relief that washed over me as I reached her side was palpable. "Charlotte, are you alright?"

When she clutched her right ankle, her face twisted in agony. "Well, I didn't fall to my death so, yeah... but I twisted my ankle."

My hand hovered over her injured foot. "Let me see." Just as I got ready to tug off her heavy water boot, she placed her hand over mine.

"We can check it out once we get out of the rain. The wind is picking up and there's no telling when a tree might take a tumble." She gave me a once over and frowned. "Plus, you're soaked. You must be freezing."

Although we were in the tropics, being wet while being whipped by heavy wind wasn't favorable. I felt chilled to the bone… until I thought Charlotte had fallen into a ravine. I forgot all about my discomfort then. The fact that she was worried about me warmed me to the core.

"I'm fine. Let's go," I said, helping her to her feet.

She took one step, let out a cry, and was on her way back down into the muddy water when I caught her.

"Do you think the ankle is broken?" I asked.

"I don't think so but I twisted it pretty badly. It hurts like a motherfucker." She gazed up at the cabin and blew out a breath. "It's going to be hell to make it up that hill on a bum ankle."

"I've got you." I already had an arm around her waist, so I bent at the knees, ready to scoop her up.

She batted my hand away. "What are you doing?"

"I'm going to carry you the rest of the way."

"No, thanks. I'll manage."

"Charlotte…"

"I said I'll manage."

She scrambled out of my hold and attempted to walk, but it didn't work out. Her grunt of pain when she tentatively put pressure on her injured ankle sent guilt shooting through me. Her pain was my fault. If she hadn't been looking back, checking on me, she wouldn't have missed her step. If I hadn't foolishly taken off into the woods alone, she wouldn't have had to come and rescue me. I had a habit of causing women pain on my birthday it seemed. Maybe I was cursed…

Refusing to watch Charlotte stubbornly cause herself more pain, I swung her into my arms without warning so she couldn't refuse.

"Jamie, put me down," she demanded.

"Stop being so damn stubborn," I chided. "You can barely walk, and we need to get inside fast." I softened my tone because I understood her reluctance to be carried. She struck me as a tough-as-nails woman who could hold her own in any situation, and I liked that about her. However, if I didn't intervene, we'd likely be swept away by the rising water. "Just relax, Wonder Woman, and let this city boy give you a hand. I owe you big for coming to save my ass."

She peeked at me through her lashes and her cheeks tinged scarlett. Her frown then melted and a smile stretched her lips. "Fine."

Wrapping her arms around my shoulders, she relaxed into my hold, and I continued the trek uphill.

16

CHARLOTTE

"The cabin's door is unlocked," I told Jamie as he hurried up the steps.

Instead of putting me down, he shifted me in his arms and reached for the handle.

I let out a laugh. "You can put me down now."

"Not until we get inside…" He pushed the door open, angled his body to get us through it, and stepped in.

As he did a quick assessment of the place, I peeked up at him, taking in the determined set of his perfectly chiseled jaw. I was embarrassed about being carried when I was the one who was supposed to be doing the rescuing, but the longer I remained in his arms… goodness. It sure felt good to be held by a strong pair. It had been a while since I had that pleasure.

Despite his status as CEO of some huge empire where I was sure he was stationed behind a desk, he was fit. I was no tiny girl and he carried my weight uphill as if I was a feather, and he wasn't even winded.

Realizing that I was getting carried away with my thoughts

and that I was staring at him, I cleared my throat. "Thanks for the lift."

His lips twisted upward. "You just can't wait to get away from me, huh?"

"That's not it." Did I sound breathier than usual? "I'm sure you're tired. It was a long walk."

He shrugged and carefully set me on my feet. "There's an entire row of these cabins up here. What's the story about them?"

"They were a part of the resort that was here before Pacific Paradise," I shared as I balanced on one foot while I stripped off my raincoat. "They were written off when the resort was bought and revamped. Now the staff use them to get away from the hotel."

Jamie grunted his amusement and pushed his backpack off his shoulders. "Why would you guys want to get away from paradise?"

"Are you kidding? Being up here surrounded by the tranquility of nature is the real paradise."

"You make a valid point. I never thought I'd enjoy a hike in the forest more than lounging in the hot tub in my suite."

I smiled at that because maybe Jamie wasn't a hardcore city boy after all. Glancing at him, I gathered that maybe we had more in common than I thought. I liked people who appreciated the simplicity and beauty of nature.

"Just last week, a few of us trekked up here to spend our weekend off away from the bustling hotel and fancy guests. Fortunately, there are still canned goods, flashlights, water, and blankets stashed in here because we planned to come back for another peaceful weekend. We should be good for a couple of days."

Jamie was still inspecting the room when I made my revelation. He turned to me with wide eyes. *"Days?"*

There was no point in even checking for a cell phone signal in these woods, so I pulled out the two-way radio I had stashed in my hiking pack and fiddled with it. I brought it along in case I had found Jamie in a worse state and needed to get him medical help pronto. Another wave of relief hit me hard because here he was doing just fine... soaked to the bone but still in one piece. I, on the other hand, was in pain.

I pulled in a sharp breath when I tried putting pressure on my foot and hopped over to a chipped wooden bench that one of the staff carved. There was no furniture in the old cabin except a few handmade chairs.

"Yup. I hate to break it to you, Jamie, but you might very well be stuck with me for that long."

There was a hint of worry in his eyes, and I wasn't sure how to feel about it. Was he worried that he wouldn't survive out here away from the luxury of the resort or was he bummed that we might be stuck together for too long? Choosing not to think too much about it, I sat down and tried the radio.

It took a few attempts before a female voice penetrated the silence.

"Kendra, is that you?" I asked, with a bit of relief.

"Charlotte?" Static crackled distorting whatever she said.

Jamie stood with his arms folded over his chest, watching me.

"I didn't catch that, Kendra, but thank God it's you."

I didn't want Josh, the hater, involved in this. He'd probably work up some devious plan to have me blamed for a guest being in danger and get me fired.

After some more static, the radio cleared. "Where are you, Charlotte? Mark has been asking for you."

I suppressed a groan as I looked skyward. Our supervisor would surely grill my ass for taking off without letting him know what was happening. However, I hoped that I'd find Jamie and have him back at the resort without incident.

"Tell him I went searching for a guest. I found him and he's fine, but making it back right now is a no-go."

"Where…" There was a series of rattling again. "…you?"

"Crashing in one of the cabins."

"Okay, I'll pass on the message and get back to you. Stay safe."

"Thanks, Kendra."

Blowing out a breath, I rested the radio beside me and started kicking off my boot. Jamie appeared and crouched at my feet to help.

"I've got it," I said. "You should get out of those wet clothes." Almost immediately, I processed what I said and regretted it. "I mean… you don't have any dry clothes, and you can't lounge around here naked…" My nervous giggle made me wince internally. *Jesus.* I was seriously anxious about being here with him, especially after last night.

He gazed up at me with a glint of amusement in his eyes. "I'll figure something out after I check out your ankle."

My breath hitched when he slid my boot and sock off to run his fingers over my ankle. "Jesus. Charlotte, this is bad."

Ignoring the tingle that ran up my spine from his gentle touch, I grimaced as I gazed at the discolored skin around the joint that was blown up like a balloon.

"It is," I sighed. I winced when I wiggled my toes. "On the bright side, it isn't broken. The swelling will go down soon."

Jamie didn't seem to see the bright side. He stared at my ankle with deeply furrowed eyebrows. The sheer despair clouding his features was unnecessary for a sprained ankle, in my opinion.

"Gosh, Jamie, I won't die from the minor injury," I joked. "You look so morbid."

His expression didn't lighten and he didn't laugh as I expected. He still held on to my foot as he murmured, "It figures I'd cause another woman pain on my birthday. I'm fucking cursed."

My eyebrows popped up. Mr. Solemn didn't strike me as the melodramatic type, so his reaction to my injured ankle was too much.

I snorted. "Jamie, relax. I'll be fine. Why would you think you're cursed?" He said he caused *another* woman pain on his birthday. What was that about? Before I could ask, he spoke.

"This is my fault. If I hadn't taken off without checking the weather, you wouldn't have had to come and rescue me. Plus, you got injured because you were looking back, checking on me…" He blew out a long breath. "I'm sorry." He met my gaze. "And it sounds like I might have caused you trouble with your boss."

I glanced at the radio and shrugged. "That's all on me. I, uh…" My face heated to epic proportions. "I might have gone about things the wrong way because I was so…"

He stared at me expectantly and I reluctantly finished, "I was hasty because I was terrified something might happen to you. I didn't inform anyone. I just ran out to find you on my own." It wasn't that I was embarrassed about being worried about a guest… I was *too* concerned about *this* particular one.

Jamie studied me for so long that the fire in my cheeks intensified. Finally, he said, "Thanks for your concern."

He looked down at my ankle, which he still cradled. "Charlotte, what I said last night… That was just me—"

Kendra's voice, warped and fuzzy, interrupted him. Jamie and I both glanced at the radio. "Charlotte, you there?"

Swallowing my curiosity about what Jamie had been about to say, I picked up the device. "I'm here."

"Mark is pretty annoyed but as long as you don't need urgent help…"

"We're okay where we are."

"Okay, you'll have to wait until the weather clears up…" I frowned as static drowned out her words again. However, I got the picture when the words, "Don't want to make a big deal and get anyone riled up…" came through.

"Thanks, Kendra, and I need another favor."

"Shoot."

I told her about Lincoln and the others who were anxiously waiting for Jamie's return. She agreed to find them and let them know he was with me and to explain our situation.

"Take care of yourself out there, Char," Kendra said and then there was silence.

Jamie's fingers unwrapped from my ankle and he stood. "I didn't get what she said about not getting anyone riled up."

"I heard enough to understand perfectly."

I took up my backpack that had all the essentials for leading guests out into the forest. There was a small first aid kit in there that had some mild analgesics… My ankle had really started to hurt.

"Since you're doing just fine, we don't want to kick up a rumpus and scare the bigwigs at the resort. That might land not just me in hot water for going on a solo rescue mission in a storm, but my supervisor as well."

He raked his fingers through his hair. "If anything like that happens, I'll be there to back you one hundred percent. I promise."

I gazed up at him with a small smile. "Thanks, but everything will be fine. The most important thing is that you're alright."

He held my gaze for so long that I practically felt the electricity crackling between us. Of course, that had me confused after what he said last night. He called me *"some woman."* That stung hard. To break the awkward silence, I held up the first aid kit. "Did you get any scratches out there?"

"I'm fine."

"Good." Looking around, I said, "We need to find those tinned goods and blankets."

"Rest your ankle. Tell me where everything is and I'll get them."

"Okay. Have you ever been camping before?"

His eyebrows dipped. "Never…"

"Hmm, well this is going to be just like camping. It'll be fun."

His skeptical expression sent amusement dancing through me. Poor, Mr. Billionaire. "Buckle up, *James Wilfred Winchester.* You're about to slum it with me in an abandoned cabin in the woods. Yippee!"

He narrowed his gaze with mock outrage at my use of his name. "Stop saying my name like that."

The corners of his lips then twitched with the threat of a smile. He looked much better than he did a moment ago when I saw utter sadness shadow his handsome features.

17

JAMIE

"I have a surprise," Charlotte said, wearing a cheeky grin.

After a couple of hours, we'd settled into the dark, furniture-less cabin. An area was set up with sleeping bags and blankets, but Charlotte and I sat on the bare floor, eating out of cans with plastic forks. For someone who'd never experienced a minute outside the lap of luxury, I wasn't too stressed about spending the night here. It was because of Charlotte. She was so chatty, chipper, and funny. I was thoroughly entertained and not once did I plunge into despair about the day.

"A surprise, huh? Is it another delicious can of..." I assessed the tin in my hand. "Mystery meat?" I grimaced and my stomach churned a little when I said it out loud because I wasn't even sure what the fuck I was eating.

Charlotte chuckled. "Oh, come on. It isn't caviar and fancy hors d'oeuvre like you typically eat but at least you won't starve to death tonight."

"True... I'm grateful. Besides, the canned peaches were a good treat." I nodded to the empty fruit cans.

"That's the spirit. You're such a trooper."

"I hate caviar by the way." I took a sip from my water bottle.

"Oh, and here I thought you feasted on caviar and champagne for breakfast, lunch, and dinner. Isn't that what rich people's meals are like?"

I lifted an eyebrow but wanted to smile because I knew she was just poking fun. Nobody except my small group of friends ever teased me as Charlotte did. "Not by a long shot. Not for me anyway."

As I gazed at her, I wondered if I should bring up the subject of last night. I was about to apologize earlier but I was interrupted. After that, we got caught up in making our little space as comfortable as possible. Now, I was wary about bringing it up for fear of ruining the lighthearted mood.

"I believe you," she said. "Your group of friends are some of the most down-to-earth people I've met. I like you guys."

My gaze locked onto her face as she peered into her canned dinner. Maybe she didn't completely hate me after last night. I was unintentionally harsh. It was just so damn hard having her right there and not being able to tell her how amazing I thought she was... because I didn't dare ruin Lincoln's big plan to get her back.

Clearing my throat lightly, I asked, "So, what's this big surprise?"

Her grin made me want to smile too. "Since your birthday meal wasn't all that stellar. You're about to get a special treat."

"And that is...?"

"A shower."

My eyebrows elevated. There was a bathroom but no running water, so I didn't see how a shower was possible. We really needed to get cleaned up. Charlotte still had patches of mud caked to her pants and my shirt had dirt stains from carrying her.

"How exactly is a shower supposed to happen?"

"Come with me, birthday boy."

As she scrambled to her feet, I remained frozen for a moment. It struck me that it was my most dreaded day of the year, yet all I'd done was smile during the few hours that Charlotte and I had been stuck together in the cabin.

Blinking out of my stupor, I jumped to my feet and helped her up. "Easy on the ankle."

"Aye, aye, doc. You know, you can stop fussing over me like a mother hen. I'm pretty sure I'll survive this sprained ankle. I mean it was touch and go there for a while..." she says, clutching her chest dramatically, "but I'll pull through."

I wanted to roll my eyes at her sarcasm and smile at the same time. Charlotte was super entertaining, so full of life and character. Why hadn't I ever met a woman like her in my circle? If I had, I certainly would have told my father to fuck off when he breached the subject of the equivalent of an arranged marriage last year.

"I've never been likened to a mother hen before," I grumbled.

My arm was wrapped around her waist and most of her weight was on me so we were pretty close. When she turned to me with a grin, the little devil on my shoulder said, *Go ahead and kiss her again. You know you want to. She's so close... so enticing...*

"I'm sure your ego will be just fine," she said with a chuckle.

I swallowed and faced forward, telling the little devil on my shoulder to shut it. When I helped her hobble to the bathroom, she broke away and disappeared into what looked like a closet.

"Hey, Jamie, give me a hand," she called.

When I entered the tiny room, there were huge water containers lined out. I didn't question Charlotte when she instructed me to lift one and bring it to the stall that had a standing shower. However, I got an idea of what was happening when I spotted a contraption that seemed to have been built onto the shower head.

She told me to put the huge container on a raised platform, which I was able to reach without the stepping ladder she brought out. She had to use the ladder to get high enough to fiddle with the strange-looking contraption. I watched her closely, ready to step in if she stumbled because I didn't like the way she balanced on one foot.

When she stepped down, I glanced at her with amusement because her excitement was so obvious.

"Check this out," she said, pulling a lever. The bottle tilted with a slight screeching sound that indicated the makeshift shower had been up for a while. Water cascaded through the shower head.

I laughed. "Wow. Very innovative."

"I know, right? It'll have to be quick and it won't be warm but enjoy your shower, Jamie. Happy birthday."

Shaking my head as I eyed the setup, I chuckled. "Thanks. Did you invent this?"

"No. A coworker who has since retired did. I miss Keanu, he reminded me so much of my dad, always resourceful." There was a wistful note in her voice. "I didn't work with him long since I've only been here for a few months, but I learned a lot from him."

I was curious about her father because of the sad look she had when she mentioned him but her expression quickly brightened.

"I see. The setup is impressive, but you should go first. Then I'll mount another bottle for myself."

"Are you sure?"

"Yeah. You need to get off your feet so go ahead and take the first shower."

"Alright. Thanks. Do you mind bringing me the clothes we found? We can spare another bottle to rinse the mud off these." She looked down at her soiled pants and T-shirt.

"Sure."

As I went to fetch the garments we'd luckily found, I thought about how Charlotte would be mere feet away from me, naked. "Christ," I muttered, trying like hell to keep my lascivious thoughts at bay.

* * *

It was quiet and dark, with the exception of the battery-operated lantern that sat in the middle of the room. It provided enough light for Charlotte and me to at least see each other. She sat on a sleeping bag mere inches from me, leaning against the wall. Her still-swollen foot was propped up on a pillow. I leaned on the wall as well, staring through the window across the room—not that I could see much in the black night. Even the moon and stars were hiding from the bad weather it seemed.

The storm raged outside, its fury unleashed on the cabin. The wind and rain battered so hard against the log structure that I feared it would crumble. I looked up each time the roof reverberated with each howling gust, expecting our shelter to be torn away.

Charlotte chuckled. "Don't worry too much. It may not look like it but this little cabin is sturdy. It has stood firm against full-blown hurricanes."

"It sounds so crazy outside it's hard to believe that it's just a tropical storm. I'd hate to be here for a high-category hurricane."

Charlotte shrugged as if she was accustomed to weathering storms. I gazed at her for a moment, wondering if I should pry into her life. Perhaps it was best if I didn't learn too much about her. It might make it easier to ignore my attraction to her. However, my curiosity got the better of me.

"Where are you from, Charlotte?"

She glanced at me. "A small town called Golden Beach in Oregon."

"What brought you to Hawaii?"

Her eyebrows rose slowly. "Are you bored, Jamie?"

"Why?"

"Because you want to talk. You weren't interested in talking last night."

I was sure she could see my sheepish expression in the semi-darkness. "About that..." I sighed. "Look, Charlotte, I was feeling out of sorts and... I'm sorry that I snapped at you."

She just nodded and went on to stare ahead without a word as if she wasn't interested in further conversation. The longer I watched her, the more the urge to make things right grew. She deserved honesty, but should I do this? Make my feelings known? I felt like I was betraying Lincoln... again. I already kissed Charlotte but being alone with her like this, I couldn't ignore the temptation, so I gave in.

"You were right. I am into you."

When her eyes snapped to my face, I almost winced because I sounded like a high schooler. While relationships have never been my thing, I dated—and *hung out with*—plenty of women, and I was usually smoother than this.

Charlotte watched me through unreadable eyes. "It doesn't matter now."

My heart plummeted. I'd ruined everything between us... before it even started.

"I get it, Jamie. When I got back to my room last night, I thought about what you said, and you were right. You can't ruin your friendship over some woman you barely know. In a few days, you and Lincoln will return home. If you and I..." She sighed. "A fling isn't worth ruining a friendship for and that's exactly what you and I would have."

She stared at me as if waiting for me to tell her she was wrong. That if we gave in to the chemistry between us, we'd have more than a fling. However, I couldn't tell her she was wrong because as she said, we'd part ways in a few days. My silence continued and she averted her gaze.

"You're not just some woman..." That was all I could say at first. Tucking my chin into my chest, I heaved the heaviest, longest sigh. "After last night, did I drive you into his arms?"

Charlotte sat taller and huffed. "I can't believe you just asked me that."

"I know it's none of my business but it's a valid question. It's what Lincoln wants. That's why he came here."

"What about what *I* want?" she hissed. "Have you or Lincoln considered that?"

18

JAMIE

I stared at Charlotte, my mouth opening and closing several times without a sound because I didn't have an answer. The fury, exasperation, and agony in her voice made me want to keep my mouth shut for fear of upsetting her more.

"What right does Lincoln have to show up here expecting to rekindle something that's been over for years without telling me?" She scoffed. "How dare he give you the impression that he and I getting back together is a sure thing when he didn't even ask me? And how dare *you* just hand me over to him!"

My eyes widened and my jaw slackened. "I did not—"

"You keep acting as if Lincoln and I are together and when you and I are simply having a conversation, you act as though I'm cheating on him. It's ridiculous! And I'm fucking pissed about being thrown into that awkward situation."

Son of a bitch. When she said it like that… Lincoln and I were both idiots. Lincoln showed up with high expectations without finding out what Charlotte wanted, and I had been behaving as if they were heading down the aisle at any moment.

"Charlotte, I'm—"

"No, shut up and let me finish, Jamie. Last night, you dismissed me when I tried telling you that I'm not interested in Lincoln as anything more than a friend. How dare he and how dare *you* decide that I'm his without even including me in the discussion?"

I nodded. "I realize that I'm in the wrong."

"And so is Lincoln," she added. "He's a great guy, but I don't want what he wants and I don't know what to tell him because…"

"You don't want to hurt his feelings. Yeah…" Neither did I. Sighing heavily, I rested my head against the wall and stared ahead. "We don't have to talk about it any further."

She looked ready to combust, and it wasn't my intention to upset her.

She sniffed softly and my attention jumped back to her. Her eyes were watery and her chin quivered.

"I feel so stupid," she whispered.

I swallowed hard to get rid of the lump of guilt lodged in my throat. "Why?"

"For getting so worked up over this whole thing. I'm not even sure why it's all bothering me so much. I guess it's because I've never felt…"

I waited but she didn't finish. Instead, she watched me with flushed cheeks and then said, "Never mind. It doesn't matter."

My curiosity remained firmly in place, but I didn't push.

She pushed back her curtain of hair. "We should change the subject, but first, tell me… If you didn't mean what you said about me being *some woman,* what exactly am I to you, Jamie?"

I held her gaze for a while. Since we were past the point of no more bullshit, I answered honestly. "You're much more. You mean something to me. It's hard to tell what yet since we've only had days but…"

Expressing my emotions like this wasn't a norm for me and it was scary as fuck. However, I had about three more days with Charlotte. I didn't have time to be afraid of opening up to her… the only woman I'd ever felt comfortable doing so with.

"There's something about you that drew me to you the first day I saw you." I shrugged. "I don't know what to do with it because we'll disappear from each other's lives in the blink of an eye."

Charlotte swallowed hard and then the tiniest smile lifted her lips. "Thank you, Jamie."

I lifted an eyebrow. "For…?"

"For being honest. I can tell you don't express yourself too much, and I know that wasn't easy."

She hit the nail on the head. "So, what's my reward for getting over my emotional repression… this *once*?" After I left Kohala and Charlotte, I was sure I'd go right back to being good ol' emotionally repressed Jamie.

Charlotte laughed. "You get an answer to your question from earlier. I ended up working here after a friend told me about the job opening."

As I held Charlotte's gaze, I considered the turn of conversation and then nodded. I supposed that was her agreeing that acting on our attraction was a bad idea since we'd go our separate ways soon. I wasn't sure how to feel about it yet, but I'd respect what she wanted.

To my surprise, Charlotte scooted closer to me. As she did, my heart picked up speed. It didn't do that with anyone else. "May I ask you something too?"

"Sure."

"I don't want to upset you or anything, but I'm curious. What do you have against your birthday?"

I swallowed hard to shove down the ball of emotion that rose in my throat. The question was unexpected, but not unwelcome, which was surprising. I usually completely shut down when the subject came up with anyone other than the four guys who already knew my issue.

Charlotte watched me with curiosity and a hint of fear as if she thought she had asked the wrong thing and I'd explode. Her apprehension got to me. I didn't want her to look at me like that.

"My mother died today, thirty-one years ago."

"Oh, Jamie..." she breathed. "Shit. I'm sorry. I didn't mean to dredge up bad memories."

I pulled my knees up and rested my elbows on them. "It's okay. I guess I should talk about it. Keeping everything locked in hasn't done me any favors."

She rested her hand on my arm and I stared at our point of contact. The little touch was hugely comforting. "What...? How...?" She blew out a breath. "You know, what? It's none of my business. I'm sorry that you lost her."

"I killed her," I revealed in a monotonous tone that stemmed from me torturing myself about it for my entire childhood and accepting the remorse and bitterness in adulthood.

Charlotte's eyes bulged and her jaw dropped. *"What?"*

"She died giving birth to me, so... I killed her."

Charlotte continued to gawk and the room plunged into silence. I was in too much despair after bringing up my mother to feel any awkwardness if there was any. I just felt... full of sorrow. I suppose it's because I never dealt with my pain. As a kid, I didn't have help dealing with it and as an adult, I simply kept it locked away only to bring it all out on my birthday.

"Jesus Christ, Jamie. You did *not* kill your mother," Charlotte finally said. "Oh, my God. Please, don't tell me you've carried that thought since childhood."

My look alone told her that I did and she groaned and muttered again, "Oh, my God."

I shrugged. "I've carried the guilt since I was old enough to understand that because of me she suffered complications. She was warned that there was a possibility she'd die if she delivered me. She refused to do what the doctors recommended—something that might endanger *my* life. She chose to endanger hers instead and in the end, she lost it to give me life. I wish she hadn't…"

Charlotte let out a long breath and plopped against the wall. She stared at me with wide eyes. "Jamie… I don't even know what I should say to you except…" She sat forward again and shuffled so that she faced me. "Your mother loved you beyond anything before she even met you because that's what mothers are supposed to do. I'm sure she wouldn't want you to torture yourself for her choice. She didn't make a mistake. You're *supposed* to be here, and maybe you shouldn't spend your birthdays in despair. I think you should go all out and enjoy it, you know… kinda like honoring her and living life to the fullest for her in a way."

My eyes locked with Charlotte's. No one had ever helped me to see things from that perspective before. I tilted my head and considered. Honor my mother. I really should do that, shouldn't I? I owed her my life. Then I revealed something that I'd never even shared with my friends.

"I've always felt too guilty to have a good time because my father blamed me for her death. Since I can remember, I've tortured myself about taking away the woman he loved. My very existence is a constant reminder of what I took from him."

Her chest heaved with a deep sigh and then she all but flung herself at me. Our position was a little awkward at first because I still had my elbows on my knees but when I relaxed after my initial surprise, I dropped my hands and pulled her closer.

Her arms wrapped around my shoulders and for once I wasn't annoyed that someone thought they had to *pity* me. That had never been what I wanted. I've always just wanted someone to tell me that they understood my pain and that they didn't think I was crazy for carrying it for so long. I knew that what Charlotte gave me wasn't pity. I could practically feel waves of empathy radiating from her and I soaked it up.

"I get it, Jamie," she whispered. "I'd probably hate my birthday too... but, please take my advice. Live fully for *her* until you learn to live for yourself."

I rested my chin on her shoulder and inhaled deeply. Even her scent was comforting. It was soft and feminine. I suppose I luxuriated in her embrace because not once since I was a child struggling with the guilt about causing my mother's death had anyone *hugged* me. Dad was a cold son of a bitch and as great as my friends were, they weren't the hugging type.

It amazed me how Charlotte gave me exactly what I needed after knowing my story for all of two minutes. She was beyond incredible. When we finally broke apart, I studied her intently, thinking that she was exactly the woman I needed in my life even if it was just for a few days. I couldn't pass on the chance to experience something I never thought I would.

Charlotte's cheeks got redder the longer I stared at her. She then tentatively tucked her hair behind her ears and smiled slightly. "You're doing that thing again where you stare at me..." Her little laugh resonated with a hint of nervousness and I thought it was cute that a woman as gorgeous as she was wasn't used to men staring at her by now.

"Yeah…" I said unapologetically. "I just can't help it."

Before she could respond, I leaned closer to softly press my lips to hers.

19

CHARLOTTE

I hesitated only a millisecond when Jamie kissed me because I didn't expect it. I thought we'd come to an unspoken agreement that we would refrain from exploring the crazy chemistry between us. However, the longer his lips stayed on mine, the less I cared about the consequences of acting on our attraction.

The fire that spread through me consumed every rational thought, leaving only an intense desire to seek more with him. Once I relaxed and kissed him back, his mouth moved over mine with a hunger that matched my own.

His palm curled around my nape, pulling me closer, and I swore fire sparked and shot through my veins. I'd never felt this consuming need for someone before. While it had me a little worried, I couldn't analyze it at the moment. Our sitting position made it hard to get as close as I wanted to properly align our bodies, and I moaned my displeasure.

As if reading my mind, Jamie shifted and then pulled me

closer to straddle him. He paused and murmured against my lips, "Wait, your ankle…"

"It's fine."

I wound my arms around his shoulders and pressed my lips harder to his with an ever-growing desperation for more. His hands roamed over my back, tracing every dip and curve. His light touch sent delightful shivers up my spine. I ran my fingers through his hair as our tongues danced. I'd never wanted to luxuriate in a kiss so much. I couldn't get enough of him.

When we finally broke apart to gasp for air, our gazes remained locked and his hands still moved over my back. I liked that he didn't seem to want to stop touching me.

"I know we just agreed that we wouldn't go further," he said. "We did, right…?"

A smile lifted my lips. "Sort of."

His sigh sounded deep and contemplative, but then he said, "I changed my mind."

"Me too."

And then there were no more words…

Each touch, however, was like a language of its own. Each one communicated longing and desire… the feelings that had simmered between us the instant we met. Jamie's hands slipped under the huge T-shirt I'd chosen from the stash of clothes we'd found. There was nothing underneath so I could bask in the delectable sensation of his fingertips on my bare skin. I arched into his touch as his lips trailed along my jawline and moved down to the sensitive skin of my neck.

When he cupped my breast to massage and run his thumbs over my hardened peaks, fluid practically gushed between my thighs. It had been so long since I'd been with anyone like this. It was as if I'd been waiting for Jamie the entire time. He paused his exploration to lift the shirt over my head. I watched him as he watched me, his eyes darker and filled with need. If it were possible for someone to devour someone else with just their eyes... That's what Jamie did.

The way he looked at me made me feel beautiful. "You're a goddess, Charlotte," he said reverently. "That's what I thought when I first saw you in the hotel lobby."

My heart stuttered and then beat faster. It was flattering to know he'd been as instantly attracted to me as I'd been to him. With one swift motion, he flipped us over and gently laid me on the sleeping bag beside him.

As he hovered over me, he said, "When I fantasized about this moment, I didn't picture it on the floor of an abandoned cabin in the middle of a storm." His eyebrows furrowed and his eyes shone with regret.

Smiling, I reached for the bottom of his shirt and lifted it. He helped me remove the garment and as I ran my palms over his chest, I said, "This is perfect."

I'd remember it forever... after he was long gone from my life. A pang of sadness struck me. I finally met the man who made my heart flutter, as I'd heard so many other women gush about, and he'd only be a part of my life for a few more days.

However, rather than wallow in despair about the misfortune, I decided that I should make the most of every moment. That didn't include worrying about the scenery of our first time together.

Jamie was still worried because a frown still furrowed his brow. So, I wound my legs around his waist and used them to pull him against me. "Stop worrying and make love to me, Jamie."

Amusement danced in his eyes before it vanished beneath something smoldering. The hot intensity of his eyes on me and the carnal intent in them sent my body temperature through the roof.

I squirmed beneath him, eager to discover what else he could do to my body.

He swooped down to kiss me again as he shuffled out of his pants and then got rid of my shorts, not missing a beat. My bare skin against someone else's never felt so incredible. His voracious kiss had me anticipating what would come next. I moaned and arched into him when he abandoned my mouth to feather hot kisses down my neck. I felt his erection throb against my thigh and it made me wetter and hungrier to feel him inside me.

"Please, Jamie," I begged in a husky voice that didn't even sound like me.

As he nipped my collarbone, I tugged at his hair, urging him to make me his… for tonight and maybe tomorrow too. Jamie groaned as he kissed his way back up and settled between my legs.

"When I pictured this moment, I didn't see myself rushing things either," he said as he slid a hand between us.

"I don't care," I replied and then gasped as his fingers teased my sensitive bundle of nerves.

Our gazes remained locked as he strummed like an instrument. The slow, teasing pace that he set had me writhing and lifting my hips to get closer to his magical touch. As his tempo increased, my moans of pleasure emerged in quicker succession.

He watched me intently as if he was completely riveted by my reaction to his touch. My face burned with the timidness of being so closely observed while in the throes of passion, but I didn't look away from him. I couldn't because his metallic eyes were like magnets holding me captive.

Jamie skillfully worked me up into a frenzy and just as I was about to explode, he positioned himself at my entrance. Without breaking eye contact, he entered me with a powerful thrust that sent my orgasm to an unbelievable level. It made me scream his name as I rode the waves crashing through me. I wrapped my legs around him, pulling him closer as he began to move.

"Jesus, Charlotte. You feel... heavenly." His voice was low and gravely, thick with emotions that I wished I could decipher.

I moaned in response, the intensity of the moment electrifying every cell in my body. We moved together smoothly and perfectly as if we'd been coming together like this for ages. So, this was what it felt like to be *entirely* connected to someone. I was a people person who made plenty of connections, but nothing like this. Nothing that ever felt as if Jamie was entwining himself around my *soul*.

"*Holy fuck!*" My voice was a tad higher pitched and it cracked a little because I was so stunned by the depth of what I felt.

My outburst made Jamie freeze and his eyes instantly swiped over my face with concern.

"What is it?" he asked.

My insides turned to mush. When I first met Mr. Reserved and Solemn, I didn't imagine he'd be this attentive and sweet.

"Nothing." I trailed a finger over his lips and then his stubbled jaw. "This is incredible."

He relaxed and captured my mouth in a kiss so scorching it sent heat down to my core, triggering my next climax. My entire body tingled, and I tightened around him as I let out a moan that echoed in the room. It resonated with desire, pleasure, and satisfaction all rolled into one sound.

His thrusts became more urgent as if he lost himself in the haze of pleasure just as I did. He hit a spot inside me that sent me soaring and I fell apart from the force of the most intense orgasm I think I'd ever had.

Jamie's groan mingled with my mewls of pleasure and he shook against me, murmuring something unintelligible. I heard the word "goddess" though and I smiled. As our breathing steadied, he gave me a quick kiss on the lips that made my heart leap before he pulled out and collapsed beside me.

The world that had disappeared around us the moment he kissed me came back into focus. The rain still pounded on the roof and the wind that sounded as if it had picked up speed howled in the night. Without the heat of his body on top of mine, the chill in the room seeped in and I shivered.

Immediately, Jamie's arms wound around me, pulling me closer. He grinned down at me. "Obviously, you're spending the night in my sleeping bag now."

I smiled. "Obviously. But there's one major problem. You look like you can barely fit in there yourself. How will we both fit?"

"I'm good at problem-solving," he said and rolled away.

I felt bereft without his arms around me, and I had to fight off the sinking feeling settling in my gut. If I missed him this much when he was merely going a few feet away, how the hell would I manage when he went back to his side of the world? I felt so intensely about him after a few days of knowing him and making love once… I might be in big trouble here.

Jamie came back with my sleeping bag. He unzipped it and spread it completely open beside the one I laid on. He then gestured for me to shuffle off his and I did. I watched as he opened it and spread it flat on top of mine. Now we had twice the space and cushion. He put the pillows and blanket in place. As he lay down, he beckoned me with a finger.

Grinning like a fool, I shuffled into the makeshift bed. "I see why you're the boss of your company. You're indeed a gifted problem solver."

I felt the vibration of his laugh as he pulled me to him and I landed against his chest.

"I should get cleaned up before we settle in," I said. I then shifted so that I was stretched along his side but still pressed closely to him.

He looked down at my thighs where our combined fluids glistened in the low lighting. Heat crept up my neck and spread into my face the longer he stared.

When his eyes met mine, something like satisfaction gleamed in them but there was also a flash of remorse. "I didn't ask…"

"It's okay. We should be fine." God, I hoped so… but I didn't regret one second of what we did.

Jamie watched me thoughtfully for a few seconds longer before announcing, "I'll clean you up."

He was on his feet before I could protest. My eyes were glued to him as he strolled toward the bathroom. I appreciated the broad set of his shoulders and back, his narrow waist, and his muscular legs. He was an incredible male specimen and I had it bad for him…

20

JAMIE

I stood on the cabin's porch, staring at the tumultuous sea below. The storm still raged on. Rain lashed against the wooden planks of the porch, but the wind had calmed significantly.

I studied the way the sea churned and roiled, sending waves crashing against the shoreline. I was like the sea yesterday, a maelstrom of emotions. I'd been tossed and battered by them for so long that I almost forgot what it felt like to be at peace.

Then last night happened... *Charlotte* happened.

"Jamie, what are you doing out here?"

I turned to her with a smile. "You're finally awake. Good morning."

She quirked an eyebrow as she surveyed the bleak surroundings. "Get back inside, you crazy person."

I chuckled. "I will in a bit. I'm just enjoying the view."

She glanced ahead at the turbulent sea and the dark sky above it and scoffed. "The view is not that great this morning."

"Go back inside," I told her. "I don't want you to hurt your ankle."

"And I don't want you to be blown away by a gust of wind or squashed by a falling tree. Get the hell inside, Jamie."

"I'm the one who usually gives orders," I said.

"Sure, but this is *my* world, remember?" she quipped.

I hummed my amusement, recalling our little tiff on the terrace of that club. "Right."

I swept my gaze over her appreciatively. I liked being in her world. Her golden hair was tousled, her eyes were still dreamy with sleep, her lips were still red from my kisses, and her skin was still flushed.

She wore only the oversized T-shirt she'd had on last night and her nipples peeked at me, tempting me to strip her naked again so I could take the delectable peaks into my mouth. She was fucking gorgeous, and I wouldn't mind waking up to the sight of her every morning. I wasn't even shocked by the direction of my thoughts.

Seeing her like this every day required a long-term relationship, which was foreign to me. However, Charlotte was pretty damn special. She had me thinking about exclusivity, but how was that possible? A long distance relationship... I didn't like the thought of that.

Charlotte stepped outside as I continued to stare at her. "Are you okay, Jamie?"

"I'm great." *Really great.*

"You're looking at me funny..." Her eyebrows crinkled into adorable lines and I laughed. "Are you sure you're okay?"

"Positive. This morning, I..." I blew out a breath. "I feel *alive*, Charlotte."

I held her gaze, willing her to understand what I meant. It was a day after my birthday, and I wasn't wading in a swamp of guilt as I typically did every year. It was because of her and what she said last night, what she helped me realize.

I didn't *take* my mother's life as Dad drilled into me since I was old enough to understand. She gave me *mine* because she wanted me to be here… and I should live my life to the fullest to show my appreciation.

This morning when I opened my eyes, I lay beside Charlotte for a while, watching her and thinking about her many adventures that I'd heard about. I decided that I'd take a page out of her book. As of that moment, I'd stop living in the box my father guilted me into staying in.

Charlotte held my gaze and then her expression softened into one of understanding. Her sweet smile touched a part of me that no one else had ever reached. "That's good, Jamie. Really good."

Of course, she got it. She got *me*. I reached for her and swept her into my arm, lifting her in the process so that she didn't put any pressure on her ankle. I kissed her deeply and even with a storm swirling around us, I felt cocooned in warmth.

When I released her mouth to rest my forehead against hers, I said, "Thank you, Charlotte." I knew she understood what I was thanking her for.

She nodded and whispered, "Come back inside with me."

I did and when I pushed the door closed, I put her down. "You know, Jamie, I'm starting to get used to you carrying me around. It's nice." She gave me one of her playful smirks and hobbled over to the wooden bench to fetch her backpack. She held up the radio. "I'm going to check in with Mark and let him know we're doing fine up here. I'll ask him to update your friends."

My friends… *Lincoln*.

Suddenly, the warm cocoon of our fantasy world crumbled.

As she spoke into the radio, she watched me with a frown. I didn't hear much of the conversation between her and whoever was on the other end because I was busy thinking about Lincoln. Now that I wasn't caught up in sexual bliss and the amazing feeling of being guilt-free for once, worry seeped in. I might lose a valuable friendship...

"Jamie?"

I turned back to Charlotte. "Hmmm?"

"I just watched you transform from Jamie to James Wilfred right before my eyes." Her frown deepened. "What's wrong?"

I couldn't help but be amused by the comparison. Chuckling, I asked, "How are they not the same person?"

"James Wilfred is much more uptight and somber than Jamie."

Stroking my chin, I murmured, "I see."

"Don't get me wrong, I like them both, but James Wilfred's scowl just now has me worried." She gazed at me with a hint of uncertainty.

"Don't be."

"It's hard not to be. What were you thinking about?"

Threading my fingers through my hair, I exhaled loudly. "The mention of my friends reminded me that I slept with the woman who Lincoln had hopes of getting back with."

Her gaze lowered to the floor and I rushed to explain, "Charlotte, I don't want you to think I regret last night. Hell, I want *more* of last night."

Her eyes flew back up to connect with mine.

"And what you said about Lincoln assuming that you'd want to rekindle a romantic relationship... You were right. He should have spoken to you first."

"But you still think we're in the wrong for pursuing what's between us?" she asked, watching me closely.

I wasn't even sure what to say. Maybe I was dead wrong for wanting her, but I had no control over what I felt.

"The only thing I regret is not telling Lincoln how I felt about you after our first kiss. He'll probably be twice as hurt when he finds out we went much further."

Charlotte shut her eyes and groaned. "So, you're definitely going to tell him?"

"I have to…" *Right?* He was one of my best friends. I couldn't keep something major from him, especially *this*. I slept with his ex-girlfriend whom he still had feelings for.

"I never meant to cause trouble between you two," she said.

"I know."

"Is there any way we could put all the negative stuff aside and just have… *one* more day?"

One more day of just us. That was what I wanted too. Well, I would have loved more than one day, but I'd take what I could get.

"Of course."

* * *

Charlotte and I ended up getting two more days instead of one. The rain stopped yesterday evening, but the terrain back to the resort was still too dangerous to tread. Both Charlotte and her supervisor thought it was best for us to wait at least another day for the water to dry up before making the journey.

However, she and I were outside, taking a walk. It was much safer because we were uphill, far from the areas that had been flooded. She said she had another surprise for me. A belated birthday present.

She was a little ahead of me, and I observed the way she

favored her injured ankle. I wasn't keen on the idea of her walking yet, but she said that she was fine.

She glanced back with a smile. "What's the matter, city boy? Can't keep up?"

"Sure, I can, but I'm enjoying the view from back here." My gaze dipped to her ass, which looked superb in shorts.

Her giggle danced around me, adding something extra to the relaxing scenery. "Perv."

I shrugged and gave her a sheepish smile. "Hey, how much further are we going? You really shouldn't pressure your ankle too much."

After three days in Charlotte's company, I discovered that the woman was as stubborn as a mule. She was also fearless, independent, and... I fixated on her ass again and then her long legs... and everything came together in a hot-as-fuck package.

"Relax, Jamie. We're here."

I came up beside her and stopped. *"Wow..."*

We looked down at a deep blue pool surrounded by lush greenery combined with the vibrant hues of tropical flora. The pool was fed by a waterfall that cascaded down an outcrop. Towering trees stretched above, creating a canopy that lessened the intensity of the sun.

"I know, right?" Charlotte smiled as she gazed at the scenery that was so beautiful it looked like a flawless painting. "Did you think the cabins are the only reason my coworkers and I steal away up here? *This* is what we really love."

I nodded. "It beats the jacuzzis at the resorts by far."

She beamed. "I knew you'd appreciate this. I was thinking we could take a dip."

"Let's do it."

I shifted the bag I'd taken from her when we left the cabin, bent at the knees, and scooped her up.

She gasped when she found herself draped over my shoulder. "Jamie, what...?"

"You are not walking on the uneven ground with that ankle," I said as I took cautious steps around rocks and thick foliage.

With a resigned sigh, she relaxed. "I think you just want an excuse to touch my ass."

My arm tightened around said area and I grinned. "I might have ulterior motives..."

She snickered.

"Still, I don't want you pressuring your ankle."

"And you always get what you want in your world, I take it?"

"I tend to."

She laughed. "Without the manhandling, I hope."

"Charlotte, you are the only person I've ever wanted to manhandle and the second I get you beside that pool, I'm going to *manhandle* you some more."

She squirmed on my shoulder and let out a soft moan that made me smile harder.

21

CHARLOTTE

"You seem different today," I observed, gazing at Jamie sitting at the pool's edge.

We had brunch—more canned goods, which Jamie hated—about an hour ago and we talked and got to know each other better. A few intimate conversations weren't enough, but I still got a better picture of who James Winchester was.

He was a man driven by loyalty and a need to compensate for something that was hardly his fault. The insight I got into his childhood made me dislike his father, a man I'd never even laid eyes on. What sane parent inflicted such psychological trauma on their child?

"It's a new day," he said, looking up at the canopied trees.

I smiled because I knew what he meant. Jamie had a new goal in life, to live for *himself*—he'd said as much. I was happy for him. He deserved to be content in his life because he was a good man. Underneath that somber, stoic armor was a heart of gold. He tortured himself when he felt like he'd hurt someone. I knew he tortured himself over the Lincoln situation, and I felt bad.

"It is." I smiled. "So, are you going to finally come into the water or what? When I suggested taking a dip, I meant more than just your feet."

I waded to where he sat with his feet dangling in the water. His lips twisted into a smile. "I'm enjoying watching you swim."

When I stopped at his feet, his gaze dipped to my bare beasts and his eyes darkened with blatant hunger.

I smirked. "I think you're only enjoying it because I'm naked."

"You are not wrong," he purred, still eyeing my tits.

When I stopped giggling, which I did entirely too much with him, I narrowed my gaze. "You don't have one of those phobias where you're afraid of bodies of water, do you? But that would make no sense because you had no problem windsurfing and you're a great swimmer…"

His eyebrows shot up. "The only crazy fear I have is of heights."

"Then what's the problem?"

"No problem, I'm simply preparing myself," he said, staring into the water.

My eyebrows snapped together. Jamie was an interesting character. "For…?"

"For anything." He lifted a shoulder nonchalantly as if staring intensely into a pool to *prepare himself* before getting in was the most natural thing in the world.

"Okay…"

He finally took his eyes off the water's surface to look at me. His eyes flickered with uncertainty. I got the impression that he contemplated telling me something. Jamie had shared things with me that I knew he hadn't with anyone else and that made me feel special. It made me feel as if this thing between us was more than a vacation fling for him.

"I can't see the bottom," he finally announced.

I blinked. The water was dark, a deep shade of blue-green.

"It's... unsettling," he added.

I stared at him with my head tilted. *"Oh..."*

He lifted an eyebrow. "Oh?"

"I get it now."

His eyes narrowed. "Do you?"

"You're a control freak. That's why you're afraid of heights too, isn't it? You find situations that you can't control *unsettling*."

Jamie's jaw slackened and disbelief flickered across his face. "Jesus, woman. You've known me all of a few days. *How* do you always get it?"

I grinned triumphantly. "Much respect for you for not getting all macho and denying it."

He laughed. "Don't congratulate me yet. I suffered through a helicopter ride because I was too *manly* to remind my friends about my fear of heights."

I laughed and rested my hands on his thighs. "It's okay, you don't have to jump in if you don't want to."

"That's the thing," he said. "I *want* to because I'm supposed to be turning over a new leaf."

"You don't have to change who you are to enjoy your life, Jamie."

He watched me through squinted eyes. "How did you get to be so wise?"

"I listened to my old man more often than not. He was always right about things..." I shrugged.

Jamie grinned, blew out a breath, and jumped into the water.

I clapped. "I'm proud of you."

"Don't be. I went over every possible thing that could go wrong in my mind and deduced that I'll be fine."

I rolled my eyes with mock disappointment. "*Ugh*, your poor brain. Here I thought you were learning to be spontaneous," I joked. I poked fun but I wanted to know why he was like that. I'd never get to see his many layers because our time together was limited.

"Hey." Jamie snagged my chin, pulling me from my thoughts. "Brooding is supposed to be my thing, not yours." He searched my face. "What were you thinking just now?"

I swallowed the emotions clawing at my chest. "I was thinking of ways to distract you from your control freak ways."

His furrowed eyebrows and narrowed eyes said he didn't believe me, so I did the only thing I knew would take his mind off talking… I wound my arms around his shoulders and pressed my lips to his.

He instantly took over, circling my waist with one arm and cupping my nape with the other hand. He deepened the kiss and *commanded* my mouth. In this case, I didn't mind his need for control because he was damn good at taking the lead in the sex department.

I moaned my protest when he pulled away. "Tell me what you were really thinking about," he demanded.

His disapproving look made me sigh. "I just don't want to talk about the heavy stuff, Jamie. We don't have much time…" My pleading look worked because he gave in and kissed me again. This time, with more urgency.

As our lips melded once again, the rising heat drove away my worries… for now. I let myself get lost in him and the feel of his body against mine. As he explored my mouth, his hand caressed my back. My skin instantly heated despite standing in the cool water. He then roamed lower, moving over my hips and further down to grasp my thighs and lifted me to him.

My legs wrapped around his waist. I was a little disappointed that he still wore shorts because I ached to feel him inside me again. Our first time together had been so incredible and so moving that he'd become my addiction. After many rounds of lovemaking during our two days stuck in that cabin, I still felt as if I'd combust if I didn't have him now.

I pulled away from his lips so I could look into his eyes. "I need you," I whispered, barely able to control the desperation in my voice. Maybe that was a bad thing. Needing Jamie probably wasn't a good idea when I'd only have him for another couple of days. Without a word, he carried me back to the pool's edge and sat me down on the towel where we'd had our picnic.

He stared into my eyes as he stood between my legs. He just *stared* until I wondered what he was thinking so intently about or what he was looking for.

"I need you too," he said.

There was the slightest catch in his voice, which could have easily been missed, but I heard it. What did that mean? I had the suspicion that it meant he needed me in more than a sexual way. Or perhaps I was getting ahead of myself…

I stopped thinking about it when he leaned close and pressed his lips to mine again. He then went on to caress my neck with light kisses and then moved down to my breasts. Waves of pleasure shot through me when he took one of my nipples into his mouth, his tongue teasing and his teeth nipping at it. I arched my back, pressing myself closer to him, wanting more.

He gave me more, moving his attention over to my other breast to lavish it with attention as he slipped his hand between my legs. My breath was caught in my throat even though his fingers barely teased me. I wiggled my hips, trying to get closer to his fingers. I knew he could work magic with them, and I was eager to experience it.

"Lay back and relax, Charlotte. Let me take my time."

My heart hammered with anticipation as I did what he said. I lay down and watched him as he hovered over me. He bent down and kissed my stomach, his lips leaving trails of fire as he traveled lower. He finally reached his destination, and I gasped as he used his tongue to trace my mound before settling on my clit.

He wasn't in any rush. The strokes of his tongue were relaxed yet powerful enough to have me writhing in pleasure.

I moaned his name over and over as he continued his slow, sensual torture. He looked up at me with hunger in his eyes and then plunged his tongue inside me. My body arched off the ground and I cried out as my hands clawed at his hair.

"How did you get so good at this?" I panted. "Never mind, I don't want to know."

I was barely holding it together. Jamie chuckled darkly and then increased his pace, driving me further into sweet bliss. His fingers replaced his tongue which went back to swirling and flicking over my sensitive bundle of nerves. The dual stimulation had me on the verge of bursting into flames.

I was lost in the sensations, unable to think or speak as he brought me to the brink and over the edge. My body shook with the force of my climax and my legs tightened around his shoulders as if I thought I could use him to keep me anchored. I barely came down from my high when he pulled me back into the water and right into his arms.

With his lips pressed to my ear, he whispered, "You taste so good... like a newly discovered delicacy that I can't get enough of. I'm fucking addicted to you, Charlotte. What am I supposed to do with that?"

I pulled back slightly to look at him, wondering if he was addressing me or just murmuring things to himself.

"I..." My response died on my tongue when he lifted me onto his waiting shaft and slid into me.

I gasped as he slowly filled me, touching parts of me no one else ever had... because it wasn't just physical with him. Could I possibly be in love with Jamie after knowing him for about a week? That was insane... right? I lost my train of thought when he moved.

I felt as if every nerve ending in my body was being stimulated. Before experiencing this level of intimacy with Jamie, sex had been generic. Just something I did to satisfy that itch or because it was what people in relationships did. *This* was... something extraordinary. Our bodies moved in perfect rhythm as if we were meant to be connected like this.

Jamie's eyes remained locked with mine and the contact heightened the intensity of the moment. As if our bodies were in tune, we shattered simultaneously. It was the first time I'd ever experienced it.

He held me close afterward for a moment before putting me back on the towel so he could hoist himself out of the water. I smiled when he stretched out beside me and pulled me into his arms. We didn't speak for a while. We simply basked in the after-sex bliss, in each other, and in the tropical warmth.

22

JAMIE

I could practically feel Charlotte's eyes boring holes into the side of my face as we approached the resort's entrance. We barely spoke all morning after we left the cabin. I think we were both disappointed about heading back to the real world after our few days of fantasy.

Does it have to stay a fantasy though? I glanced at her. Now she was the one staring straight ahead, so my gaze lingered on her as my mind raced with possibilities of a future. What if we could work something out? I could travel to Kohala more than once a year…

Before I could open my mouth to tell Charlotte what was on my mind, she said, "The welcome party awaits."

I looked ahead and all thoughts about making arrangements to see each other again came to a screeching halt. Lincoln was the first one I saw. He broke away from the group and barreled toward us. The rest of my friends followed and then I saw a man who I'd glimpsed a few times before. He must be Mark, Charlotte's supervisor.

No one looked too worried since Charlotte had kept her boss updated. However, Mark looked pissed. His scowl intensified the closer he got and his gaze narrowed on her. My first instinct was to protect her from whatever consequences might arise. Although, I didn't see why there should be any consequences when she'd had the balls to brave a storm to save my ass.

However, as I prepared to tell Mark to back off, Lincoln swept in. He clapped me on the shoulder. "Jamie, it's good to see you. You had us worried."

"Thanks. Charlotte took good care of me out there."

I could have bitten my tongue. Those words only sounded suspicious to *me* because I knew just how Charlotte took care of me. My gaze skated away from Lincoln's smiling face to meet Charlotte's. I looked away from her too so no one would notice if I happened to gaze at her with stars in my eyes.

However, I almost exploded when Lincoln swept Charlotte into a hug. My molars ground together from the force of the jealousy *and* irritation that sizzled through me. For one, he was too affectionate considering that they weren't a couple. Plus, now that I knew Charlotte didn't entertain thoughts of a rekindled romance with him, I was annoyed on her behalf.

Thirdly... Charlotte was *mine* dammit. I caught up on myself and realized that I was snarling at Lincoln. I quickly shook off my possessiveness and jealousy and relaxed my expression.

However, Alex must have caught on because as he tilted his head to study me, his eyes narrowed with suspicion.

When Lincoln finally put Charlotte down—he held on too long for my comfort—the others greeted her. They then turned their attention to me. Questions were fired at me, which I vaguely answered because my attention was split.

Mark had pulled Charlotte away, and I could tell from their

body language that he was reprimanding her. His hands cut through the air in a series of angry gestures as he spoke, while Charlotte listened with a tight expression. She then nodded and turned to walk away and Mark followed.

"What do you think that was about?" I asked.

Everyone turned to watch the two disappear inside.

"He's pissed that Charlotte took off to find you without notifying the necessary persons that you were missing," Lincoln replied.

I sighed. "I'm not a fucking child."

"Still, if anything had gone wrong, the resort would be in hot water," Spencer reasoned. "You know how these things go…"

"Yeah, the smaller guys always suffer the consequences when the bigger guys want to cover their asses," Michael said.

I frowned. How many times had we been involved in giving the *smaller guys* the shitty end of the stick without remorse? To get where we were, I was pretty sure we'd all had our ruthless moments. I wouldn't allow anyone to use Charlotte as a scapegoat to cover their asses.

"Don't worry about Charlotte, guys." Alex raised his eyebrows at me. "Jamie is going to fix everything, I assume."

I ignored the knowing look he gave me. "Damn right, I am."

"It's alright. I'll talk to Charlotte's supervisor—"

"*I'll* fix things for her," I growled, cutting Lincoln off.

His eyebrows snapped together and he eyed me as if I'd gone insane. Spencer and Michael wore matching *what-the-hell-is-wrong-with-you* looks. Alex just shook his head and smirked as if he knew exactly what had gotten into me.

* * *

"You dog," Alex said as he barged into my suite. "You slept with Charlotte, didn't you?"

Gawking at him and then at the open door, I hissed, "Keep it the fuck down, will you?"

He tutted and closed the door. "Not only did you sleep with her but you're in love with her."

I jumped up from where I sat on the arm of the sofa. I was going through the barrage of emails I couldn't check while I was stuck in the woods. Slamming my phone down, I scoffed. "I can't deny sleeping with her but love? I've known her for a week."

He snorted. "Yet you wanted to murder one of your closest friends for touching her. I saw the way you looked at Lincoln when he hugged her."

My gaze lowered to the floor. I wasn't proud of that.

"And you went into straight-up demon mode to protect her job."

Folding my arms over my chest, I muttered, "I don't know what you're talking about."

"I followed you to the recreation office."

"Seriously?"

"I thought you were taking off to see Charlotte, so I followed to talk some sense into you." Alex shrugged. "You know, to tell you to back off and end whatever you've got going on with her because you can't hurt Lincoln like that."

My jaw tightened but I stayed quiet.

"I saw you go into the supervisor's office. You came out wearing your stone-cold mask. He came out looking as if he'd seen a monster. I'm guessing he did... *you*. You must have gone into ruthless CEO mode. I can only imagine what you said to that poor man to have him look so terrified."

I illustrated how I'd destroy his very existence and orchestrate the ruin of this resort, that's what I did. And I never made empty threats. The Winchesters' reach was extensive. Mark saw the error of his ways… for the way he dealt with Charlotte today.

"Charlotte doesn't deserve to lose her job. She loves it here."

Alex's scrutiny of me made me uneasy. Was he judging? Categorizing me as a betrayer?

Combing my fingers through my hair, I walked over to the table where a bottle of my go-to poison, Stroh, sat. I poured some into a glass and threw it back.

Alex grunted and joined me. With his glass in hand, he flopped onto a chair and said, "Well, clearly the guilt is killing you." He lifted his eyebrows when I took another shot.

"I don't feel guilty for liking Charlotte, but I am an asshole for not telling Lincoln about us," I acknowledged.

"*Like* her?" He snorted. "You've fallen for her. How could you do that to Linc?"

"I did not fall—"

"I know the look, Jamie." His features darkened. It was like I was looking at a different person. Gone was the laid-back jokester. Pain flickered in his eyes but then it was gone and his expression softened again. It was as if he stomped down on the emotions that had been dredged up and buried them even deeper. "You know out of the five of us, the one who knows that look well is me."

I didn't comment on that because I knew what thinking about *her* did to him. "Fuck, Alex, I don't know if I'm in love, okay? Because I don't know how it feels." I threw my arms up. "Maybe that's sad. The whole lot of us are goddam pathetic when it comes to matters of the heart."

He chuckled and lifted the glass in agreement. "I suppose that's why we make such great friends." His amusement vanished, replaced by a scowl. "And I'd like for it to stay that way, so don't fuck around with Charlotte when you know Lincoln wants her back."

My molars clamped together. "We weren't *fucking* around."

"*Jeezus.*" Alex massaged the bridge of his nose. He got up and pointed at me. "Fix this, Jamie."

Before I could tell him that I had no idea how to fix it, he stormed out. Blowing out a breath, I eyed the bottle of liquor. I ditched the glass and went for the bottle, turning it to my head. Maybe if I got drunk enough, I'd somehow find clarity to deal with my current situation.

Michael's face flashed in my mind. He wore his usual bored expression. The ever-cynical man would say something like, "Clarity in the bottom of a liquor bottle? That's a hell of an oxymoron... you moron."

I laughed because I knew my friends well. I knew their likely responses to things, so I knew Lincoln would be hurt when I told him about Charlotte and me.

Shit.

23

CHARLOTTE

My hand hovered in the air, my knuckles centimeters away from Jamie's door. Showing up in the guests' domain wasn't a usual practice but I had to see Jamie... even if it was midnight. To my surprise, the door swung open before I knocked, and Jamie and I came face to face.

I slowly lowered my hand as we stared at each other. He seemed surprised to see me too.

"Charlotte, I was just coming to see you."

"Really?"

We hadn't seen or spoken to each other since we hiked back to the resort last afternoon. We'd taken our time trekking through the forest because although we didn't speak, neither of us wanted to head back to the reality of our situations. I suppose neither of us wanted to admit or accept that this was the end of our... whatever there was between us.

He exhaled. "Yeah. I'm sorry I didn't find you earlier. I meant to, I just..."

"It's okay. You don't have to explain. I get it." I imagined he had a lot to think about concerning Lincoln.

His expression softened. "You always get it."

"I always get *you*." I shrugged.

Jamie made a low groaning sound and his face twisted into a grimace. He then murmured, "You know, what? Fuck it."

"Fuck wh—?"

He swallowed my gasp when he pulled me to him and captured my mouth. As stunned as I was that he kissed me right in the hallway where any of his friends could come out of their rooms and see us, I melted against him and kissed him back with fervor.

"I told myself that I wouldn't touch you again until I spoke to Lincoln," he whispered against my lips. "But here you are and I can't resist."

He maneuvered us inside, closed the door, and pressed me against it. He didn't have to do much to get me hot for him. I found that all he had to do was be present and my reproductive organs went haywire. When he kissed me like this, deep and with so much passion, fluid gushed between my thighs. However, I came to see him about something important.

"Jamie..."

"Hmmm?" He hummed, yet he only kissed me harder. He slid his hands behind me to cup my ass and pull me closer. He tasted like liquor and smelled of it, and I wondered if he was drunk.

Tearing my lips away from him, I peered into his eyes. "How much did you have to drink?"

His lips twisted into a wry smile. "A lot... more than usual. It's okay though. I'm sober now... mostly. That's why I was just now coming to see you."

I sighed, feeling responsible for him behaving unlike

himself. I might not have known him long but my instinct told me he wasn't one to overdo it with alcohol because he was a control freak. Right now, he was in a situation that he couldn't control and I had a lot to do with it.

Cupping his face, I studied him and affection hit me hard in the chest. The attraction I'd had for Jamie when we first met blossomed into something much more potent... and frightening.

"Oh, Jamie... I'm sorry."

"For what?"

"Everything."

"I'm not sorry," he said, his hold on me tightening. "Meeting you, getting to know you..." He sighed. "This has been the best week of my life."

My heart warmed, melted, and ached all at the same time. "I came to say goodbye," I whispered. "When you didn't come to see me, I was worried that you'd leave without saying goodbye." I learned that they were leaving tomorrow... in a matter of hours.

He tucked my hair behind my ear. "I wouldn't do that."

We stared at each other. I supposed he wasn't sure what else to say. However, I had something to say, so I ducked out of his hold and hurried to the open door that led to the balcony.

Jamie hesitated but followed.

"It's been a strange evening," I said, lifting my face to inhale as the night breeze brushed my face.

"How so?"

I turned to him. "Well, my department threatened to fire me."

"I'm sorry. It's my fault."

I shook my head. "No, my actions are all on me, Jamie. I was so worried about you that I didn't follow the proper protocols. I wasn't thinking clearly..." Because I'd gotten too emotionally involved with a guest. "But my job is fine. Hours later, Mark called me back to his office. He said he spoke to the higher-ups and told them what an asset I was to the team and that I deserved a second chance."

"You are and you do," he insisted.

"Uh-huh." I watched Jamie closely... suspiciously. "Mark seemed terrified for some reason, and he apologized profusely. I mean to the point of being pathetic really."

"You don't say." He held my gaze, his expression giving nothing away.

"Did you have anything to do with everyone's change of heart?"

He rocked back on his heels. "I might have paid Mark a visit and told him that you were great at your job and that my friends and I are eager to come back here and spend our money because you helped us have the time of our lives."

"A glowing evaluation, huh? That's all you said to him?"

His innocent expression as he nodded said it all. My eyes narrowed to slits. I bet he threatened the hell out of Mark. I didn't know the nuances of Jamie's business, but I imagined that a billionaire from an affluent family had a lot of pull even outside of New York. I didn't typically rely on anyone to fight my battles, but in this case, I was grateful. Jamie fighting for me made me that much more certain that he saw me as more than a fun summer fling, and I was relieved.

"Thank you."

"You're welcome." His eyes smoldered as he gazed at me as if he'd kiss me again at any moment.

However, I couldn't get distracted now. "Have you spoken to Lincoln?"

Shoving his hands into his pockets, he shook his head. "No.

He disappeared, and I didn't bother searching for him because I hoped to avoid a conversation with him until we got back to Manhattan."

"I see." Twisting my hands in front of me, I revealed, "He disappeared because he came to see me. He finally told me…"

Jamie glanced at me. "And…?"

"I told him the truth. That I don't see him as more than a friend and that he shouldn't have assumed that I wanted the same thing he did when we reconnected."

Jamie's eyes widened slightly. "You told him about us?"

"No. I wasn't sure if you'd want me to or if it's even my place…"

He blew out a breath. "I should be the one to tell him."

I nodded. "He was pretty upset. He said he was going to take a walk on the beach to clear his head."

Jamie stared into the distance and his eyebrows furrowed. I knew what he was thinking… He hated that his friend was hurt. So did I.

"So, I guess this is it…" I said, swallowing the lump in my throat and forcing myself not to show my despair. "You'll be back in the Big Apple by tomorrow, and I'll be a distant memory… if not forgotten." That was meant to be delivered with a hint of humor but I failed miserably because my voice quavered.

Jamie whipped around, his eyes fierce and gleaming with outrage. "You think I'll forget you just like that? Fuck, Charlotte, you're…"

There was a loud knock, and we glanced inside at the suite's entrance.

"Jamie?" Lincoln called. "Are you still awake? I need to talk to you, man. And we'll need that Stroh you like to drink."

Jamie sighed and tucked his chin into his chest.

I nibbled my lower lip and actually searched for an escape as if we weren't on the freaking twenty-first floor. Once Lincoln saw me in Jamie's room, it would ruin Jamie's *preferred* time to reveal our secret.

"Shit, Jamie. I'm sorry."

He lifted his hand from his pocket to stroke my jaw and give me a slight smile. "It's okay. I was going to tell him anyway. No time like the present."

True, but I didn't want to be faced with the possibility that I'd ruined a friendship. If they had a falling out, I wouldn't be able to live with the guilt. Dread settled in my gut and I grabbed Jamie's hand when he moved toward the door. I couldn't find the words but I was sure that he saw how apologetic I was in my pleading eyes.

"It'll be okay, Charlotte… one way or another." He then pulled away and went to let Lincoln in while I stayed rooted to the balcony.

When Jamie opened the door, Lincoln brushed past him, threading his fingers through his hair. "Jamie, I just made a fucking fool of myself, so bring on the liquor in droves. I'm such an idiot," he hissed.

Jamie didn't say anything.

Lincoln continued, "I talked with Charlotte, and—"

"Lincoln," Jamie began. "Stop. I know…"

Lincoln's eyebrows furrowed. "What do you know?"

Taking a deep breath, I stepped back inside because I didn't want to stand in the shadows like a coward while they talked about me.

Lincoln did a double take at me and then he turned to Jamie.

"What the…? Charlotte…? What are you doing…?" he sputtered and then stopped. I could practically see him doing the math in his head. Finding me in Jamie's bedroom at this hour—or even at all—said it all, I suppose.

Lincoln rounded on Jamie and snarled. "Motherfu—"

"Lincoln, this isn't..." My words trailed off when he looked at me. I swallowed hard because the disbelief and hurt on his face made guilt clog my throat.

"Are you two... a *thing?*" he asked.

An awkward silence fell over the room like a suffocating blanket. I glanced at Jamie with bewilderment. What exactly were we?

As Jamie opened his mouth to reply to break the silence, Lincoln said, "So *you're* the reason why she kicked me to the curb." He glared daggers at his friend.

Jamie's scowl was just as fierce. "So you're just going to disregard everything she told you? Her *primary* reason for turning you down. It was never something she wanted, Lincoln."

"How the hell do you know what Charlotte and I talked about?" Lincoln glanced at me with accusation, and I averted my gaze. "You two are unbelievable. What is this, Jamie? Did you get a kick out of stealing the woman I had my eyes on from right under my nose?"

"It was never like that, Lincoln," Jamie denied.

The longer I listened, the less guilt I felt and the more pissed off I got. "Hold it right there." I stepped forward and both men looked at me. "First, you two aren't going to talk about me as if I'm not standing right here."

Jamie blew out a breath and Lincoln's jaw clenched. "Lincoln, I understand that you're hurt and angry but you're turning this into something it isn't."

"Well then, Charlotte, tell me, what exactly is it?" His full attention was on me and he had his arms folded over his chest while his eyes drilled into me.

Jamie angled himself between us and gave his friend a seething look. "This is between you and me now, Lincoln. If you want to direct your anger at someone, it should be me."

"It's okay, Jamie. I'll say what I have to say." I scowled at Lincoln. I'd never been one to back down from anything and he knew that. "Lincoln, I didn't *cheat* on you with your friend so stop acting like it. We broke up years ago, and I didn't expect you to want to rekindle our romance."

"So you didn't get the hint during our messages and phone calls?"

"No!" I threw my arms up. "What hint? You said you wanted to come to Pacific Paradise to unwind and to see an old friend. How the hell was I supposed to decipher that you wanted to get back together from *that*?"

He dropped his hands and nodded. "Okay… I see I should have been direct from the beginning."

My indignation melted away too. "That would have helped, and I'm sorry that I avoided you when I realized what you wanted. I should have womaned up and told you I wasn't interested."

The slightest hint of pink tinged his cheeks and his gaze slid away from me. I was sure women didn't turn him down often.

"Maybe I messed up," he said. "But that doesn't mean Jamie isn't a complete asshole for going after my ex." He shot Jamie a pointed look. "You knew about my past with her and you still went after her."

Jamie's deep sigh resonated with remorse. "When I first saw her and felt something…" He rubbed the back of his neck. "I didn't know who she was, I swear." He addressed Lincoln but he looked at me and I held his gaze, my heart turning into a puddle.

"Are you two serious?" Lincoln growled.

I jumped a little, tearing my gaze away from Jamie's hypnotic one.

"I should have known something was going on between you two. The secret conversations and Jamie making googly eyes at you." Lincoln scoffed in disgust. "Right in front of me… the *disrespect*."

That made Jamie wince. "Disrespecting or hurting you wasn't our intention. I thought about telling you, but you were hellbent on getting Charlotte back and I wasn't sure how she felt about you…" He sighed heavily and shoved his fingers through his hair.

My sentiments exactly. This conversation was incredibly awkward. It was like we were caught up in a love triangle that wasn't *really* a love triangle… weird.

A frown creased Lincoln's brow as he gave us disapproving looks. "I don't care about what you intended. Don't expect me to be happy about my best friend hooking up with my ex-girlfriend behind my back. Don't expect me to be forgiving either."

I watched with a sinking feeling as he stormed out, leaving Jamie and me in tense silence. I couldn't come between their friendship.

Jamie turned to me. "Charlotte, I'll talk to him. I can get through to him…"

"No, if you go home and never mention me again, the whole thing will blow over. He'll eventually forgive you as long as…" I swallowed.

"As long as there's no us?"

I nodded sadly. "Why ruin your friendship over something that won't work out anyway? You live in Manhattan, and I'm here. You're..." He was a billionaire and I was... nobody. Completely different worlds...

Jamie stared at me, waiting for me to finish and when I didn't, he asked, "What makes you so sure we wouldn't work?" There was a distinct echo of hurt in his voice, but I ignored it. "Sure, there's the distance, but—"

"Jamie, we've already hurt Lincoln. The least we can do is respect him. He clearly can't stand the thought of us. He's your best friend. Parting ways is for the best. You know it."

There was a heavy silence as I watched Jamie fight whatever emotional battle raged in his mind. Then his expression went blank and I almost snorted my amusement. He knew how to turn off his emotional switch like a pro and I hated that for him. I hated that whatever life he lived back in Manhattan required him to hide his emotions behind a brick wall.

He finally lifted his head to meet my gaze. "I guess this is goodbye then."

"Yeah. I suppose it is." With a last lingering look, I walked away from what I thought would have been something great had we had a chance to explore it.

24

JAMIE

The atmosphere in my office was tense. It had been for a while and it was my fault. I'd never been overly friendly and chatty with my employees before, however, despite my typical aloofness, I wasn't a tyrant.

Since returning home from my birthday trip two weeks ago, I'd been intolerable... That's what I overheard my assistant telling the secretary in the lobby. She was right. I'd been miserable since I said goodbye to Charlotte. The worst part? Lincoln didn't give a shit that I parted ways with her for good. He was still pissed at me and barely said a word to me on our way home.

He was back in LA and was ignoring my calls. The others were upset with me at first because they thought what I did to Lincoln was messed up. However, after I explained the finer details of everything that transpired in Kohala, they understood that I didn't *steal* Charlotte from Lincoln. However, they all agreed that I should have said something and not have Lincoln discover what was going on when he found Charlotte in my room. That was a terrible way for him to find out.

Thinking about everything got me all riled up again and as I rounded the corner and burst through the doors of my private office, I directed my attention to my assistant. "Where the hell is the report I asked for, Darcy? " I held my phone and scowled. "I haven't gotten the email yet."

My assistant flinched and scrambled to pull up the requested document. "I-I'm sorry, Mr. Winchester. I was preparing the letter for…" She inhaled and exhaled loudly. "I'll email you the report in a few minutes." Her fingers flew over her keyboard and her shoulders were hiked up.

Jaw clenched, I marched toward my door, my every step probably brimming with agitation. When I stepped into my office and closed the door, guilt pricked me in the chest. My assistant didn't deserve to suffer because of the shit going on in my personal life. Charlotte would likely tell me I was being an asshole or that I'd transformed into *James Wilfred*. The memory of how she teased me about my name made my lips twitch. I hadn't smiled since I got home.

Releasing a puff of air, I yanked the door open. "Darcy?"

Her head popped up and her eyes were the size of saucers as if she expected me to go off on her again.

"I'm sorry," I said. "It's been a rough day." She lifted an eyebrow, and I gave her a sheepish smile. "I mean, it's been a rough couple of weeks. Take your time with that report. I'll wait."

She nodded and her shoulders relaxed.

Closing the door, I massaged the bridge of my nose. "I need to get a grip."

I couldn't go around snapping at employees because Charlotte pretty much told me to get lost. She had a valid reason for doing so but still… it stung. I thought we'd at least exchange phone numbers and agree to keep in touch.

Walking to my desk, I flopped down on my chair and swiveled it around to face the window. As I gazed at the sleek glass skyscraper buildings beside mine, my thoughts drifted to Charlotte as they usually did. I'd resigned myself to seeing her in my memories. Her smile, her laughter, her warmth… the way she always understood me.

The memories were like a knife twisting in my gut because I'd never experience those things with her again. She was clear when she said goodbye. She wanted nothing to do with me. In her mind, she was protecting my friendship with Lincoln. I bet she didn't realize how much she'd hurt me.

This was a first for me—getting my feelings hurt by a woman I'd been romantically involved with. That meant I was more into Charlotte than I even realized. I think I was… *heartbroken.*

"Jesus," I breathed as I rubbed my tired eyes. Didn't that kind of heartbreak come from being in love…? *"Jesus,"* I muttered again.

I didn't get to drive myself up the wall trying to figure out the depth of my feelings for a woman I spent barely a week with because my cell rang. The name on the screen made me sigh.

Still, I answered. "Dad."

"James, are you at the office?"

His stern voice boomed into my ear. The sound of his voice always made me tense. I even sat up taller in my chair, ready to receive whatever order he had to dish out. Dad always made it sound like he was giving suggestions but he gave you hell if you said no. So, essentially, he gave *orders.* And I always followed them…

"Where else would I be, Dad?" My fingers drummed out a rapid agitated rhythm on the desk.

"Working hard as always. Good. Good. I trust you're ready to meet Gwendolyn."

My fingers stopped drumming. "Gwendolyn..." Who the hell was Gwendolyn?

"Gwendolyn Calloway," Dad sighed. "You said I could arrange an introduction with her when you got back from that silly trip with your friends."

I massaged my forehead. A trip to escape the emotional despair of my birthday was silly... the cold, clueless bastard. "Did I agree to that?"

"You never gave me a response so I took it to mean you agreed."

My molars clamped together so hard, I thought they'd shatter. Of course, he assumed my lack of response was a yes. I did everything he said up to this point. That was on me. However, Charlotte helped to significantly lessen the guilt I felt about Mom and the obligation I thought I had to please Dad.

"No," I said.

"No?" The mixture of shock and confusion in his tone sent a sliver of amusement through me.

It was like I said, I had nobody to blame for Dad's constant expectations of me but myself. I'd never said no to him.

"I changed my mind about getting hitched to some woman I don't know because you think she's suitable."

"But... You..."

Spinning my chair around, I threw my feet onto my desk. It was time to take charge of my life and stop living to please my old man. "When I'm ready to get married... *If* I ever am, I'll choose my own bride."

"The Calloways—"

"Are in the same social sphere. They come from old money and will help to extend the Winchester reach… Yeah, I got it."

Boy, did I get it. I'd been hearing the same shit about the kind of woman I should tie myself to since I hit puberty. There had never been any mention of love or even *like* for the other party. It was all about keeping up appearances and doing what was right for the Winchester legacy.

After experiencing what I did with Charlotte, I decided that if I were to commit, I'd rather it be with someone I had a meaningful connection with.

"I've grown the Winchester empire to multi-billion dollar status, Dad. I think I have the mental capacity to find my own dates. You don't have to do it for me."

Dad huffed, and I imagined his eyes bulging and his face turning red as it usually did when he was pissed—when someone said no to him. Plus, he hated sarcasm. My lips twisted into a slight smile because it felt damn good to tell him no and not be hit with guilt.

"James, what has gotten into you?" he asked calmly.

He never let his emotions control him… and that was a part of the problem with our strained relationship. I loved the old man but he'd die before he showed me a sliver of affection.

I considered his question. "I'm learning that I deserve to be happy, Dad." There was more to life than being his dutiful soldier.

He fell quiet. I guess he was trying to work through his shock to formulate a response.

Before he did, my phone beeped. When I glanced at it, I saw Michael's name. "I have to go, Dad. Important business call. You understand, right?"

"Son—"

I switched over to Facetime. Michael's, Spencer's, and Alex's faces popped up on the screen.

"Well, well, if it isn't Benedict Arnold," Alex greeted.

I sighed and looked skyward while Michael chuckled. If there was one person who could make the grouch laugh, it was Alex.

"I'm not a traitor," I said.

"He's bloody dramatic, isn't he?" Spencer said.

"*Dramatic?* That's what Michael and Spencer keep telling me," Alex grumbled as he glared at me. "But I don't think I'm wrong."

"You joined the call so you can't hate me all that much," I threw back.

"Of course, I don't hate you. I'm upset because I warned you, didn't I? You know who hates you? Lincoln."

My jaw tightened. "Michael, how is he?"

His eyebrows shot up. Michael lived in LA so he and Lincoln saw each other more often. "He's been… broody. On the bright side, I doubt he really hates you as Alex thinks."

I scrubbed a hand over my face. I was tempted to fly out to LA and force him to talk to me.

"How are you, mate?" Spencer asked, watching me closely.

"I've been better. I'll be fine once Lincoln calms down and talks to me. I'd be on cloud nine if I could talk to Charlotte."

There was a chorus of groans and *"Oh, god," "Bloody hell,"* and *"Are you serious?"*

I'd always been comfortable expressing most things I felt around these guys. That said a lot because I clammed up tighter than a vise around everyone else… except Charlotte.

"I can't stop thinking about her," I defended.

"I told you he was in love," Spencer said.

"I'm not." I frowned. "I didn't get enough time with her to be sure…"

"Then spend more time with her," Michael suggested. "It's not fucking science. She might be the one."

That resulted in a string of expletives from Alex. "I can't believe this, Michael. *You're* encouraging foolishness? Weren't you the one who agreed with me that romance is a load of crap and there's no such thing as *the one?*"

"I changed my mind." Michael shrugged. "Jamie was happy. I've never seen him glow the way he did after being stranded with Charlotte in the woods."

"I didn't *glow*," I scoffed.

Spencer roared. "You glowed… like a pregnant woman."

I rolled my eyes but said nothing. At least two of my friends understood.

"The one might not exist for everybody," Michael reasoned. "Definitely not for me. But maybe Jamie is one of the lucky few…" He stroked his chin. "All I'm saying is that if he has strong feelings for Charlotte, it's worth exploring. It's unfortunate that he had to catch feelings for Lincoln's ex, but if she's who makes him happy…"

"Blimey, did someone slip something into his drink in Hawaii?" Spencer mused.

We all gawked at Michael. I'd never heard him sound like this.

"I'm sure Lincoln will come around," he continued. "After all, he and Charlotte were no longer together." A phone rang in Michael's background. "I've got to go, fellas. Jamie, I'll keep you posted on Lincoln's mood and let you know when it's safe to try talking to him again."

"Thanks, man."

After Michael disappeared, I directed my attention to

Spencer. "What do you think? Should I reach out to Charlotte?"

Spencer rubbed his jaw. "Go for it."

"*Spencer,*" Alex seethed.

"I'm going to go before Alex labels me a Benedict Arnold as well. Later, gents."

Alex and I were left on the line. I stared at him for a moment. Finally, I asked, "What's your *real* problem with this entire situation?"

"What other problem could I have other than one friend betraying the other?"

"I didn't betray—"

"So you keep saying."

I huffed. "I think I know what's going on. You think that Lincoln's heart is broken and it hits too close to home. You got your heart broken by—"

"Don't fucking say it," he snapped.

I snapped my mouth shut and took in his darkened expression. Perhaps it was best not to jump down that rabbit hole. "Then *you* say it. Say *something*. I don't want two of my best friends pissed at me."

"I hate that our group dynamic isn't the same, okay? That's my problem. I've never had much of a family until I met you assholes in college."

I smiled at that. We forged a bond that was like any blood-related family.

"We just had one of our group chats and Lincoln is missing. I don't like it." He sighed.

"Me either. I'll try my best to fix things with Lincoln but I can't just forget about her, Alex, and I need your help."

"Nope. I know where this is going." He shook his head emphatically. "Absolutely not."

"I confess… I called the resort but they said she wasn't there.

I don't know if she got fired after all or if she quit. We never exchanged phone numbers…"

"Jamie, no. Lincoln is angry with you. I'm not about to help piss him off further."

"I just need to talk to her. The way things ended doesn't sit well with me. Come on, Alex."

"You can find her. You have the resources."

"I know, but you can do it faster." By faster, I meant the very next day. His resources outdid mine by far when it came to these things. "Please, Alex."

He heaved a sigh. "Fine. I'll do it. After that, I'm taking a break from all of you asshats and your emotional shit. I'm serious, don't call me."

I smirked when he ended the call because I knew his break from us "asshats" wouldn't last. He'd forget he was pissed at me in two days tops, and he'd call me with some ridiculous story about some shenanigan he got himself into.

Putting my phone down, I turned to face the window again. As I stared out, I wondered where Charlotte was and what she was doing. Was she thinking about me as I thought about her?

25

CHARLOTTE

Jamie.

He haunted my thoughts like a ghost. No matter how hard I tried, I couldn't let him go. In my defense, it had only been about two and a half weeks since we parted ways. Realistically, it would take much longer than that to get over someone I felt a strong connection with. I resigned myself to reliving every moment we had together since we met in that hotel lobby.

Maybe Jamie hadn't even thought of me once he got back to Manhattan. He was probably back to dating models and socialites or whoever billionaires dated. He and Lincoln were probably as tight as ever and they'd already forgotten the tension I caused between them. I hoped the latter was true, but thinking about Jamie dating made me want to throw something and scream with rage and jealousy.

"Charlotte, honey, are you alright?"

I blinked and turned to Mom. It was then I realized that I'd been staring out the kitchen window for... I wasn't even sure how long, but my feet were tired.

"Yeah. I'm fine." I forced a smile as she eyed me dubiously. I came home last week for a short vacation. Admittedly, I couldn't stand to be at the resort with memories of Jamie swirling around everywhere I looked. I thought a week away would help.

"Somebody is awake and wants to see Aunt Char."

My smile turned genuine fast when I looked at the sweetest face ever. It was my nephew and he wore a gummy smile as he reached out to me. He was only eighteen months old and my sister was about to pop out another one. Vicky certainly wasted no time.

"Come here, handsome," I cooed.

"Aunt Cha," little Max squealed.

I laughed because I loved being his Aunt *Cha*, but I hated that he hadn't seen me for seven months.

Mom smiled from ear to ear as she got to work on breakfast while giving me and Max happy glances. I sat in a chair and rocked him on one knee, pretending to be a space shuttle because he loved the hell out of the little game. His cute baby laughs filled the kitchen, which drew out my giggles.

Just then Vicky waddled in, clutching her swollen belly. "Goodness, Char, he only laughs like that with you. Not even his father can get him to squeal with joy like that."

I grinned at Max. "That's because you and I have a special bond, right, Maxy? You're an adventurer at heart." I chucked his chin. "I can already tell."

"It's because you're great with children, Charlotte," Mom said, pointing a spatula at me. "I've been telling you that you should have at least one little one already. What are you waiting for? You love kids." She swept the spatula around to encompass the scene of me and Max.

I stifled a sigh as I glanced at Vicky, silently pleading for her help.

My sister rolled her eyes and said, "Mom, lay off. Charlotte came home for a break. Stop stressing her out."

"I don't see how talking about a family is stressful," Mom grumbled.

Vicky gave me a look that said *just ignore her*. I did because I was in enough emotional turmoil. If I had to deal with Mom pressuring me, I'd likely lose it. I managed to tune Mom out enough to not hear much of what she prattled on about. However, I knew the topic was about my lack of enthusiasm to settle down and give her more grandchildren.

"Charlotte, are you alright?"

My head snapped up and I glanced at Vicky who was behind the counter helping Mom. I absently bounced Max on my knee still, but I had been in a completely different world. A world where Jamie and I were back in that cabin contentedly stranded together, basking in our fantasy bubble. I suppose I was so hung up on him because of the way things abruptly ended between us. We didn't even get a chance to see if we were good together.

As I swallowed a devastated sigh, the doorbell rang, resonating through the house.

Mom's eyebrows snapped together. "I'm not expecting company…"

Vicky, who was just visiting for the morning, shrugged.

Since they were both busy, I stood up and settled Max in one arm. "I'll see who it is."

As I walked through the living room and foyer to the door, I tickled Max because I loved hearing him laugh. His little giggles made me smile and my lips were still stretched in amusement when I opened the door.

My grin tumbled from my face as my jaw dropped and my eyes all but popped out of my head. Standing on Mom's porch was the man who I thought I'd never see in real life again.

"J-Jamie?" I stuttered.

Was he real? My brain almost short-circuited as I computed if he was because what in the world would he be doing in Oregon? And how would he know where to find me?

Jamie stared at me just as I gawked at him. His gaze then shifted to the toddler in my arm and his eyebrows elevated.

"He's not mine…" I said stupidly. "I mean… He's my nephew."

Jamie blinked and met my gaze once again. "You're probably wondering what the hell I'm doing here…"

It was my turn to give him a raised eyebrow stare. "Actually, I'm wondering how you found me," I replied when what I really wanted to do was throw myself into his arms.

Sure, I was reeling from shock and confusion but I was happy to see him. My heart hammered against my rib cage as I took him in. He looked different than he did on vacation. He was clean-shaven and immaculately dressed. He looked good.

"I, um…" He rubbed his nape and cleared his throat. A flustered Jamie was adorable because I was sure he rarely lost his cool. "I called the resort asking for you because we never exchanged phone numbers."

I went back and forth between regretting not asking for his information and convincing myself that it was for the best.

"They said you weren't there." His brow creased. "You didn't lose your job, did you?"

I glanced at Max who was tugging at my necklace. "No. I took a short break. I'm going back to work next week."

"Oh... good." He blew out a breath. "I wanted to see you. I remembered you told me where you were from and I tracked you down..." The slightest tinge of pink highlighted his cheeks. "Not like a stalker..." He then frowned. "Although hunting you down might come off... *Shit*," he breathed. "I'm regretting showing up at your mother's place without calling first to find out if you wanted to see me. I was trying the whole spontaneity thing." Uncertainty clouded his eyes as he frowned at me. "Please tell me you want to see me or I might die of embarrassment."

I pulled my lip between my teeth to hold back my amusement at the otherwise stoic Jamie practically having a meltdown on Mom's porch. He hunted me down and showed up, and I was happy about it. A giggle escaped me and I almost burst into tears because of the barrage of emotions that hit me.

I stepped outside and cupped his face with my free hand. As soon as I lifted my face to him, his mouth came down on mine. The kiss was short because I held a baby in one arm but it was so good. I wanted to kiss him deeper and savor our reunion.

However, I pulled away and breathed. "I'm happy enough to see you that I don't care *how* you found me."

"Thank fuck, or this would have been beyond weird."

"Jamie!" I hissed, putting a hand over Max's ear.

Jamie winced as he glanced at my nephew. "Sorry..."

"I'm *really* happy to see you. I—"

"Charlotte, sweetie, who's at the door?"

Crap. It wasn't that I didn't want to introduce Jamie to Mom, I just would have liked to warn him about her craziness first. Mom appeared in the doorway and glanced at Jamie with a polite smile.

"I thought it might be Lincoln," she said, glancing at me. "You did tell him what I said about wanting to see him, right?"

My jaw tightened as I glared at her. "Things didn't work out with him, Mom," I bit out, hoping that my sharp tone was warning enough to tell her to shut it.

Jamie didn't react to the mention of Lincoln or Mom being kinda rude and dismissive. Of course, if he felt any way about it, no one would know because he was a pro at hiding his emotions.

"Oh… And who is this?" Mom asked.

"This is my friend, James. Jamie, this is my mother, Faye."

Mom's eyes narrowed. "A *friend*?"

I groaned inwardly. "Mom, can you give us a minute?"

Maybe I could arrange a meet-up with Jamie in town far away from my mother.

"Wouldn't your friend like to stay for breakfast?"

I turned to Jamie and tried to tell him with my eyes that he'd better refuse.

A devious smirk curled his lips and he said, "Breakfast sounds lovely, Mrs. Brooks."

I glowered at him.

"And I'm not just Charlotte's friend. I'm dating your daughter, ma'am."

My jaw nearly brushed the floor as I stared at him in disbelief. The angelic smile that appeared on his face made me want to throttle him. Mom just about swooned at the news… the *false* news. I frowned at Jamie, wondering what he was thinking.

"Dating? I didn't know Charlotte had a significant other." She clapped her hands as she pretty much mowed me over to get to Jamie. She shook his hand with enthusiasm and gazed up at him with adoration. I guess Lincoln was forgotten and my new *boyfriend* was now the apple of her eye. "My, you are so handsome."

Jamie grinned and my eyes narrowed on him. He was enjoying every minute of this.

"And none of that *Mrs. Brooks*. You can call me Faye."

"It's a pleasure to meet you, Faye."

Mom slid her arm through his. "Come inside, James. You can meet Charlotte's sister, Victoria." She escorted him through the door as if he were royalty.

Did Mom *have* to be so excited about me being in a relationship that Jamie totally lied about? She made me look pathetic for goodness sake. Jamie's Cheshire cat grin when he glanced back at me made me shake my head.

26

JAMIE

Charlotte led me up the stairs and down a hallway. My head moved as if it were on a swivel, taking in everything about the Brooks' home. The ambiance of the place was warm and welcoming and there were tons of photos on the walls that illustrated sweet and fun family moments. The walls practically exuded love, and I soaked it up because I didn't know what a *normal* loving home was like.

Charlotte wrapped her hand around my wrist and tugged me into a room. As she closed the door, she let out a long sigh. "Please allow me to apologize for my mother's behavior. She's a bit much to handle on a first meeting."

My chuckle filled the room that I discovered to be a bedroom… Charlotte's childhood bedroom it seemed. There were posters of popular bands from the nineties and nature scenes from exotic locations adorning the walls.

"Don't worry about it. Faye is quite the entertaining character."

Charlotte pushed the door closed, leaned against it, and huffed. "She pinched your cheek and called you *adorable*, Jamie."

"So?" I shrugged.

"I was horrified. You're a grown man! Her mission in life is to embarrass me."

I smiled at the memory of Faye gently pinching my cheek and tutting at me as if I were a kid. I was caught off guard at first but it warmed my heart and made me laugh because I never had a mother to do that kind of thing.

"Actually, I liked it. I like your mom. I wish I had a mom to embarrass me."

Charlotte's annoyance was wiped away in an instant and she pushed herself off the door and groaned. "Right... I'm sorry. Now I feel bad for being irritated by Mom's smothering affection."

"I like your sister too. You guys seem close."

"We are."

"I've always wanted that..."

Charlotte watched me with a frown. However, she didn't make me feel bad by watching me with pity for too long like most people did. Instead, she narrowed her eyes to slits as she took a step toward me.

"Why would you tell my mom that we're dating? You know that's not true."

There it was. I'd been waiting for her to dig into me about that. She had to hold her tongue while we had breakfast with her family, but I had caught her seething looks. I still couldn't believe I had shown up, met her family, and shared a meal with them... all before asking Charlotte to date me.

This spontaneity thing wasn't me, but if it got me what I wanted—Charlotte in my life—I was all for it. "It could be true..."

A frown tugged at her eyebrows. "What?"

I'd never had trouble going after or saying exactly what I wanted until now. Suddenly, my nerves felt frayed. Never in my life had I asked a woman to date me exclusively before.

"I mean, if you're interested, of course," I said lamely.

She continued to gawk, and I raked my fingers through my hair. "I'm asking you to be a part of my life, Charlotte."

Her eyes widened. "In what way?"

As I stared at her, I couldn't remember ever experiencing this level of vulnerability. The worst that could happen was that she'd say no. However, it was hard to come out with my answer because if she did turn me down, I'd be devastated.

Covering the distance between us while holding her gaze, I said, "In every way."

I heard the catch in her breath as she continued to study me through wide eyes. "You mean, like…"

"I want us to date and see where things go."

Charlotte blinked and the surprise in her eyes gave way to a cautious curiosity. "Are you serious?" Her tone was a mixture of disbelief and a hint of vulnerability. She then laughed. "What am I asking? You hunted me down."

"If that doesn't show you how serious I am, then I don't know what will," I said.

We stood centimeters apart, gazing at each other with mutual longing. I cupped her cheek and ran my thumb over her soft skin because I had to touch her.

"I spent every minute of every day since we parted ways wondering if I made a huge mistake walking away from you. I concluded that I did."

Her eyes shone with that curiosity that I got to know during our short time together in Hawaii.

"When I decided to make a change in how I lived, that

included following my heart. My heart tells me that you and I have something special, Charlotte."

"Jamie…" My name fluttered from her lips as a soft sigh and her expression softened as she planted her palms on my chest. Immediately, I placed my hand over one of hers. "This is crazy."

"What's so crazy about it?" There was no denying that we clicked. I thought we had at first sight of each other.

"Our different lives. Lincoln…"

The latter put a slight damper on my determination to explore what was between us, but it wasn't enough to allow me to give up.

I sighed. "Pursuing you further is probably wrong considering that Lincoln and I have yet to talk. He's been avoiding me."

She scoffed and pulled away, taking a few steps back to put distance between us. "*What?* Then why are you here telling me you want to date?"

My jaw clenched. "Because I can't get over you, Charlotte."

Silence ensued as we stared at each other. Her eyes were wide and filled with conflict, which mirrored the turmoil I felt inside too. While I was reluctant to upset my friend further, I simply couldn't walk away from Charlotte. I tried and I failed.

"Maybe I'm being selfish." I shrugged. "But what I felt with you in a few days… I've never felt with any woman my entire life. That's worth exploring and you know it because I know you feel the same way."

The unshed tears I'd seen in her eyes when we parted ways weeks ago told me she hadn't really wanted to say goodbye.

She made a little groaning noise and her shoulders sagged. "Well, then, if you're being selfish, then I guess I am too." With that, she was in my arms before I could catch my next breath.

Her body fit perfectly against mine. Satisfaction surged through me as I fitted my mouth over hers.

Her lips were soft and pliant. I deepened the kiss and it became ravenous in an instant. I'd gone too long without kissing her, without being wrapped in her warmth like this. I couldn't get enough of her taste. I pressed her against the door, my hands roaming hungrily to touch every part of her that I could. Just as I made my way under her blouse to cup her breasts, she moaned into my mouth and pulled away.

"What are we doing?" she panted.

Feathering kisses along her jaw and bending to reach the delicate column of her neck, I whispered, "I'm hoping you'll let me fuck you right here against this door." I found the front clasp of her bra and was about to snap it open when she socked me on the arm.

"No. We're in my mom's house and my childhood bedroom for goodness's sake."

My arousal dampened… a *little*. I still wanted to have her in every way. "We can be really quiet…"

"Jamie."

I sighed, backed off, and grumbled, "You're supposed to be the fun, spontaneous one."

She smirked. "Get over it, you fiend."

"I missed you, Charlotte." I gave her a once-over and plenty of dirty things played out in my mind as I did. "Missed feeling your skin against mine… missed being buried *deep* inside you…"

She made a slight moaning sound, and I bit the inside of my cheek to hold back my smirk. However, I couldn't contain it when she glowered at me and said, "I know what you're trying to do."

"It was worth a try."

She smiled at me and my heart melted. "Do you want to get out of here? I can show you my favorite hang-out spots growing up. We can... talk and figure things out." A frown then marred her gorgeous face. "Do you even have time? Do you have to get back home today? How are we—?"

I pressed a finger to her lips. "I don't want you to worry about anything, and I've got plenty of time."

* * *

Charlotte beamed at me from across the table and I stared at her in amazement. She was one hell of a woman. I mean, she'd gotten *me* to want to... date. We were still in the honeymoon stage of a relationship, but it was a big step for me. This was going to be my *first* serious relationship. I'd keep my fingers crossed and hope I wouldn't fuck up.

"It gets less weird over time when you stare at me like that. I suppose I'm getting used to it." She grinned broadly and sipped the smoothie she'd ordered. After spending the morning driving and walking around Golden Beach, Charlotte's hometown, we stopped at her favorite diner for lunch.

"I can't help staring at a beautiful woman," I said, dunking a fry into ketchup and *not* eating it. I wasn't hungry because I was full of anticipation about *us*.

Charlotte's cheeks bloomed a rose pink and her long lashes fluttered down to hide her eyes. Her shy blush was a contrast to the confident woman who was so full of life and humor. When her lashes lifted and her gaze met mine again, I detected a hint of worry.

"How are we going to do this, Jamie?"

I paused while lifting my drink. Of course, I knew what she

meant. "We'll make it work." Hopefully, the confidence in my tone would reassure her.

"How do two people date when they live five thousand miles apart with an ocean between them?" Her teeth sank into her lower lip as she watched me expectantly, waiting for my answer.

"Your job in Kohala isn't permanent, is it?"

"No, but…" She glanced around the diner. "Even if I'm not in the middle of the Pacific, I'll be here in Oregon… still on the opposite side of the country."

Blowing out a breath, I placed my hand in the middle of the table with my palms up. She caught on and immediately placed hers in them. "We've *just* decided that we're going to be a couple. How about we not think too much about the barriers and focus on the present? I'm here with you now."

Still, she gnawed at her lower lip. "When do you have to head back to Manhattan? I imagine you're a busy man."

"I can spare a couple of days."

Disappointment clouded her eyes but she nodded. "That's something. We'll make the most of it."

I watched her for a moment, troubled by the hint of uncertainty I caught shadowing her eyes. She didn't think this could work.

"Is it possible for you to take another week off work?" I asked.

"Sure…"

"Come to Manhattan with me. We'll have a few days here and then another week together."

"Jamie…"

"I've seen your world. It's only fair that you spend some time in mine."

She smiled, no doubt recalling our conversation about living in different worlds. It was true in a way. Charlotte and I led opposite lives, and we never would have met if not for that spontaneous trip to Kohala. I had Lincoln to thank for that, which was pretty fucked up considering how things went down. However, I couldn't dwell on that right now...

I traced little circles on the back of her hand. "We'll visit each other's worlds as much as we can until things change and one day our worlds become one."

Her eyes, which had been fixed on my fingers moving over her skin, flew back up to meet mine. Yes, I knew what I implied... that this might turn out to be something permanent. Maybe it was presumptuous of me but for once in my life, I felt that going beyond dating was a possibility. It was both a scary and exciting thought.

Charlotte swallowed hard, her wide eyes still fixed on mine, but she didn't disagree.

27

CHARLOTTE

For someone who traveled and saw as much of the world as I had, I was a little overwhelmed by Manhattan. I mostly visited exotic locations with beaches, jungles, mountains, and deserts. Not big, bustling cities with never-ending traffic and skyscraper buildings.

It wasn't just the city setting. I wasn't accustomed to anything that Jamie seemed used to. I'd certainly never flown on a private jet. Of course, he had a private jet and he was carted around in fancy chauffeured vehicles.

I took my eyes off the city sidewalk that was busy with pedestrians and glanced at him. He tapped away on his phone as he'd been doing intermittently since we boarded his jet. I bet he was dealing with important business… billionaire CEO stuff.

The thought drove home just how different we were. He was somebody important and I was… a woman who flitted from job to job without a steady home and just enough in her bank account. What was a man like Jamie doing with me?

My heart started to sink from the weight of my negative thoughts.

Jamie glanced at me and immediately tucked his phone into his pocket. "Charlotte, what's wrong?"

Just like that, I had his full attention. It showed that I indeed meant something to him. The fact that he was so tuned in to my expressions and moods already was a great sign. Jamie constantly showed me that it didn't matter to him what I had or didn't have. For someone with as much money and power as he had, he was one of the sweetest, humblest men I'd ever met.

He spent three days with my family, and they had no idea how wealthy he was because he was so down to earth. He got his hands dirty helping Mom in her garden, and he helped my sister's husband paint the new nursery. My nephew even puked on what I suspected were his super expensive pants and shoes and he laughed it off.

When Jamie looked at me with such concern, his world didn't seem so daunting.

"Nothing is wrong."

Sharp silver eyes moved over my face. "You sure?"

"Yeah. I'm just taking everything in."

After a moment's hesitation, he smiled and purred, "I can't wait to get you home."

The drop in his octave made my pussy muscles clenched. That was the same tone he used when he whispered dirty things in my ear while he was inside me. Plus, his suggestive smirk reminded me of the crazy amount of sex we'd had in the motel room he stayed in back in Golden Beach. It was like we tried to make up for a lifetime of not being together. Then there was the flight to Manhattan during which Jamie inducted me into the mile-high club…

Sweet goddess of the best sex of my life. I squirmed on the SUV's posh leather seat because my panties got too wet for my comfort. Jamie's smirk grew and his gaze dipped to my thighs. The devil knew what was happening to me. I tried to glower at him but failed.

"We are not having any more sex," I announced. "Seriously. We need at least a day's break."

His eyebrows shot up as if he was saying *we'll see*.

* * *

The elevator doors swished open and Jamie stepped out with me wrapped around him like a vine on a tree. He held me in place with one hand while carrying my bag in the other. Once we were inside his apartment, he dropped the bag and grabbed my ass with both hands. I moved my hips against him, aching for us to be connected in the most intimate way.

He didn't miss a step as we kissed wildly. One touch from him in the elevator and I forgot about the break I'd mentioned. It wasn't even that much of a sexual touch. He'd merely wrapped an arm around my waist as we waited for the lift to ascend and planted a chaste kiss on my forehead.

The gesture had been so sweet that I lost it and jumped him like a cat in heat, and here we were, stumbling through his apartment, tearing at each other's clothes in a frenzy. I managed to push his blazer off and then he lifted my shirt over my head. He had to put me down to get my pants off and that was when I got a better look at his place.

The penthouse apartment was the epitome of luxury. The expansive open-plan layout was expertly furnished. Each piece of furniture seemed to be made just for the area they occupied. For example, the plush beige sectionals that adorned the sunken lounge area were perfect for the space. The room was bathed in natural light coming from the floor-to-ceiling windows.

My gaze zeroed in on the view of the skyline. "Wow, that view is incredible," I whispered as Jamie tugged my pants down my thighs.

He paused long enough to look at me and then at the windows. "Yeah? Then you should enjoy it while I enjoy you."

I laughed at the thought of craning my neck to look outside the entire time we made love. It was ridiculous. However, I understood when he swept me off my feet and carried me to the windows. As soon as my feet touched the glossy hardwood, he spun me around to face the glass.

The sprawling canvas of skyscrapers practically touching the clouds and the sun receding to disappear behind the horizon was set before me.

"Better?" Jamie whispered in my ear.

Smiling, I glanced up at him and nodded. I then angled my face for a kiss and he captured my lips in a bone-melting kiss. While our tongues mingled, he palmed my hips, moved his hands around to caress my stomach, and then upward to knead my breasts. Each flick of his thumbs over my nipples made me moan as electric-like currents shot down to my core.

The fire between us built back to a frenzy the longer we kissed, and Jamie released my mouth to free himself from his pants. His movements were quick and jerky as if he couldn't wait any longer for us to be joined. The rustle of his pants dropping to the floor made my stomach flutter in anticipation. He grasped my hips and pulled me back against him, pushing my underwear aside at the same time.

His cock pressing against my entrance made me moan and press myself into him, begging him to slide home. "Are you ready for me, Charlotte?"

"More than ready." My voice echoed with desperate need.

He hummed and slid a hand between my thighs to run his finger over my mound and then between my folds. I sucked in a sharp breath as I shivered. "So wet for me," he purred with satisfaction.

"Only for you. Please, Jamie. Now." Only he could get me to the point of shameless begging. I pushed back, demanding that he give me what I wanted. He pushed into me with a slow, smooth thrust. The delicious sensation of being filled by him made my eyes roll back. He stayed still as he feathered kisses on my neck and shoulder. I angled my head to give him better access.

He thrust again, his movement gentle as he gave me time to adjust. "Is this okay?" he asked, lips pressed to my ear.

The way he handled me with utmost care was almost orgasmic. "It's perfect. More."

He moved, pulling out almost fully before plunging back in. I let out a guttural moan and my body trembled with pleasure. As he sped up, I wound an arm around his neck to anchor myself against his rougher movements while I pressed a hand to the cool glass. I gazed out at the spectacular view while Jamie drove me to sheer bliss. Each powerful thrust brought me closer and higher until I shattered into what felt like a million pieces around him.

He erupted with a roar of pleasure and as he shuddered against me, he nuzzled my neck and whispered, "You are a fucking dream come true, Charlotte."

My heart shimmied. I'd never been called a man's *dream come true*. It made me feel special… empowered. I was glad when Jamie scooped me up into his arms because my knees were in danger of giving out from the force of my orgasm and the emotions pulsing through me. I was in love with Jamie after barely spending a week together on an island and within a few days of us officially dating.

Holy shit. I hoped like hell that he didn't break my heart. He had the power to completely shatter it because I'd never felt so intensely about anyone. I clung to him as he strolled down the steps and dropped onto one of the sofas with me still in his arms. I sat across his lap and snuggled against him. We made quite the pair with me in just my bra and him in his boxers and button-down shirt.

However, we were so comfortable wrapped up in each other that we both began to doze off. I felt so content with Jamie that I almost blurted out that I loved him. Somehow, I held my tongue and then I fell asleep in his arms.

28

JAMIE

My eyes opened to sunlight filtering in through the spaces between the drapes. The arm I had thrown over Charlotte's middle tightened slightly because I couldn't get enough of holding her like this. It felt good waking up beside her. I propped myself on one elbow to look at her. She still slept soundly, her chest rising and falling in a steady rhythm.

The soft glow of the sun illuminated her serene features. Her long lashes created crescents on her flushed cheeks. Her full lips were slightly parted and still showed signs of my hungry kisses last night. Her golden hair fanned out on the navy satin sheets. She was a beautiful sight and as I stared at her with a tenderness that surprised me, I thought that maybe I did love Charlotte.

I had tried to be realistic... denying the notion that I had fallen for her within a few days of meeting her. The affection that hit me in the chest from just watching her sleep told me that maybe tumbling into love this fast wasn't so fictional after all. When I blew out a breath of mild disbelief, Charlotte stirred and rolled over to face me.

Her eyes fluttered open and as soon as she saw me watching her, she smiled. "Good morning," she hummed, her voice husky with sleep.

"Morning." I smoothed a finger over her cheek and pushed strands of her hair out of her face.

"Are you okay?" she asked as she stretched.

"Of course. Why?"

"I opened my eyes to find you watching me with a frown."

"An expression of wonder," I corrected.

She chuckled softly. "Well, what were you *wondering* about?"

"How you burrowed into my heart so fast."

She blinked, probably stunned by my honesty.

"Maybe I'm taking the whole new attitude on life and finally seeking happiness too far…"

I smiled when she continued staring at me with the typical curious glint in her eyes. That was one of the things I liked about her. She never interrupted but waited patiently to hear what was on my mind. She always showed me that she was genuinely interested in what I felt and what I had to say.

"When you encouraged me to live free and stop feeling guilty about something I had no control over, you probably didn't mean diving head first into romance."

Her lips twitched and stretched into a grin. "Hey, I'm having a good time so I'm not complaining. Do you think we're moving too fast?"

"No." I rested my head on my palm and held her gaze. We were in the middle of the extra week we had together and I enjoyed every second with her. It felt natural having Charlotte in my space and a part of my life as if we'd been together for ages.

She lifted a hand to stroke my jaw. "What else are you thinking about?"

I reveled in this intimacy between us. We didn't have to indulge in sex—amazing sex—to feel entirely connected. I felt the bond when we just talked like this.

"When I showed up at your mother's place and saw you with your nephew in your arms, I… liked how you looked."

Her lips parted but no words came out and her eyebrows furrowed. "Okay…"

My heart picked up speed because I was a little nervous about making the admission. "I've never thought about settling down and starting a family, never had the desire to. But I met you and experienced a real connection and lately, I've been thinking about going the distance. You know, a permanent partner, kids…"

I inhaled sharply and flopped back onto the pillow to scrub a hand over my face. Fuck. Charlotte must have cast a spell on me. *I* was considering marriage and kids. And I was expressing myself *freely*. Who had I become?

Charlotte appeared in my line of vision. She grinned. "Why are you embarrassed about what you want, Jamie?"

"Because I've never sounded like this. My entire life feels different with you, and I like it. I want to hold on to it… to you."

Her rich espresso eyes became molten. "Goodness, you are the sweetest, most romantic man I've ever met."

My eyebrows popped up with disbelief and I almost laughed. Romance, sweet, and *me* in the same sentence sounded strange. But maybe I was those things… with *her*.

"You just always say the right things," she gushed, bringing her face closer to mine. "You make me feel like we can work when I start having my doubts."

I cupped her face and pressed my lips to hers. "I want you to stop having doubts."

"I'll try."

Gazing up at her, I decided that it was time to lighten the mood. I said, "Alright, I spilled my heart and guts now you tell me something. Something about you that I don't know yet."

She sniggered. "Okay... what do you want to know?"

"Everything."

Her pert, adorable nose wrinkled. "Where do I start...?"

"Start with how you became so adventurous. Why did you start traveling and working such interesting jobs? How on earth did you become an adventure and sports instructor?"

Grinning from ear to ear, she settled back into my arms and rested her head on my shoulder. "It wasn't really a career choice. I sort of just fell into it. I have a master's in education and a bachelor's in archeology."

I glanced down at her in shock. "Really?"

"Uh-huh." She smiled. "I took every step to become just like my dad. He was a professor of archeology, and he's been *everywhere*."

"Are you telling me that your father was like Indiana Jones?" I saw a plethora of posters, postcards, and what looked like all kinds of exotic souvenirs in her childhood room. Her father's job and travels explained them.

Her eyes rolled around as if in consideration and then she burst out laughing. "You know what? You might be onto something. I suppose Dad was like Indiana Jones, minus the hat and tweed jacket... and he was just a *tad* nerdier."

I laughed. "Your father sounds like a hell of a man." The light and adoration in her eyes when she spoke of him said it all.

"He was." Her eyes met mine. "You would have loved him, Jamie. He was so smart and full of life."

I smiled at her. Clearly, she was everything like her old man.

"When he got sick and couldn't travel anymore, I saw how sad it made him." She sighed. "He told me that I should take advantage of my health and youth and see the world, to do whatever makes me happy. I took a break from my studies and started traveling so I could return home with amazing stories like the ones he used to regale me with as a kid."

"So you two switched places?" I asked, idly trailing my fingers up and down her arm.

"You can say that. I needed money to fund my traveling so I took up jobs in each country I visited so that's how I ended up working in places like the Maldives and Morocco. The light in Dad's eyes when I told him about where I'd been and the adventures I was a part of… that made *me* happy, so I stuck with it for years until he died."

"You traveled and lived for him when he couldn't…" I deduced.

"Exactly. It might sound crazy to everyone else but it made perfect sense to me."

"No, I get it." That was where her encouragement for me to live for my mother came from.

She lifted her head to meet my gaze. "After that, I just couldn't bring myself to get an office or classroom job. I spent so long living uninhibited that I… I guess I don't know *how* to go back to normal," she finished with a little laugh.

I stared at her with amazement. "You're incredible and fearless, Charlotte."

"I have plenty of fears. Speaking of… I've been wondering why the heck you have a top-floor apartment when you're terrified of heights."

I chuckled. "I'm only terrified of heights when my feet aren't secured on solid ground."

"I detect a story here." She folded her hands on my chest and rested her chin on them to gaze at me expectantly.

The interest in her eyes made me smile. I'd never shared the origin of my fear with anyone. "When I was eight, I had a friend over for the first time. We were feeling rather invincible after watching *Tarzan*."

"Oh, no…" she moaned.

I grunted my amusement. "We gave the nanny and the other staff the slip and made it outside beyond the estate's walls. My friend dared me to climb the tallest tree and swing from the limbs like Tarzan, and I accepted the challenge with bravado. Naturally, it didn't end well for me. I ended up with a broken arm and a concussion. I woke up in the hospital to a pissed-off Dad."

Charlotte winced.

"Falling into thin air with nothing to hold on to and nearly choking on the fear of possible death as I rushed to meet the ground was terrifying as fuck. The loss of control over my body and what felt like my entire existence wasn't something I wanted to experience again."

She nodded. "I understand."

"Plus, Dad made me feel like the biggest idiot alive with his lecture about me being a Winchester, therefore, following my friends and fucking up wasn't an option. I lost the privilege to have anyone else over after that. Hell, I wasn't even allowed to have friends." My eyebrows creased at the memory of what Dad said after that. "He asked me if it wasn't enough that I killed my mother. He said I was a fool for trying to kill myself as well."

"Oh, Jamie…" She sighed. "Why would he…? That was incredibly harsh to say to an eight-year-old."

I shrugged. "I never allowed myself to lose control of any situation after that. I lost all desire for spontaneity. I became uptight really." I gave her a wry smile. "And I prefer to not *hover* in the air by any means or method."

She studied me through narrowed eyes. "So that's why you distracted yourself with sex and then work while we flew from Oregon."

"I hate flying. Unfortunately, I have to do it often for work. I mentally freak out a little every time."

She stroked my cheek. "Thanks for telling me."

I felt like I could tell her anything. I felt no fear. I forgot about my father's expectations, Lincoln's anger, and *everything* when I was with her. We talked some more, sharing things we never did with anyone else. I got to know Charlotte and I soaked up everything she told me.

We ended up having a late breakfast, and I decided to not go to the office. I wasn't willing to spend a second of our limited time away from her.

29

CHARLOTTE

"Are you sure it isn't too much for you to take off again?" Jamie asked.

I studied him on my phone screen. His hair was neatly cut and he wore one of his insanely expensive suits. He said he just got done with an important meeting. I liked that he kept me updated with his every movement. It made me feel as if our relationship could survive the distance between us.

We had been dating for over three months now. However, I only saw him in person a handful of times. After my last visit to Manhattan, he was the one who came to Kohala. Unfortunately, those visits were brief.

"I'm positive," I said.

My job wasn't one where I was restricted to a one-week vacation every year. I could take off as much as I wanted if I could afford it. Maybe I couldn't really afford another two weeks off but I was desperate to be in the same room as Jamie. I missed him so much and two weeks with him sounded like heaven. Besides, he was taking care of my travel expenses, and I never spent a dime when I stayed with him in Manhattan.

"Good. I have lots of plans for your birthday."

I beamed. "I'm happy to be spending it with you. I can't wait."

"Neither can I." He looked away from his phone when a knock sounded on his door.

I heard a female voice say, "Mr. Winchester, your one o'clock is here. He's heading up from the lobby."

"Thanks, Darcy."

When he returned his attention to me, I smiled. "Busy day?"

He blew out a breath. "Yeah. I have to go. We'll talk later."

"Bye, Jamie," I said, not caring if I sounded too dreamy or adoring. He had that effect on me. I felt as if I floated on clouds each time we spoke.

"Bye, Jamie," Vera and Kaia sang as they appeared over my shoulders to wave to him.

He chuckled—maybe because of their sing-song, saccharine chorus. "Bye, ladies."

When I hung up, I playfully nudged Kaia who made kissing noises, and then repeated, *"Bye, Jamie,"* in the tone I'd just used.

"Shut up," I said, rolling my eyes.

She giggled and Vera joined in.

"You're so in love," Kaia remarked.

I gave her a pointed look but didn't bother to deny the obvious.

Vera watched me closely, wearing a little smirk. "I guess you've changed your mind about not wanting to settle down."

"Hey, I recall saying that I wouldn't turn away Mr. Right if he appeared," I reminded her.

She raised her eyebrows. "So Jamie is Mr. Right?"

Kaia's head swiveled as she glanced at us. "Of course, he is," she answered before I could say a word. "Jamie is *perfect*."

I laughed. "How do you know that, Kaia?"

"Well, he's so kind to me. He's helped me out a lot with my dad. I took his advice to meet Dad halfway and things have been great between us. Together, we came up with the perfect solution."

"What's that?" Vera asked while I listened with pride. Jamie was going to make a great father someday.

"Since I want to travel and see the world, I've joined this medical volunteer program in South America. I'll be there for six months aiding doctors and nurses in impoverished areas, so I'll get a feel for the whole medical scene while exploring a new country."

Vera nodded. "That's a great idea."

"Dad was so happy when I told him I was willing to try out medicine to see if I liked it," Kaia continued enthusiastically. "I never really gave it a chance. I just opposed the idea because I felt like Dad was forcing me into it. If I like the experience, then I might go to medical school after all. I mean, I don't have to be stuck working in a hospital, I can still be a doctor and travel as Jamie said. Plus, he insisted on being my sponsor for my six-month trip."

Kaia turned to me. "He's so cool, Char. If he treats me, a practical stranger, so great, I can imagine how well he treats his girlfriend."

I grinned. He treated me like the most precious thing in his life. "You're right. He is perfect." And I couldn't wait to be with him in a few days...

"Mhmm," Vera hummed. "So have you guys worked things out with Lincoln?"

My mood plummeted. "I haven't spoken to him since he

found me in Jamie's hotel suite. I've heard Jamie on the phone with him a few times, but their interactions always sound so tense. Jamie doesn't talk about it. I guess he doesn't want me to worry."

Vera quirked an eyebrow. "Does he know you two are a couple?"

"No…" I nibbled my lower lip and gave Vera and Kaia a sheepish look as they exchanged glances. "Jamie and I have kept our relationship on the down low for Lincoln's sake, but we'll have to tell him soon. I think that Jamie wants to stop hiding us from his friends. He's said as much."

We both agreed to date in secret until we were certain of the direction we were heading in. After months together with our feelings growing… We were sure.

* * *

I flew into Jamie's arms the moment I spotted him in the crowded airport. He lifted me off my feet and my legs wrapped around him. I think we both forgot where we were as we kissed.

"I missed you so much, woman," he growled against my lips.

"I hope you're going to show me how much when we get back to your place."

"What makes you think I'll wait that long? I'll fuck in the back of my—"

"*Jamie.*" My smile broke through even as I swatted him on the arm.

He grinned wickedly and that's when I noticed people watching us.

"Oh, my God. We're in the middle of an airport," I muttered

as I wiggled out of his arms. He didn't look too happy about our broken connection.

"Let's go," he said, reaching for the suitcase I had abandoned. "I can't wait to get you all to myself."

Hand-in-hand, we weaved through the crowd, already lost in the bubble that enveloped us when we were together. Everything else faded into the background.

* * *

"Happy birthday, gorgeous," Jamie purred into my ear as he embraced me from behind.

My eyes fluttered closed and I leaned into him as he ran his lips down the column of my neck. "I feel like it's been my birthday for two weeks straight."

Seriously... Since I touched down in Manhattan, Jamie had been spoiling me rotten. I had been to the most upscale restaurants in New York, shopped until I damn near dropped in the most expensive boutiques, and been primped and pampered non-stop.

Last night, we arrived in Vancouver because Jamie had a business meeting tomorrow. I was celebrating my birthday in a beautiful city and in a hotel that cost an arm and leg per night. I opened my eyes to gaze out at the view of the heart of Vancouver from our suite's balcony. I'd been having a great time with Jamie, getting more than a taste of his billionaire lifestyle.

"You deserve to be spoiled and pampered," he said, pulling away.

I then felt something cool settle around my neck. I gasped when I looked down and saw an exquisite necklace. The pendant was a mesmerizing opal that swirled with greens, blues, and oranges. They changed with the light's angle. A halo of diamonds surrounded the gem. The stones were so brilliant I bet they could be seen from space.

I ran a finger over the platinum chain and turned to face Jamie. "Jamie, I can't accept this…"

The skin between his eyebrows puckered. "You don't like it?"

"I do. It's just…" My face prickled with warmth. "You've already spent a fortune on me." The gown that he got me for the gala he was taking me to this weekend cost more than I made in months. Then there were the other gifts—more clothes, jewelry, and shoes.

"I haven't spent nearly enough," he refuted.

I let out a shocked snort. "You don't have to buy me expensive things, Jamie."

"I *want* to." As he fingered the sleek necklace, the warmth of his touch soaked into my skin. "I saw this and it reminded me of you. Beautiful and unique."

My heart melted like hot butter. It took getting used to… being indulged like this… I took a deep breath and decided to accept it.

"It's lovely, Jamie. Thank you," I whispered as I leaned in to kiss him.

His lips were warm and soft and the way they moved over mine made my entire body tingle with need.

He pulled back to gaze at me with blatant affection. "I want to celebrate all of your birthdays with you. I want to spend money on you, make love to you, and indulge you in every way. Charlotte, I…"

I saw the adoration in his eyes and my breath hitched. He was about to say the three magical words. My heart raced as I prepared to say them back.

However, he didn't get the chance because his phone rang. Jamie blew out an annoyed breath and reached into his pocket for the device.

I smiled and whispered, "It's okay," when he gave me an apologetic look. I understood that he was juggling work while giving me his time.

Jamie's expression shuttered when he looked at the screen. His change of mood made my eyebrows snap together. I assumed it was work until he answered.

"Lincoln, hi." His gaze flickered briefly to me and then he sighed heavily. "I know… But you've been ignoring my calls…"

I folded my arms around my middle, feeling awkward as I listened to his side of the conversation. While we'd been on cloud nine, enjoying being with each other, Lincoln was a dark cloud that lingered in the background waiting to overshadow our happiness.

"What am I supposed to do when you won't even give me the time of day?" Jamie asked as he raked his fingers through his hair.

His growing agitation sent a sliver of guilt through me, which I hadn't felt in a while. I was the cause of this strain on his important friendship. That thought made me turn away from him to stare out at the sprawling cityscape beneath us.

"Well, I'm glad you're ready to talk because I'm coming to LA soon. There's something I have to tell you, and I don't want to do it over the phone."

I turned back to Jamie when I heard that. My feelings about him finally letting everyone in on our romance were mixed. On one hand, I was happy that I was important enough for him to want to go public. On the other hand, I was terrified that stepping out of our perfect, secret bubble might ruin things. Would his friends judge our relationship? Would I be accepted into

Jamie's high society circle? I was so lost in thought that I didn't hear the end of Jamie's conversation with Lincoln.

I jumped when a pair of arms wrapped around my waist from behind. I'd been clutching the balcony rails for dear life as my anxious thoughts ran wild.

"I'm sorry about that," Jamie said.

"No need to be sorry about a conversation with your friend." *Who happened to be my ex-boyfriend...* Whenever Lincoln appeared in our perfect picture, awkwardness was never far behind.

"You're upset."

"No…"

"Don't lie to me, Charlotte," he sighed as he stepped back and turned me to face him.

With reluctance, I met his gaze.

"Tell me what you're thinking," he demanded in that bossy tone that always made me roll my eyes.

However, the concern and pleading in his eyes soften the moment. I didn't want to weigh him down with my negativity when he was still clearly upset about his conversation with Lincoln.

"It's…" I swallowed, fighting the urge to be honest and tell him about my fear… The one where our relationship ended when he realized that I wasn't worth the risk to his friendship or his posh life. "I just hope things work out between you and Lincoln, that's all."

30

CHARLOTTE

The grand ballroom of the hotel was abuzz with activity. People sipped champagne, chatted, and laughed. There was so much bling in the room that my eyes dazzled, and I could practically *smell* money. I took in the crowd of super-wealthy folks, a little dazed. That flutter of nerves that plagued me when I first stepped into the room was coming back. I wasn't one of them and they could probably all tell…

However, my feeling of insecurity came to a halt the second Jamie was back in my sight. He wore a smile as he approached carrying the two glasses of champagne he left my side to get. I grinned back. He was so handsome in his tux… absolutely swoon-worthy. I didn't miss the envious looks I'd gotten from some of the ladies.

They were miffed that they weren't the recipient of Jamie Winchester's attention. I'd read so many blogs about him being one of New York's—and the country's—most eligible bachelors.

When I read a few of them to him, he'd been so embarrassed. His humility was one of his many endearing qualities.

I took the glass he offered and smiled broadly when he wrapped an arm around my waist and proceeded to sip from his glass. His hold was possessive and I liked it. It showed me that he was proud to have me on his arm despite me not moving in his social circle.

"Are you having a good time?" he asked.

"I always have a great time with you."

He glanced at me. "Good because I hope to take you to more of these pointless shindigs. With you by my side, I don't *suffer* through them like I usually do."

My heart skipped a beat as it always did when he implied that we were in this for the long haul, but I played it cool. "Pointless? It's a charity gala."

"For which I could have simply written a big check. However, it's important that I keep up with the social expectations of a Winchester," he sighed.

The annoyance in his voice made my chest tighten with sympathy. After being with him for months and getting immersed in his world, I'd glimpsed the less glamorous side of his billionaire lifestyle. He had so many obligations, such as showing up to high society events like this when he really didn't want to.

Keeping up with his affluent surname seemed exhausting and I understood why he'd been so somber when we first met. The man could barely get a moment to let loose and relax. The social expectations, the endless meetings and appearances, the constant scrutiny... Camera lights nearly blinded me when we showed up to the gala, for goodness' sake. Jamie warned me that we might end up in the paper or on society blogs. I didn't even know how to feel about that...

Jamie's life made me realize that I shouldn't envy the wealthy folks in the room or feel too bad about my life. At least I was genuinely happy. Most of them seemed to be putting on fake smiles for their peers and the cameras.

It was a good thing Jamie and I met. I could make sure he remembered to enjoy himself from time to time. Glancing at him with a smile, I said, "How about you and I sneak off to get away from this crowd? They're so stuffy." There was a dance floor and no one was even putting it to use.

He chuckled. "Most of these people wouldn't be caught dead having fun. Some of them might even be allergic to it." He nodded to an older woman who stood in one corner, watching everyone with disdain.

Laughing, I looped my arm around his and tugged him to the double doors we had entered through. Before we exited, we deposited our empty glasses. He followed my lead, his laughter mingling with my giggles.

"Where are we heading?" he asked.

"I don't know. Let's just walk until we find somewhere where no one can see us."

We wandered through the hotel's corridors holding hands. Every now and then, Jamie pulled me close to feather kisses along my jaw and shoulders as he whispered about the things he wanted to do to me when we got home. My giggles filled the hallway and I felt carefree… and in love.

Eventually, we stumbled outside into a secluded courtyard at the back of the hotel. It was dimly lit by lanterns with plenty of shadowed areas created by the massive plants in the garden.

Jamie pulled me into a dark corner. "This is perfect," he said, looking up.

I followed his gaze. "What are you looking for?"

"Security cameras. If we stay in this corner, we'll be completely hidden."

My eyes narrowed but a smirk played on my lips. "Completely hidden to do what?"

His wolfish grin made me snigger as his head came down and his mouth crashed against mine. I loved seeing him this relaxed and playful. Fire practically gashed between us the instant our lips connected. I got lost in our kiss, forgetting where we were and savoring the way his tongue slipped between my lips to tease and taste me.

He pinned me between the wall and his hard body as he parted my legs with one of his. I was so hot with need that I grounded my hips to rub my crotch on his thigh in a desperate need to satisfy my growing arousal.

Jamie groaned as his lips left mine to trail down my neck. "Jesus, woman," he growled. "Now I'm going to have to take you right here."

"What did you initially have in mind?" I panted, tilting my head to give him better access.

He paused to meet my gaze. His gray eyes were darker, appearing like molten silver in the moonlight. "I had no intention of fucking you against a wall. Now, I'm going to…"

The dark promise in the purred declaration made me whimper. This side of Jamie, the domineering sex god, never failed to make me bend to his will. Why wouldn't I want to when I knew how skilled he was at handling my body?

"I've never done anything like this before," he mused as his hand moved up my thigh, exposed by my dress's daring split. "But you make me feel so adventurous and daring."

"Well, I'd hope you don't make a habit of fucking women against hotel walls at charity galas, Jamie," I breathed and then moaned as his fingers slipped into my panties. The thought of him with another woman like this made me see red, and I actually glared at him despite the pleasure he brought me with his touch.

He watched me with a little smirk. "You're so hot when you're jealous."

All I could do was moan in response because his fingers were working magic between my legs, and I was seconds away from erupting. When I did, his lips locked on to mine again, muffling my cry of pleasure as I shuddered against him. He then lifted me and yanked my underwear to the side with enthusiasm.

"Don't damage my dress," I warned. He paid such a hefty price for it, it almost seemed a sin to destroy it.

"I'll buy you a dozen more," he growled as he freed himself from his pants.

Our bodies were flushed against each other, his hard length pressing against my core, and I panted with excitement.

"It's okay now, right?" he asked.

With the heat of my blush flooding my face, I nodded. I'd decided to get on birth control since Jamie and I tend to get caught up in spontaneous sex—like now. We'd lived on the edge for too long by not using protection, and I knew our luck might run out eventually. Based on when I started the contraceptive, it would take about seven days to become effective. Luckily, we were beyond that.

"Good," he purred as he slid home, making us both moan with satisfaction. As we rocked against the wall, I practically clawed at him, trying to get my hands on anywhere I could touch him. Each of his thrusts sent shockwaves through my body, building me up until I was nearly dizzy with pleasure.

"Oh, God..." I breathed as tingles shot up my spine and spread through my bloodstream.

"I like it better when you call *my* name, gorgeous," he grunted.

With a little laugh that bordered on a moan, I said, "Oh, *Jamie*."

His eyes danced with laughter even though they were dark with desire. He then declared, "I love you, Charlotte."

His eyes widened as if he hadn't meant to say it just yet. Those magic words sent warmth flooding through me and set off my orgasm. If anyone was in the vicinity, they definitely heard my scream of bliss. I shook uncontrollably as he followed me over the edge. We stood there, pressed against each other, catching our breaths. Jamie had his forehead resting on my shoulder.

When he finally looked up and captured my gaze, he gave me a sheepish smile. "I didn't mean to make the announcement. I mean, I *meant* it, but I had a much more romantic scenario planned." His eyebrows crinkled. "It certainly didn't include a wall and a dark corner…"

I grinned and I swore that his obvious dismay made me fall deeper in love with him that very moment. He always made me feel so cherished.

"It's okay. Right now is perfect." Cupping his face, I planted a kiss on his lips. "I love you too."

His long exhale echoed with relief and then he kissed me again, slow and deep. My heart was full and my body buzzed with sexual satisfaction. The night with Jamie was perfect.

31

JAMIE

My phone buzzed incessantly. Muttering a curse, I reached for it with my free hand. Charlotte was tucked neatly in my other arm. I'd never tire of how she clung to me in her sleep. I felt loved and needed. She belonged in my arms and I wanted her there for the rest of our days. How long was it appropriate to wait after pronouncing one's love to propose marriage…?

My phone buzzed again, jerking me from my runaway thoughts. I was probably getting ahead of myself. Four months of dating, mostly long-distance, was probably too soon to ask. Not for *me*… for Charlotte. I was already sure what I wanted with her.

When I glanced at my phone's screen, my hackles immediately rose. It was barely seven and already my peace of mind was being disturbed.

"Dad," I answered with little enthusiasm.

"James, what is the meaning of this?"

I tiredly rubbed my eyes as I wondered what his problem

was this early. When I gently tried to disentangle myself from Charlotte, she stirred and opened her eyes. "Jamie?"

I planted a kiss on her forehead. "Go back to sleep. I'll be back."

When I stepped out of the bedroom, I sighed. "What are you talking about, Dad?"

"Was that her you were talking to?" he demanded.

My steps faltered. There was only one *her* whom he could be referring to… but I had yet to introduce Charlotte to my old man because he can be a massive dick.

"What's this about, Dad?" I asked hesitantly.

"It was brought to my attention that there's a video out…" His tone was calm. Too calm, which meant he was pissed.

Video? My mind raced and then came to a screeching halt. *Holy fuck.* Had I missed a security camera last night when Charlotte and I…?

Taking a deep breath, I mentally prepared myself for a PR shitstorm. I was great at playing cool, so I did. "You'll have to be more specific."

Dad sighed deeply as if gathering his patience. I then heard a beep and I checked my phone. He had sent a link from some entertainment site. I put the phone on speaker and hesitated before pressing the link. If it was a goddamn sex video of Charlotte and me, I'd lose my shit. Not because of me but because it would mean that I failed to protect her from my world of nosey fucks who watched my every move because I was a *Winchester*.

However, as the video played, my dread dissipated and I flopped onto a sofa out of sheer relief. The only thing the security cameras had captured last night was Charlotte and me strolling hand-in-hand through the hotel's corridors laughing and stopping to make out after every few steps.

I grunted my amusement when I finally took the time to

read the headline. *Love is in the Air: Hotel Cameras Capture Billionaire's Romantic Night.*

The article beneath the video went on to talk about how great it was to see two people so "joyfully in love" and how refreshing it was to see such "sweet displays of affection." Charlotte and I did indeed look happy.

"I'm not seeing an issue here, Dad... or did you call me to congratulate me?" I looked skyward, knowing damn well that I shouldn't push the old man's buttons.

"*Congratulate...* ? James, Winchesters do *not* prance around hotels *necking* with random women."

My jaw tightened. "She's not a random woman. Her name is Charlotte, and she's—"

"She's, what, James?" Dad snapped. "Who is she?"

"The woman I love."

Dad laughed. "You're a Winchester."

Fury boiled in my veins. If I heard "You're a Winchester" one more time, I'd likely explode. I'd been hearing it since I was fucking born... as if I'd ever likely forget!

"You can't fall in love with a nobody. What's her last name? Does she have a penny to her name? She could be another gold digger, James."

"Jesus, Dad—"

"Look, I understand that you have needs. You're young. There's nothing wrong with fooling around and scratching that itch, but you don't take your playthings to important events and get captured on camera. You have your fun and then find someone *suitable.*"

The faint whisper of a sigh had my head snapping up and around. *Fucking hell.* Charlotte stood behind me, wearing the most forlorn expression, and it nearly ripped my heart out. She only had on one of my shirts, her skin was flushed, and her hair was tousled. She looked beautiful and *miserable*.

Scrubbing a hand over my face, I snapped at Dad, "You don't get to dictate my life. Not anymore."

"James—"

I ended the call and shot to my feet. "Charlotte... I'm sorry you had to hear that."

She said nothing. She just looked down at the floor and exhaled. When she met my gaze, her eyes were troubled. "You don't really think I'm after your money, do you?"

"Of course not." I walked to her and rested my hands on her shoulders, wishing that I could reassure her with my touch.

"Are you just having fun with me?" Her voice quavered.

"How can you even ask me that? I *love* you, Charlotte."

"But I'm not—"

"Don't even say it," I huffed, wanting to throttle my father. "You're suitable for *me*. I don't care what my father says."

"It's hard for *me* not to care, Jamie. I don't want your father to hate me..."

"He doesn't know you, Charlotte. Once he gets to, he'll see how perfect you are."

Skepticism was practically written on her face and I stifled a sigh. "Look, Charlotte—"

My phone went crazy again. No doubt, the video and maybe some pictures had circulated and the entire world now knew that Charlotte and I were a thing. It hit me then that Lincoln would find out from the goddamn media before I had the chance to tell him.

* * *

"Remember when I said I didn't think Lincoln hated you?"

I raised my eyebrows at Michael's question as I stared at my phone sitting on my desk. "Uh-huh."

"Well, if he didn't, he probably does now."

Massaging my temple, I nodded. "Yeah..."

"How could you let him find out about you and Charlotte like that, Jamie?" Michael chided.

"I already got crap from Spencer and Alex, man. Can you cut me some slack?"

He huffed. "Dating Charlotte in secret... I get it. I like to protect my privacy from the media too, but you should have said something to Lincoln at least."

"How the fuck was I suppose to do that when he wouldn't even stay on the phone with me for a full minute when we did talk?"

"Good point," Michael murmured.

"Besides, I wanted to tell him in person. I didn't think about Charlotte and me going *viral* for Christ's sake."

"Hmmm. So... you love her, huh? I can tell from those pictures and that video." Michael chuckled. "She must really be something for you to gaze at her with stars in your eyes."

I shrugged as if he could see me. "I do and she is."

I wasn't the least bit embarrassed about everyone seeing how I felt about Charlotte from just a few pictures.

"Well, good luck fixing things with Lincoln, you poor bastard. I'm rooting for you."

I snorted. "Thanks. I'll talk to you later."

Ending the call, I rested my head on the back of my chair and gazed up at the office ceiling. I had to fix things with Charlotte too. She hadn't been her usual perky self since she overheard my conversation with Dad yesterday. I only had a couple more days with her before she returned to Kohala, and I didn't want her to leave doubting our relationship.

32

CHARLOTTE

I stared out the window of Jamie's penthouse, not really seeing anything. Too many worrisome thoughts flitted through my mind for me to properly enjoy the view. My time with Jamie had started so perfectly. I had a blast for my birthday, we shared our feelings… We had been on the right path. How could things change so quickly? Now, doubt overshadowed our happiness.

I couldn't ignore everything his father said when those had been my fears from the beginning. How many times had I said our worlds were too different for us to work? How many times had I wondered what he was doing with me when I felt he was out of my league? When I heard his father call me a "nobody," it hit me hard.

"But he loves you," I whispered, hoping that the reminder would ease my doubts.

I glanced at the clock hanging over the gigantic flat-screen TV that took up almost an entire wall. Jamie wouldn't be back for a couple of hours. He had to run to the office for the morning. He'd been reluctant to leave because he wanted to talk more about what I heard yesterday. I hated that our time together was ending on such a bad note.

Jamie's landline rang, pulling me from my thoughts. I glanced at it, wondering if I should answer. Maybe it was him calling to check on me. I'd left my cell in his bedroom, so maybe I missed his first call. I hurried across the room to answer the phone.

When I didn't hear Jamie's voice, I hesitated. "Hello...?"

"Miss Brooks, good afternoon." It was the security in the lobby. I was familiar with his voice. "There's a Gwendolyn Calloway here..."

"Mr. Winchester isn't here," I said. Of course, he must know that since he saw Jamie leave this morning.

"She's here to see you."

My eyebrows shot up. First of all, who the hell was Gwendolyn Calloway? I figured she must be one of those personal shoppers Jamie hired to bring me tons of clothes and jewelry to try on. I shook my head at his need to spoil me at every turn.

"Er... Send her up..."

I waited in the foyer for the elevator to arrive. As soon as I heard the ding, I slapped on a smile, expecting to see a woman dressed in designer slacks and heels, carrying arms full of clothing bags and shoe boxes. However, the woman who appeared was empty-handed except for a clutch purse. There were no shopping bags on the elevator's floor either.

My eyebrows furrowed as I took in the lithe brunette who had stilts for legs. She wore a dress that clung to her body and heels that looked like they could slit somebody's throat. She wore minimal makeup that enhanced her naturally gorgeous features.

"Uh... hi..."

She must be a close friend of Jamie's if she was visiting his home. He was so private and cautious about who entered his domain.

The woman assessed me as a queen would a peasant, and I dropped the hand I had extended, which Miss Snooty Pants ignored.

"Charlotte, I presume?" She looked down her nose at me.

I resisted the urge to roll my eyes as my snarky side surfaced. "Gwendolyn, I presume?" I threw back in an equally superior tone.

Her smile was cold enough to freeze my tits off my chest. *Jeez.* Jamie's friend sure was a bitch.

"Jamie isn't here," I said. "Maybe you can come back later."

"I'm here to speak to you."

"About…?"

"The video that's making its rounds on social media. The photos from the charity gala…"

Gwendolyn brushed past me and flounced into the living room, her heels clicking on the hardwood. I frowned. Jamie hadn't seemed upset about those, but had he hired a PR person or something? Rich CEOs did that to control narratives in the media, right?

"Okay… What about them?"

I almost collided with Gwendolyn, the snob, when she stopped abruptly and turned to face me. "Look, Charlotte, I'm sure you're a nice woman and you probably don't know."

"Know what?" I felt so lost and stupid. What was I missing here?

Gwendolyn gave me a pitying look. "I'm James' fiancée."

A sound escaped me, a little snort of shock mixed with amusement. I stared at the woman, waiting for her to laugh and say "*Gotcha,*" but Gwendolyn looked as serious as a heart attack… like the one I was on the verge of having.

"Of course, he didn't tell you. *Men.*" She shook her head. "That's why we girls have to stick together. I know James lied to you—"

"*Jamie,*" I corrected.

"Excuse me?"

"If you're his fiancée, why do you call him James? He doesn't like it. You should know that."

Gwendolyn stared at me as if I were crazy. Maybe I was. This woman claimed to be Jamie's betrothed, and I was defending what he preferred to be called by those closest to him. I guess I was in shock.

She blinked. "*James* and I have been engaged for over a year. It's always been in the books for him to marry me. Our families are… equals. *I'm* his equal. And you're…"

And you're a nobody… I knew that was what she wanted to say. I swallowed hard.

"Where the hell have you been this entire time, then, *fiancée*?"

Jamie and I had been dating for months, and I'd never once seen or heard any sign of another woman. Even if Jamie was an expert liar, surely I would have seen *something…* I glared so hard at Gwendolyn that she should have burst into flames.

She clutched her chest. "I should be the one upset here, Charlotte. Imagine being on the other side of the world and getting news that the man I'm to marry is parading around with another woman." She scoffed. "It's humiliating, yet here I am trying to help you."

"Oh, really? And how the fuck are you helping?" I wanted to break down into tears because after what I heard from his father yesterday, I was inclined to believe that Jamie would be engaged to some pretty, rich socialite.

Gwendolyn clutched her chest as if she was too refined for the word "fuck" to harass her ears. "Charlotte," she said with saccharine gentleness. "Men like James who have money, power, and so many responsibilities... They like to have their fun before settling down with *their* kind."

The fuck? My molars ground together at that. What the hell was I? An alien species because I didn't have a well-known last name or money? Plus, Jamie wasn't like that... *Was* he? *Oh, God.* I fought off a wave of nausea.

"I can only hope that he's had his fun and gotten the need to spread his wild oats out of his system," Gwendolyn continued. "His father assured me that he has."

I swallowed the bile rising in my throat as I held Gwendolyn's gaze. I'd never break down in front of her and allow her to see how utterly heartbroken I was. Instead, I gave her a look frigid enough to rival hers.

"Take my advice, Charlotte. Walk away now and don't stick around to be humiliated later when he tires of his latest... adventure." Her words dripped with disdain. "I'm trying to look out for you. Men like James always choose their legacy over a fleeting romance. In our world, you're the fun fling, but I'm the wife."

In their world... God. All my insecurities surfaced to bite me in the ass. Would this woman show up here and blatantly lie? I doubted it. Gwendolyn Calloway had stuck a knife in my heart and savagely twisted it, but I'd never let her see how hurt I was.

Keeping my composure—barely—I said steadily, "Thanks for your *concern...*" *You frigid bitch,* I added silently and bitterly. However, I should be mad at Jamie not her, so I kept my temper and sharp tongue on a leash. "But you don't have to worry about me, *Gwen*. I'll gladly leave you and James to your future marital bliss. You two certainly deserve each other. You can go now."

She seemed taken aback by my response and that satisfied me. Gwendolyn and I had a staredown. She watched me as if she was uncertain about how to react. When my eyes narrowed to slits, she angled her chin up, wheeled around, and sashayed out. I didn't move, didn't blink, and probably didn't even breathe until I heard the elevator doors open and close. Then, I crumbled.

A sob escaped me, but I dashed the tears away with annoyance. I had to keep my shit together at least for a little while until I was out of Jamie's house.

* * *

I was in the safety of my room so I could let my tears flow, and I almost flooded all of Oregon. It was hard to return to Kohala and get back to work as if I didn't get my heart torn out of my chest and trampled into the dirt.

Mustering smiles for my friends and guests at the resort just wasn't possible for the time being, so I took an extended leave and had been holed up in my childhood bedroom for two days. My mother had stayed out of my way for the most part. I suppose she didn't know how to handle a sad and distressed Charlotte. She had only ever dealt with perky, defiant, and smart-mouthed Charlotte. I'd tell her what happened when I was ready because I could tell she was worried about me.

I'd barely slept or eaten as I wallowed in the sting of betrayal. All I'd done was cry and stare at my phone when it lit up with Jamie's name flashing on the screen. Coward that I was, I packed up and fled Manhattan before Jamie got back from his office and I'd ignored all his calls. The adult thing to do would have been to confront him, but how could I when I was too miserable and hurt to speak?

The phone stopped lighting up for the gazillionth time, and I tentatively picked up the device as if it were an explosive. Several notifications for texts and voice messages flashed, tempting me to read and listen.

With a groan, I gave in, knowing they were all from Jamie. His urgent texts led me to listen to the voice messages. He sounded frantic in some of them, begging me to call him back because he was worried about me.

My heart ached even more. How could he still sound so genuinely concerned? In one message, he said he loved me, and if he didn't hear from me, he might *go off the deep end. Love?* He was engaged to be married! Yet, he still sounded so believable. Jamie Winchester was cold-blooded. Just as I was about to listen to another of his messages, he called again. My heart thumped as I stared at his name. Taking a deep breath, I accepted the call but said nothing at first.

"Charlotte?" Jamie asked. "Are you there?"

I swallowed.

"Jesus, Charlotte, answer me. *Please.*"

Clearing my throat, I spat, "What do you want, Jamie?"

He hesitated. I guess he wasn't expecting my tone. "Are you alright?"

"I'm fine."

"Where are you?"

"None of your business. *I'm* no longer your business."

"What the hell is going on, Charlotte? Are you mad at me? Still, you can't just *disappear*. I almost reported you as missing, woman," he growled. "That is, until security told me you left with your suitcase. *What. The. Fuck?*"

"You have some nerve being angry. I'm the one who has the right to be pissed. And I can't believe you'd think I still want anything to do with you."

Jamie paused. "What? Is this about what my father said? Charlotte..."

My control slipped. "No, it's about your fiancée, you... you... jerk!"

"My *what?*"

I scoffed. He still felt the need to keep up his act. Unbelievable. "You are a lying, cheating asshole, Jamie Winchester. A real piece of work."

"*Whoa.* I might be an asshole *sometimes* but a lying, cheating one...? *What* are you talking about?"

Beyond agitated, I got up from my bed and paced. "Your wife-to-be showed up at your place, Jamie. She and I had a nice chat."

He laughed, but I detected little humor and plenty of disbelief, which had me perplexed. "Charlotte, is this some kind of joke?"

"Oh, my gosh! Drop the act, Jamie. The jig is up. I met Gwendolyn."

"*Who?* I don't know..." There was a long pause and then he groaned. "Oh... shit. I can explain..."

It was my turn to laugh. "Yeah, I bet if given the chance, you'll spin your lies to perfection. Congratulations on playing me for a fool for months. Screw you, Jamie."

"No, Charlotte, wait—"

I hung up because I couldn't bear to hear his voice any longer and a tiny part of me was afraid he'd talk me right back into his charming web—I was that weak to him. And that knowledge brought on fresh tears...

My pity party was interrupted by a sharp knock.

"Charlotte?"

I sniffed, wiped away my tears, and scowled at the door. "I'm busy, Mom."

"Being miserable I know, but there's someone here to see you."

I rolled my eyes. "I told you not to call Vicky." For one, my sister had her hands full with her family. Secondly... I was too humiliated to share my pain with anyone at the moment.

"It's not Vicky."

My heart stuttered, came to a halt, and then began to race. Was it *Jamie*? I sprang up off the bed and looked around as if I could find a place to hide from him. How could he possibly be here? I just spoke to him... but he could have already been in Golden Beach by the time he called...

"Wh-who is it?" I stuttered.

"It's Lincoln, sweetheart."

What?

When I didn't answer, she asked hesitantly, "Should I tell him you're not up for visitors? He's come such a long way..."

"Uh..." I combed my fingers through my hair, blew out a breath, and opened the door, coming face-to-face with Mom. Her gaze moved over my face to take in the tear stains and my puffy red eyes.

Her soft sigh echoed with sympathy. "Did you and Jamie break up?"

I lifted a shoulder. "Something like that."

"I'm sorry, sweetie. You really love him, don't you?" Her eyes raked over my face again. "I've never seen you like this."

My chin quivered and fresh tears filled my eyes. "Well, aren't you going to badger me about what happened? Or ask what *I* did wrong because I'm not a *proper* lady who wants to settle down? Because I tried and it didn't work." My voice cracked and tears slid down my cheek.

"Oh, Charlotte... *no*. I..." Mom grimaced. "You've always been perfect the way you are. I've just always worried about you, and I might have said some things... I'm so sorry."

I dropped my face into my hands and let out a sob. "I know. I'm sorry. I didn't mean to snap."

She sighed and pulled me into an embrace, and I felt... better. Slightly. For once, she wasn't lecturing me about my life choices.

"Thanks, Mom," I whispered.

She pulled back but kept her hands on my shoulders. "I can tell Lincoln to leave..."

"You're really not going to ask what happened?" I asked incredulously. Knowing Mom, the curiosity was killing her.

A ghost of a smile appeared on her lips. "Something tells me you're not ready to talk about it."

I shook my head. "I should go speak with Lincoln. It must be something important..." It had to be if he traveled all the way from LA.

"I'll keep him entertained for a while," Mom said. "You take a few more minutes."

"Thanks, Mom."

Goodness, I loved her to the moon, especially when she was so understanding.

33

CHARLOTTE

I tentatively descended the last step into the living room as I warily watched Lincoln. He sat with his elbows on his knees, twirling a glass of water in his hands. When he spotted me, he put the glass on the coffee table and stood up. His massive frame seemed to take up the entire space.

"Lincoln..." I greeted with a mixture of confusion and apprehension. Was he here to pick a fight? Maybe berate me for being with Jamie behind his back? I was sure he'd seen the video and pictures by now. It wasn't like him to pick a fight, but he'd been so upset about everything that I wasn't sure...

"Charlotte, hey. I should have called before showing up, but I was worried."

My eyebrows snapped together. "About me? Why?"

Sharp green eyes locked onto mine. They carried sincere concern that I didn't expect. I assumed he harbored resentment about the way things happened between us. "Yes. I thought you were missing."

"What?"

"Jamie called me."

"And you answered..." I smiled slightly. "That's great. Does that mean things between you guys are okay now?"

His lips twisted into a wry grin. "I don't know. We haven't spoken much. However, yes, I answered when he called the other day, frantically searching for *you*. He said you disappeared. Trouble in paradise?"

I took a step back and glared. "God, Lincoln, if you came here to gloat..."

"You know me, Char. I wouldn't do that no matter how upset I am."

Air was expelled from my lungs in a whoosh. "Yeah. I know you."

"You look like hell, kid," he said with his typical tone of humor as he studied me intently.

I snorted. "Thanks."

"It's none of my business what happened between you and Jamie, but are you... okay?"

I gave him a look that said *hell no*, and he frowned.

"So did you come here on his behalf or what? Because I already spoke to him and he knows that I simply left. I'm not missing."

Lincoln nodded and shoved his hands into his pockets. "I'm here to see for myself that my friend is alright."

"We're still friends even after I've been dating Jamie in secret for months?"

"A heads-up would have been nice, but I've had plenty of time to think. You and I were long over before you and Jamie started." He yanked one hand out of his pocket to rub his nape. "I might have overreacted."

I sighed. "I guess it wasn't fair to you that we kept it a secret." He nodded, and I gestured to the sofa. "You might as well make yourself comfortable. You know Mom won't let you leave this house without making you eat dinner first."

Lincoln laughed as he sat. "Faye does love to feed everyone."

I flopped down beside him, not feeling as awkward as I thought I would. I was right, no matter what, Lincoln and I would always care about each other. We'd always been great friends and maybe that was the problem between us to begin with.

"May I ask you something, Char?"

I turned to him, tucking my legs under me. "You came all this way just to check on me. You can ask me many things."

He smiled, and I returned it.

"Why Jamie and not me?"

My lips parted, and my eyes widened slightly. "Wow… just right in there, huh? No easing into it."

He shrugged. "You know what I liked about us as a couple? We were honest with each other, no matter how hard it was to be."

I nodded. "True."

"It was so easy between us," he said. "That's why I don't get why you weren't interested in trying again."

My chest heaved with the force of my inhalation. "That's just it, Lincoln. Have you ever thought that maybe it was so easy between us because there was no passion?"

He blinked and then sat back. However, he didn't deny it.

"We just sort of worked because we had things in common. I've always felt more like your bestie than a girlfriend. There's your answer, Lincoln. I wanted to be with Jamie because I… I felt… We were…" I swallowed the ball of emotion rising in my throat. If I had to verbalize everything I felt with Jamie—the intensity, the consuming passion, the heart-fluttering moments, the intrigue, and the *love*—I'd burst into tears.

Lincoln took pity on me. He grunted. "It's okay. I get it."

"Thanks." I sniffed and dashed at a tear that escaped. "Since we're being honest, why did you travel from LA just to ask me why I chose Jamie? I know it's more than curiosity."

It was a rarity to see the gentle giant blush, and I folded my lips to hide my amusement.

"Who is she?" I asked.

I feared he might have caught whiplash with the speed he turned his neck to gawk at me. "What? Who...?"

I rolled my eyes. "Years ago, when we got together... I saw the pain in your eyes. I knew I was a rebound, but you were just so cool that I let it slide and things turned out to be good between us for a while."

"Jesus, Char, you were never a rebound. You're one of the most amazing women I know."

"Who you dated to get over whomever you were trying to forget..."

He stared at me with a slack jaw and then he scrubbed a hand over his face. With a resigned sigh, he confessed, "I heard she's getting married. That's why I got it into my head to fly all the way to Hawaii to win you back. I... wasn't thinking clearly..."

"Oh, Lincoln..." I shuffled closer and placed a hand on his shoulder.

"I'm a fucking idiot," he hummed. "I'm so sorry for the way I blew up at you and Jamie when my heart wasn't even in the right place. I just thought that if she's getting married, then surely I can get out of the past and find my happiness too."

My heart constricted. I always knew he was in love with another woman, but I never pried. "You can still find happiness, Lincoln. You will. You deserve it."

He hung his head and grunted in response. However, in true

macho fashion, he shoved away his emotions and focused on mine. Turning to me, he said. "So do you. I know it's awkward for your ex to ask what happened between you and your current…"

I snorted. "*Hella* awkward."

He gave me a sheepish smile. "I'm asking because I genuinely care about you and Jamie. I think I need to tell him that. Let him know I'm no longer pissed."

"Well, what have you been waiting for?"

He lifted a shoulder and smirked. "I thought I'd let him suffer a bit more for going after my ex-girlfriend. He broke the bro code."

"*Lincoln.*" I swatted his arm, and he chuckled. I then instantly plunged back into despair. "Then again, perhaps he deserves to suffer."

He raised an eyebrow in askance.

"I met his fiancée," I sighed. "I know about your *bro code* or whatever, but you could have given me a heads-up that Jamie was just looking for a good time before he tied the knot. Why didn't you say something?"

Lincoln's features twisted into confusion. "His what?" His laughter boomed. "Char, I'd know if my best friend was engaged. Jamie Winchester has been running in the opposite direction from that kind of commitment since I met him… until you, anyway."

I sat taller. "What…? But… that woman."

Lincoln stroked his chin. "If by *fiancée* you mean the woman his father has been trying to convince him to marry, a woman he's never even exchanged a word with…"

I sucked in a breath. Lincoln said he had yet to speak to Jamie, and I believed him. He was no liar. So Jamie didn't commission Lincoln to come here and lobby for my forgiveness. Plus, Lincoln seemed genuinely lost.

"What the hell happened, Char?" he asked.

I dropped my head into my hands. "I walked away from Jamie because I thought he was playing me. I thought he was engaged. Damn it! I knew there was something off about that woman."

I mean, if I found out that my fiancé was cheating on me with another woman, I'd be livid. Gwendolyn Calloway had been too calm, detached even, for someone who was supposedly hurt about her lover's affair. I told Lincoln everything and then he set the record straight.

Jamie had never been in a serious relationship until me and had only *considered* doing what his father demanded in the far future. However, he met me...

"Jamie is head over heels for you, Charlotte," Lincoln said.

"How do you know? You've been avoiding him... *us* for months."

He combed his fingers through his hair. "I'm not blind. Even in Kohala, I saw how he looked at you. And he's no cheater. I've known him for over a decade. Jamie is one of the most loyal people you'll find."

I fell back against the couch's cushions and covered my face. I felt terrible and *stupid* for running without hearing Jamie out.

"What am I supposed to do with this revelation, Lincoln?" I asked, uncovering my face.

He scoffed and stared at me as if I'd gone insane. "You can call Jamie and you two could talk..."

I felt like he wanted to add *duh!*

I threw my hands up. "Okay... so Jamie isn't really a cheating asshole. He's incredible, and I really love him."

"But?"

"His father doesn't approve of me. I'm not wealthy like he is. I live halfway across the world… The odds are stacked against us. We probably wouldn't have worked out in the long run. Maybe this whole fiasco with that Calloway woman was a sign."

Lincoln shook his head. "Charlotte Brooks backing down from a challenge… I never thought I'd see the day."

"I have to protect my heart," I returned.

If Jamie and I moved forward after this, it was only a matter of time before his father lashed out or some other hindrance arose. Maybe it was best if we left things as they were. Jamie and I were good together for a while… We were *perfect*. However, perhaps we should leave well enough alone.

34

JAMIE

I walked into Dad's home office, barely holding my fury in check. My father had done some fucked up shit over the years. Hell, he was the major cause of me carrying the heavy burden of guilt because he convinced me that I killed my mother. But *this*... this took the cake.

After Charlotte hung up on me yesterday and I recovered from my shock, I processed what she said about speaking with Gwendolyn Calloway. Since I'd never officially met the woman, I wondered how she even got it into her head to go to my place. Then it hit me...

Dad wasn't pleased that I was with Charlotte and not a woman he chose. He'd called me several more times after our first chat and expressed concern about the Winchester legacy being tarnished.

I'd say that I was pretty smart since I'd grown said legacy to new heights that Dad never could, yet I couldn't comprehend *how* my being with the woman I loved would tarnish it. If Charlotte and I had children, they'd still be Winchesters… so what the fuck?

I looked up Gwendolyn Calloway, who I hadn't even crossed paths with yet because she spent so much time in Europe. When I paid her a visit, she took one look at me and broke. I've been told plenty of times that I can look terrifying when I fully transform into "ruthless bastard mode…" I believe those were Alex's exact words.

Gwendolyn confessed to everything. Dad encouraged her to "get rid of" Charlotte who was a danger to our possible marriage. Gwendolyn was inclined to go along with Dad's scheme because her family's wealth had dwindled significantly, and it was imperative that she marry someone like me.

I'd listened with disdain as she prattled on, apologized, and then had the nerve to throw herself at me. I had then—not subtly—told her that if she even dared to cross my path again, her daddy's dwindling bank account would be the least of her worries. I didn't get off on scaring women—or anyone for that matter—but I was fucking livid.

Today was Dad's turn to receive the brunt of my anger. He looked up from whatever he was reading at his desk and plucked his glasses off his nose.

"James, I expected you."

"Mhmm."

He smiled slightly. "You're angry. You tend to speak very little when you are. We're alike in that way." He gestured to the chair in front of his desk.

I ignored the invitation and strolled over to the pictures of my mother adorning his wall. I stared at the smiling woman who had tightly curled strawberry-blonde hair and sparkling green eyes. She was beautiful, not just on the outside but on the inside too. I could tell by the warmth projected from her eyes when she smiled. Every day, I wished I'd gotten the chance to know her. My heart constricted, but I tore my gaze away from my mother's image and lasered in on Dad.

"I might look like you, Dad, but I'm nothing like you, so don't say we're alike in any way. I think I inherited everything else that counts from my mother because I'm not a wicked, conniving, son of a bitch."

Dad's nostrils flared. "You will address me with respect, son."

"And you will shut the fuck up and listen to me for once in your life!" I roared.

I inhaled and exhaled, getting a grip on my temper. I'd never spoken to him like this, but I was done with his bullshit and I needed him to know that.

Dad's jaw slackened and despite my rage, I felt a sliver of amusement. He'd been on his high horse for so long that he probably didn't know what it felt like to be defied. And maybe I played a part in making him feel so powerful, but I'd remedy that soon enough.

"I had an interesting chat with Gwendolyn. She told me what you did."

He at least had the decency to look a little guilty. "James, what I did was for the best—"

"I believe I told you to shut the fuck up, old man."

The way his eyes bulged and his face reddened... I hoped he didn't have a cardiac arrest. My intention wasn't to kill the old goat, just to put him in his place once and for all.

"This is my fault," I said. "You thinking that you can control my life is on me, and I'm taking accountability. Since I was a kid, I've done everything you demanded of me because I felt bad. You were a miserable bastard when Mom died, and I carried the guilt of thinking that I ruined your life. But it's time

I let all of that go. And you know what? I forgive you for being an awful parent who psychologically tortured me by blatantly blaming me for her death."

Dad went pale as he stared up at me as if I'd just driven home how fucked up he was and he realized it for the first time. However, I didn't care much what he was feeling, just as he never cared about my feelings.

"I've let you get away with a lot, even thinking that you still run this Winchester show." I waved my hand to encompass his office, which was in a sprawling mansion. "But let's be honest, I'm in charge now. You know it… everyone knows it. When you go out of your way to ruin the *one* great thing I had in my life… You just fucked yourself epically, Vincent."

He pulled in a puff of air and sat back. I'd never addressed him by his name. I'd always tried to respect my father even when he failed to give me the same courtesy because, as I said, I was nothing like him.

"James, what are you doing here?" he asked.

"I'm finally standing up and showing you who the real boss of this family is, old man. Your time in charge has long passed. I might have given in to your demands over the years, but I've always been in control where it counts. I control the purse strings, the connections, and every goddamn thing. So, if you don't want me to be a heartless bastard like you and cut you off from everything you value, you'd better follow *my* demands."

Dad's face went through a series of emotions from disbelief, to anger, and ultimately resignation. He was an ass, but he wasn't stupid. He knew the reality. There would be no EcoEnergy Solutions without me. I dedicated my entire life to the family business and made it flourish like neither he, nor Granddad, ever could. If I walked away, the legacy and the empire he held so dear would crumble.

"And what are your demands, son?" he asked softly. He gazed upon me with a shadow of apprehension in his eyes and something akin to respect.

"From now on, you stay out of my affairs—business and my personal life. If you have something you want to *suggest* business-wise, then you'll be humble and respectful about it and I might hear you out. It's time to accept that you're not in charge anymore." I planted my palms on his desk and practically snarled. "If you ever involve yourself in my relationships or dare to tell me who I can or can't be with, then there will be hell to pay."

I pointed a finger at him. "When I introduce you to Charlotte…" If I could get her back because she wouldn't even answer my calls. "You'll welcome her with open arms. Hell, you'll kiss her goddamn feet if I tell you to. Got it?"

For a moment, there was silence between us. We had a stare-down, something like a battle of wills.

Dad finally understood the gravity of my fury and how done with his shit I was. He exhaled long and hard before nodding. His gaze then shifted to a family picture of him and Mom.

She was heavily pregnant and grinning, and he had a palm placed possessively over her stomach… over me. There was softness and love in his eyes, things I'd never seen. Dad hadn't always been a cold prick. He loved his wife with his whole heart and that was his only redeeming quality. I couldn't help feeling bad for what he'd lost.

"James, I…" He swallowed and pain shadowed his face, which was an older, more weathered version of mine. "I was so caught up in grief that I didn't realize…" He sighed, shook his head, and met my gaze. His eyebrows were deeply furrowed.

I blinked, shocked by what I knew was his version of an apology. The emotions he exhibited made me feel as if Dad and I had a chance of fixing things between us... *maybe*. Without another word, I nodded in acceptance and walked out.

* * *

I stared at the elevator doors, anxiously waiting. Lincoln called and said he was ready to talk. Not just a series of grunts and one-syllable words over the phone... a real conversation. I wasn't sure if I should be relieved yet because he might very well be coming to tell me that he still hated me and wanted to end our friendship for good. That would be the icing on my crap cake, wouldn't it? Losing my girlfriend and one of my best friends...

When the doors opened and Lincoln and I made eye contact, I exhaled softly, bracing myself for whatever was to come. He stepped into the foyer. I watched him watch me. His expression was unreadable, and I kept mine neutral.

Lincoln looked me up and down and then shook his head. "Jesus. You poor, sad bastard. You look like you forgot to take off your Halloween makeup last night."

I let out a laugh that sounded a little like a sigh. Lincoln showed up with his humor front and center. We might be alright after all...

"Let's hit the bar, Winchester. You look like you could use a few strong ones." He brushed past me, dropped his travel bag, and made my place his like he always did when he visited.

I rocked back on my heels and took a relieved breath. We'd definitely be all right. Joining Lincoln at the bar, I watched him inspect the bottles of liquor. This bar I had in one corner of my massive living room had been a group consensus about five years ago.

"So I guess you know why I look like shit…" I said, taking a seat.

He selected a bottle, picked up two glasses, and nodded. As he poured, he said, "I do. Charlotte broke up with you."

I snorted. "There wasn't much breaking up. She just disappeared before I got home. Which one of the guys told you?" I guess we were saving the conversation about our relationship for later.

"None of them. Charlotte told me what happened."

He pushed a half-filled glass in my direction, and I stopped it. Every muscle in my body tensed as I looked up at him. He wore the tiniest smirk while he sipped his liquor and watched me over his glass.

"You spoke to her?"

"Yeah. I went to see her."

My fingers tightened around my glass, threatening to shatter it. My jaw was clenched so tightly that it hurt when I bit out, "You saw her, did you? What else did you talk about with her?" With *my* woman… who wouldn't even answer my calls.

"There it is." Lincoln chuckled. "The jealous monster. Man, you really have it bad for her, huh?"

"Lincoln…"

"Relax, Jamie. I went to check on her after you called, sounding frantic about not knowing where she was. I reached out to Pacific Paradise, and they said she was still on vacation. I knew there was one other place she was likely to be."

"And you couldn't have told me you were going to see her?" I glowered.

He shrugged. "We weren't on speaking terms."

"Because you were being immature."

"I admit that I was." He watched me through narrowed eyes. "I can tell what you're thinking. I didn't reach out to Charlotte to try to win her back. I was genuinely worried. At the end of the day, she's my friend."

My shoulders, which had hiked up to my ears, slowly relaxed.

"How is she?" I asked longingly… desperately.

I tossed my drink back and winced as it burned a path down my esophagus.

"About as miserable as you are."

I tucked my chin into my chest. "She thinks that I—"

"I know, and I set her straight."

I sat taller. "Then why the fuck hasn't she called me or answered any of my texts?"

He stroked his jaw and frowned. "I think that's something you two should talk about. I don't want to get in the middle…"

I slammed my glass onto the counter. "Goddamn it, Lincoln. You're already in the middle. Tell me so I can fix things with her."

"She's scared, Jamie. Okay? She told me about what your father said."

"He won't be a problem. I dealt with him."

Lincoln tilted his head, and he lifted his glass. "Hmmm. It's about time. Cheers."

"Lincoln," I growled.

He sighed. "She knows the truth but is still reluctant to jump back into things with you, man. She's felt insecure about your different lifestyles from the beginning. The entire mess with Gwendolyn is a sign that you two won't work."

My heart sank into my ass as I gawked at Lincoln.

"I told her that was a crock of shit, by the way." He shrugged. "But she wouldn't listen to me. She insists on protecting herself from further hurt."

I dropped my head onto the bar, my forehead making a thudding noise on the surface.

"Bashing your head in won't help, Jamie," Lincoln said. "You'll need your brain intact if you're going to get Charlotte back."

I snorted, fully aware of the irony of the situation. My lover's ex-boyfriend, who had been angry with me for pursuing her, was the one trying to help me win her back after our alleged breakup.

"Why do you care?"

"As I told Charlotte, I care about the both of you. I was a jackass for prolonging the tension between us. You didn't steal Charlotte from me. She chose *you*. Besides, she and I aren't compatible."

My eyes narrowed to slits. "So you just found clarity all on your own?"

His sheepish smile sent amusement coursing through me despite my misery about Charlotte.

"No. Michael told me to stop being a petty bitch and not throw away my friendship because of my wounded pride. Yes, the ass actually called me a *petty bitch*."

I chuckled and grabbed the glass Lincoln had refilled. "To Michael, the hardass who has never led us astray." I suppose he was wiser than the rest of us because he was the oldest of the group and he was an actual father.

He tipped his glass, and we drank.

"I'm sorry about how things happened," I said.

"Me too. Now onto more important matters..."

My eyebrows shot up.

"Charlotte is heading back to Kohala tomorrow. You and I are going to meet her there."

"*We* are?"

"Hey, you're going to need a wingman and I'm a damn good one."

I rolled my eyes. "Doesn't matter how good you are. She's pissed at me and won't even answer my calls. Popping up at her job might upset her more."

"We're not popping up at her *job*. We're going to Pacific Paradise as *guests*, and you'll just happen to show Charlotte that you're the man for her."

"Well, I *know* that I am, but how do you suggest I *show* her?"

Lincoln's sly smirk made my eyes narrow with suspicion. Whatever brilliant plan he was working up in that brain of his… his expression told me that I wouldn't like it. Still, I'd do anything to get Charlotte back.

35

JAMIE

"Fuck you, Lincoln! I'm not jumping out of a plane!" My outburst gained us the attention of the guests walking past.

Some watched us with curiosity and some with amusement. Lincoln and I stood near the building where we were told that Charlotte would be today.

We arrived at Pacific Paradise Resort yesterday, but she had no idea we were there. Immediately after we arrived, I was ready to find her and launch my we-shouldn't-break-up petition. However, Lincoln suggested surprising her by showing up at her work area today.

That way, she wouldn't be able to dodge me. He had a point. I knew Charlotte well. She'd find ways to evade me and run away from a conversation if she knew I was here. But surprising her on a plane and jumping out of it with her…? Lincoln had lost his mind.

"Do you want Charlotte back or not?" he asked.

"Of course, I do. But how is skydiving the way to get her back?"

"Alright, hear me out…"

My derisive snort echoed. "Hearing you out got me into this mess in the first place. *Skydiving*, Lincoln? *Me?*" I had to fight the urge not to vomit and pass out when he made me board yet another helicopter to get here.

"Facing your fear like this will impress the hell out of Charlotte."

Yes, I wanted to impress the woman who was amazing and crazy enough to jump out of planes, but… "I'm no good to her dead," I grumbled. "And that might be my fate if I go along with your insane plan. I might very well die of a heart attack midair."

"When did you get so dramatic?" Lincoln sighed and then clasped my shoulder. He looked me in the eye and said, "Jamie, Charlotte is adventurous, spontaneous, and a risk-taker. You need to show her that you can match her energy. Show her that you're the right man for her to risk her heart with."

Because she felt that being with me was a risk to her heart… right. If I conquered my fear and took this risk for *her*, she'd see that she could follow suit and take a risk for *me*. Was our logic crazy? Maybe. Would it work? Hell if I knew. Was I desperate enough to win Charlotte back? I sure as hell was.

Wiping away the beads of sweat that had formed on my forehead by merely thinking about free-falling through the air, I squared my shoulders. "Fine. I'm ready to show Charlotte that I'm the perfect man for her."

"Awesome. She's going to be stunned when she finds out we're her students."

"If I die, I'll haunt the hell out of you for the rest of your life, I swear," I murmured as we started walking again.

Lincoln chuckled, and I couldn't help smiling because I was relieved that we were back to our easy relationship.

"I didn't know Charlotte was a certified skydive instructor," I mused. She never mentioned it. She continued to fascinate me to this day.

"Yeah." Lincoln nodded. "She has been working on it since she and I..."

He glanced at me and didn't finish. We were still navigating the awkwardness of him having once dated Charlotte.

"She got into it years ago just to get the experience. It was on her father's bucket list, but he never got the chance to try it. She did it so she could tell her dad what it was like soaring through the sky. She said getting paid to jump out of planes was just a bonus. I guess she makes extra with the skill working here."

I nodded, fighting the sliver of jealousy that Lincoln knew so much about her past. *I* wanted to be the one to know everything about her. As we entered the building, my heart hammered for reasons beyond the impending skydive. I hadn't seen Charlotte in three weeks and had barely spoken to her.

The anticipation of our reunion had my stomach in knots. I waded through mixed emotions. I was happy to see her because I missed her. On the other hand, I was pissed at her. She walked out on me without a fair trial. It was disappointing because I thought the bond we'd forged would have ensured at least that.

I pulled in a deep breath as we approached. She had her head down as she stared at a clipboard she held. Her face was hidden by her blonde mane. Hearing our footsteps, she looked up with a smile. I knew her well enough... knew her genuine smiles to know that was a practiced one for guests.

"Hello, welcome..." Her eyes widened when she realized that it was us. "*Jamie? Lincoln? What...?*"

"Hey, Char," Lincoln drawled. "Surprise."

She glanced at him and then her gaze slid to me and she proceeded to gawk. I stared back, watching the range of emotions flicker across her face—shock, alarm, confusion… and was that pain that I glimpsed clouding her eyes for a moment?

She swallowed. "What are you guys doing here?"

I had yet to say a word, and I couldn't even muster a response. The barrage of emotions that hit me upon seeing her was overwhelming. Charlotte broke my heart when she walked away from me.

Lincoln gave me a pointed look as if telling me to get my shit together and say *something*. When I didn't, he jumped in and said, "We're your students for today."

"Yeah, I got that… I mean, what…?" She blinked. "Wait, the *both* of you?" Her eyes zeroed in on me. "You're joking, right?"

My eyebrows cinched into a scowl as I gathered my wits. "No, Charlotte. Since you won't answer my calls, I figured I'd come here and jump out of a fucking plane to get your attention."

Lincoln groaned softly.

I didn't mean to snap. I just gave in to the fury brought on by her refusal to talk to me even when she knew the truth.

Charlotte stared at me, her eyes sparking with irritation. And there she was… The feisty woman I knew and loved. God, she was gorgeous.

The tension became almost palpable the longer we glared at each other, and I wanted to pull her against me and kiss the hell out of her.

Lincoln scratched his head as his gaze flickered between Charlotte and me. He cleared his throat and muttered, "Well, this is getting uncomfortable."

Charlotte ended our staring contest. "Fine."

Jumping into professional mode, she launched into a speech about the skydiving process—the paperwork, the hour-long safety training, and gearing up...

The entire time, I was caught up between disappointment that she hadn't launched herself into my arms to tell me how much she missed me and nerve-wracking apprehension about going through with Lincoln's ludicrous plan.

Hours later, we walked to the small aircraft. We were donned in jumpsuits, harnesses, goggles, and altimeters. The closer we got, the harder it was for my legs to move. *Jesus.* Was I really going through with this?

I was bathed in cold sweat and trying not to hyperventilate and we hadn't even taken off yet. Charlotte watched me through narrowed eyes as she had been the entire time we took to prepare. It was like she was testing me, waiting to see if I'd cry timeout and hightail it back to the resort.

I refused to give her the satisfaction. Squaring my shoulders, I moved with purpose.

"This is awesome," Lincoln said excitedly. "It's been too long since I've done this. The others should be here to experience the exhilaration of free falling. How are you feeling, Jamie?"

Free falling. The words echoed in my mind like a frightening mantra, and I almost doubled over to lose my breakfast.

"I'm stoked," I choked out.

Charlotte let out an exaggerated sigh. "Alright, *enough.*"

We stopped to look at her.

"Lincoln, can you give Jamie and me a moment?"

"You got it." He gave me an approving smirk before sauntering to the plane. He was convinced that his plan was working. I wasn't so sure...

Alone with Charlotte, we held each other's gaze for a moment until she asked, "Jamie, what are you doing?"

"I thought it was obvious." I pointed to the plane. "I'm about to skydive."

"Don't be a smart ass." She rolled her eyes. "You're terrified. You're pale and sweaty… I'm afraid you might not survive long enough to even jump."

I scoffed and glared. "What? You think I can't keep up with you, Miss *Adventure*?"

She sighed heavily. "Alright, you've got my attention. That's what you wanted, right? You're here, so we'll talk… You don't have to go through with this."

"Are you saying that you'll give us another chance? I'm *assuming* that we're broken up since you left me high and dry without a word."

She planted her hands on her hips and looked skyward. "I don't think it's a good idea for us to go any further."

My jaw tightened. "And you get to make that decision for us? I don't even have a say? I fucking *love* you, Charlotte."

"I know. It's just…" She blew out a breath, her expression tortured.

"You're a coward," I said.

She scoffed.

"Well, I'm going to show you what a coward I'm *not*." Clutching my helmet under my arm, I walked off.

"Jamie, you don't have to do this."

I ignored her and marched on the plane.

"Well?" Lincoln asked as I stepped inside. "Are you two back together or what?"

"*Nope.*"

He frowned. "And you're still going ahead with this?"

"I am," I confirmed, my resolve hardening. If I could take a leap of faith, she'd see that she could take one too.

"I've never seen you this determined," Lincoln mused as he watched me with what looked like admiration. "Love is a hell of a thing, isn't it?"

I glanced at him, confused by the undertone of longing and *knowing* in his voice. Had he ever experienced the consuming intensity of love? If he had, he never told me.

Charlotte joined us and started chatting with the pilot. When we were airborne, Charlotte kept eyeing me with concern. I imagined I looked like I'd keel over at any moment.

"Alright, Jamie. Let's go over this one more time…"

I'd been attached to Charlotte for our tandem skydive because it was my first time. Lincoln was qualified to dive on his own since he'd done this the amount of time required to gain that independence. So, my best friend and my girlfriend—if she didn't turn me down again—were both nut jobs.

My stomach churned with nerves as we got ready to jump.

"The most important thing is to trust me and follow my lead," Charlotte instructed, her voice steady over the roar of the engine.

"I do trust you, Charlotte," I shouted. "And you can trust me too."

She huffed and shook her head. However, I saw the tiny smirk she tried to hide. She wasn't all that annoyed with me for still trying to win her back even when I was on the verge of passing out.

She ignored my comment and carried on with professionalism. "Once we jump, keep your arms crossed until I tap your shoulder, then you can extend them. Keep your legs bent back toward me."

I nodded, trying to commit her words to memory, but my mind was a blur of emotions. The plane reached the right altitude, and the door opened, revealing the vast sky and the earth far below.

"Holy shit," I breathed.

Don't pass out. Don't pass out. That certainly wouldn't impress Charlotte. I glanced at Lincoln, who gave me a thumbs-up, and I groaned.

The beating of my heart was loud in my ears as Charlotte and I moved toward the door. We were strapped together, her body pressed against mine. Charlotte looked at me, her eyes searching mine.

"Ready?" she shouted over the noise.

Fuck no. But I nodded anyway because there was no going back now.

"Breathe, Jamie," she said, making me realize that I was holding my breath.

We stepped out into the open air and tumbled into a free fall. Terror gripped me in its clutches, but I reminded myself that I was doing this to prove something to Charlotte and that was what helped me stay conscious. I had to show her that I was willing to face any challenge with her.

The things you do for love...

36

CHARLOTTE

"Jamie, are you okay?" I stood over him as worry pricked me in the chest.

We had a smooth landing but as soon as we touched the ground and I unstrapped us, he rolled onto his hands and knees and started to dry heave as he released a string of expletives.

"For the love of God, Charlotte. You actually enjoy shit like this?" He looked up at me with an expression of disbelief. "You're crazy!"

I grinned because he was talking and *reprimanding* me, so he'd be fine.

Lincoln walked over to us, wearing a grin. "That was incredible. You okay, man?"

"Fuck you, Lincoln," Jamie hissed.

Lincoln chuckled and clapped him affectionately on the shoulder so I gathered they spoke to each other like that all the time. "You see how he conquered his fear for you, Charlotte?" Lincoln said.

I snorted my derision. *Men.* "I know you talked him into this, Lincoln. How could you when you know he's terrified of heights, *particularly* free-falling through the air?" I gave him the dirtiest look I could muster.

"Ah, you're ready to rip my head off for your man." Lincoln smirked. "So you love him too, and my plan worked. Great." He helped Jamie to his feet and held us both by the shoulders. "Now, you crazy kids are going to kiss and make up while I head back to the resort." We got pats on the shoulders before he took off.

I watched him walk away slack-jawed. Did my ex-boyfriend just *demand* that I get back together with his best friend? I guess things were alright between them…

I turned my attention to Jamie, who was still a little pale.

He wiped away beads of sweat from his forehead. "Well, Charlotte, *am* I your man?"

"You jumped out of a plane to prove *what?*" I growled because I was still so worried about him. He really didn't look good.

"To show you that I'm your guy. To make you see how committed I am to you." He raked his fingers through his hair. "I faced my fear for you. Surely, you can face yours for me. I know you're apprehensive about the differences between our lives but I jumped out of a plane with you… I'll face any challenge that arises against us even if I'm terrified. You can trust me with your heart."

The mentioned organ turned to a puddle in my chest as I gazed at him. "It's not just my fear, Jamie," I confessed. "I don't want to make your life difficult. I don't want you to constantly have to fight people in your circle because of me… because I'm not suitable for you. I don't want you to end up resenting me."

"Charlotte, that's impossible. You're perfect for me. I feel *alive* when I'm with you. I don't care what anyone else thinks. Skydiving is one of the scariest things I've ever done, but losing you is much scarier. I need you in my life."

My resolve deflated with a sigh. "I know, Jamie. I heard you."

"What?"

My smile wobbled as I covered the distance between us. "When we were in the air, I heard you shout that if you died, you'd die happy because you got to experience a little bit of life with me."

"Oh… Yeah…" He rubbed his nape and gave me a sheepish look. "I swore I was going to kick the bucket up there."

Chuckling, I cupped his face. "Jamie, you are most certainly my guy."

Relief lit his eyes, and I practically felt the tension seep out of him. I tipped on my toes and angled my face toward his. He swooped down, wrapped his arms around me, and kissed me as if we'd been separated for years rather than a few weeks.

*   *   *

"Jamie…"

He lifted a hand to tuck my hair behind my ear. We lay in the massive bed in his suite, facing each other after yet another round of love-making. We'd been going at it like crazy for three days now… We had a lot of lost time to make up for.

"Hmm?"

"I'm so going to get fired," I joked.

Seriously… I'd been neglecting work to hang out with Jamie after he decided to stay in Kohala for a few more days. Lincoln had suggested that he stay in paradise for a while and spend quality time with me.

The finger he stroked my cheek with stopped. "You'll be

fine. I'll threaten your boss again. Hell, when I'm done, you'll be running this resort."

"*Jamie.* You will do no such thing."

He smirked, but I was under the impression that he was serious... the devil.

"I don't mind losing this job," I said, sitting up to gaze out of the open balcony door. The morning breeze that floated in brushed my skin and ruffled my hair. "Because I've been thinking about making a change."

Jamie sat up too and watched me expectantly.

"I want to move to New York... for my next adventure." I smiled at him. "I can't bear to be apart from you. I don't want to do the whole long-distance thing anymore. It's time for me to stop flitting about every few months and set down some roots."

Jamie grunted. "And here I was thinking about quitting my job and abandoning my home to *flit around* with you every few months."

I laughed. "As if your inner control freak would allow you to do that."

"What makes you think I wouldn't do anything for you?"

My breath hitched when he captured my gaze. He was serious. *Be still my heart.* "Well, you don't have to turn into a roaming hippie to be with me, Jamie. I'm serious about moving to New York. It's time I explored a steady life and relationship... with you."

His eyes darkened in the way they did when he was satisfied and he tugged me onto his lap. "Tell you what. We'll spend half of the time living a steady life in Manhattan... or wherever, and half of the time being *roaming hippies.*"

I sniggered at that. "Really?"

"Yes. I want you to be happy, Charlotte, and you live for new adventures. Plus, I want to see the world with you. I want to do things like mountain climbing and exploring jungles together. I need you to show me how to have some fun."

I grinned broadly, loving the sound of the life he wanted for us. It was hard to tell what the future held, but I wanted to live in the now and enjoy it with him. "Half and half. I love it."

"There's one condition," he said.

"Oh?"

"No more skydiving... for me, anyway."

I chuckled. "Deal."

In a swift motion that caught me off guard, he rolled us onto the bed and pinned me beneath him. "Let's kiss on it."

* * *

I walked through Jamie's penthouse as I said goodbye to my mother. She was checking up on me after my move to Manhattan. Jamie and I were officially living together. Charlotte Brooks, shacking up long-term with a guy... *Holy cow.* It was scary and thrilling at the same time.

We were so in love and committed to each other that it didn't feel like we were moving too fast. I found Jamie in his room, leaning against the window and gazing into the night as he spoke on the phone. I didn't say a word to interrupt. I just walked over to him and wound my arms around his waist.

Without hesitation, he wrapped an arm around me and held me close. I smiled and pressed my cheek to his chest to look out at the stars. It was just nice to be close to him, to touch him.

"Alex, why are you asking about that company? You know *she* owns it."

I frowned, wondering who *she* was.

"For Christ's sake, Alex. What are you up to?"

A smile lifted my lips. Alex was always up to something. I

listened to Jamie's side of the conversation until he said, "Yeah, I'll email you the info in a few days. Just… *behave*."

He sighed and shook his head, and I knew that Alex responded with something crazy.

When he hung up, I asked, "Is Alex okay?" I hoped he was. I liked him. I liked all of Jamie's friends.

"He's fine. I'm just suspicious about what shenanigans he's up to this time. But never mind that…" He threw his phone onto a chair and lifted me into his arms. "Right now, I need to focus on much more important matters."

Wrapping my legs around his waist, I grinned. "What's that?"

"Making love to my woman."

I smiled as he laid me down and kissed me passionately. As usual, we got completely lost in each other.

ALSO BY ALINA PARKER

Checkout other books from Alina Parker at www.alinaparker.com . All these books are independent reads.

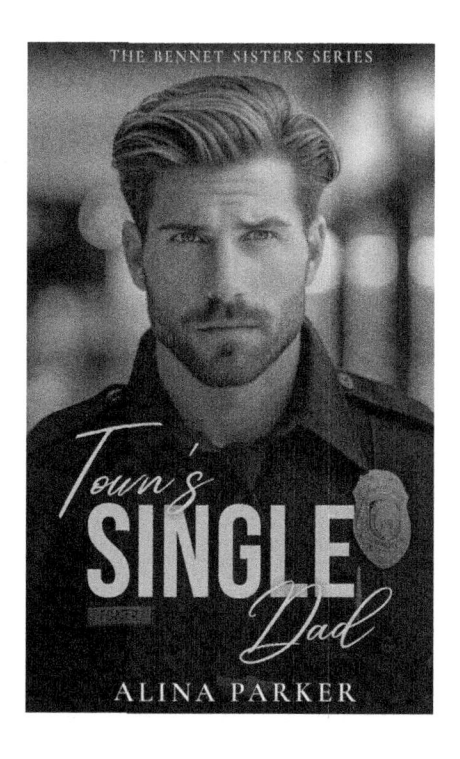

Town's Single Dad: A Friends to Lovers Small Town Romance (The Bennet Sisters)

Best friends should never sleep together, *right?*

It's a recipe for disaster.

But when your best friend is a wickedly charming bad boy who's always been your protector and is hot as mine is, it's hard to resist.

Crossing the line of friendship tore us apart.

He wanted more and I couldn't give it to him. So, Nic Wilder left me behind in our small town, and I thought I lost my best friend for good.

Fourteen years later, he's back.

He isn't the same man that left. He's now the police chief, a single dad, and the most eligible bachelor in town.

One thing hasn't changed— the sexual chemistry simmering between us.

We shouldn't cross the line again. I want my best friend back and we need to remain just friends.

It doesn't matter if I've wondered what would have been if I'd given in to him years ago. It doesn't matter that I secretly want to explore the explosive chemistry between us.

We're just friends… until I give in and we become more.

We shouldn't do this. Not again. Everything might be ruined— for good this time.

I've seen firsthand the havoc that friends turned lovers can wreak. Prime example— my parents.

But there's no resisting the sparks between us.

Nic slowly demolishes every emotional wall I've built.

I'm falling for him and I'm terrified. He has the power to break me.

He says I can trust him with my heart.

Should I?

Am I ever going to leave my fears behind and have a chance at my Happily-Ever-After? Or am I about to destroy myself and the only true friend I have?

Town's Single Dad is filled with emotional drama, breath-taking love scenes, a smoking hot single dad, and a town of nosy folks. If you like second chance friends to lovers romance, you are in for a treat! Read this stand-alone novel from Alina Parker and get ready for a satisfying HEA.

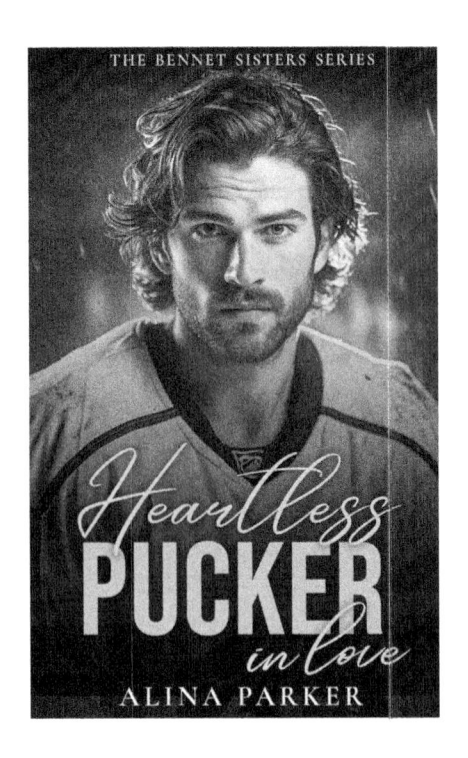

Heartless pucker in Love: An Enemies to Lovers Sports Romance (The Bennet Sisters)

An NHL star(aka my arch-enemy) gives me an offer,
Travel the world as his nurse until he recovers
Get enough money to support my town's free nursing home
And try not to kill him on his private jet.

Julian met with a motorcycle accident, and I'm his nurse.
Taking care of him is going to be hard,
He broke my heart in high school & I wrote him out of my life.

Now he's a big-shot hockey star and a womanizer.

With his charming ways and a body sculpted by the gods, I can see why so many women find him irresistible.

But not me. I'd rather die than stay near him.

And that is precisely why he offered me a job as his private nurse.

I run a community nursing home in my small town which will shut down if I don't get enough money to run it.

My plan is to take his high-paying job, travel the world with him until he gets better.

And save my nursing home while staying (almost) sane.

My simple plan is blown to pieces by my traitorous body. I end up in Julian's bed and… Oh, my sex god! It isn't just the amazing sex. He's slowly stealing my heart.

I have to keep my feelings in check, even though he makes me feel safe.

I'm a small-town girl, and he's a rich, famous star. I'll never hold on to him.

He broke my heart before.

He says I can trust him this time, but should I?

If it happens again, I won't be able to pick up the pieces.

If you love enemies to lovers romance with a dash of sports, this is the perfect book for you. You'll love Julian and April's chemistry! Read as part of this series or as a stand-alone book.

Note: Formerly published as "My Pucking Enemy"

Unsure in Love: A Billionaire Accidental Pregnancy Romance (The Bennet Sisters)

Love is BS. The only side of love I've seen is selfish and toxic.

Until I met Damian. a self-made billionaire with silent charm.

I wasn't supposed to fall in love with him, and I sure as hell wasn't supposed to end up pregnant with his baby.

It all started with a passionate night. To be fair, I made the first move.
I never knew, he was a *billionaire* who will leave me with a baby.
I am a (mostly) happy small-town girl, I am not after his billions.

In fact, I hate men…

My father abandoned me and my family when I was a kid.

I can't imagine having the same fate for my child, I wanted to find my father and get to him for what he did…

I hired a top-notch private investigator agency to find him, But guess what, who is the owner of this multi-billion-dollar company?

Yes, its *Damian*…

He takes on the mission to break through my emotional walls with the finesse and resilience of the ex-military man that he is.

He has made me feel loved, protected, and desired—things I never thought I could feel.

I'm falling and falling hard, but I'm terrified.
Can I allow myself to fully trust him?
Do I even deserve a chance at happily ever after?

For once in my life, I feel the kind of love that songs are written about—the kind that keeps you up all night with giddiness. But can it survive the secret I'm carrying? Or is my past about to rear its ugly head and destroy everything?

"Unsure in Love" is a standalone and can be read independently or in series. There is no cheating or cliffhangers. And of course, a guaranteed Happily Ever After.

Grumpy Boss in Love: An Enemies to Lovers Billionaire Office Romance (The Bennet Sisters)

Walking down the wedding aisle,

I never imagined I'd say "I do" to the man I despise the most—Elliot Sinclair.

He was my former professor and my current boss from hell.

My plan was simple:

Complete my marketing course, save up and start my business.

That was until Elliot came into my life, on a mission to torment me!

First, he made college a living nightmare,

then he became my boss(-hole) at the internship of my dreams.

But desperation has a way of pushing us to do the unthinkable.
So here I am, entering a contract marriage with him.

He needs to get married to secure a property,
and I need his big-shot name for my future marketing agency.
Two weeks is all we're in for—just a quick hitch and unhitch.

But when we exchanged our "fake" vows,
We never prepared for the wedding kiss or the steamy nights that followed.
It felt so right that I started falling for the grumpster,
and the way he looks at me hints that he feels the same.

But just when things get real, he calls me into his office with a bombshell:

"We need a new contract. The last one didn't cover sleeping together."

"Grumpy Boss in Love" is a heartwarming and passionate tale of Ruby & Elliot who discover that sometimes, the most unexpected partnerships lead to the most profound love stories.

Join Ruby and Elliot on a roller-coaster of love and hate that will make you laugh, cry, and ultimately fall in love with them.

Note: You can read this book as a standalone or as part of the series. No cheating and of course a guaranteed Happily Ever After.

Snowed Inn Love: A Forced Proximity Billionaire Romance (The Bennet Sisters)

In a howling blizzard, a stranger walked into my inn

My inn was closed, but I allowed him inside...

It's embarrassing enough that I have been on a dry spell for over a decade.

If the universe has sent a gorgeous-as-sin man my way.

I'm going to take my chances.

I'm super awkward around strangers.

Especially when he is a hunk built like a Viking god.

I mean, I giggle in bed; I get nervous when I need to make small talk.

Holy fudge. I can't even curse like normal people.

But he rolled with it, he made me feel more comfortable than any man before him.

He was my angel that gave me multiple nights in Heaven.

But when the snow cleared, so did his lies.

He is no angel; he is a ruthless billionaire who wants to take over my inn.

And he is going to stop at nothing to get what he wants.

Snowed Inn Love is a standalone book that can be read independently or in series. It contains no cheating and ends on a satisfying HEA.

His Fake Wife: An Enemies to Lovers Billionaire Romance (Thorne Legacy Book 1)

How NOT to screw yourself

1. NEVER go for a fake marriage with your childhood enemy

2. DON'T sleep with him.. EVER

3. Absolutely do NOT get pregnant with his baby!

When my father died, he sold his company and just about everything else to his best friend.

I would have been cool with that if he hadn't made another deal—

Marry his best friend's son, Adam Thorne.

Forget marriage, I can't even stand that man for five minutes. Only reason I agreed is because of a deal he proposed:

Help him change his image as a rake and I get back everything my father sold. I can work with that.

Make him look good (and avoid killing him) and in two years, I'm free.

Begin the countdown to my freedom!

Only, a few months in, Adam starts getting under my skin in a more...sexual sense. I'm getting to see firsthand why women's panties—including mine—just drop for him. Our simple arrangement is about to become way too complicated when I tell him about the baby!

I wonder, Do I really want to be free?

THIS IS A STANDALONE ENEMIES TO LOVERS ROMANCE WITH NO CLIF HANGERS, NO CHEATING AND OF COURSE A HEA!

Formerly published as "Fake it for Billionaire Enemy"

His Best Friend's Sister: A Billionaire Forbidden Romance (Thorne Legacy Book 2)

If my over-protective brother asks, don't tell him I slept with his billionaire best friend and don't even mention that I might have gotten pregnant while doing it...

My brother thinks that Nate is exactly the kind of guy that I should stay away from, even though he is his best friend. Nate is a total womanizer, he goes through women like underwear.

I had a silly little girlhood crush on him that died long ago. 10 years later, he's back in town for a company he bought. My brother convinces me to take an internship at Nate's new company to complete my course.

He's an uptight control freak who lives in suits and ties.

I'm a wild child— totally not his type.

And I am not looking for romance.

Like Nate, I am so over relationships.

I took on a foolish mission to get him to "loosen up". I wanted him to enjoy life.

I tried to keep my distance, but his toe-curling O's… are irresistible.

I know! Sleeping with him is completely wrong but it felt so right…

If my brother finds out, he is going to kill us both!

Will we be able to hide our secret affair now that we were expecting the unexpected?

If you love a captivating forbidden billionaire romance full of passion, promise, and a touch of the feels, then this story has just the right amount of scorching heat, emotion, and drama. With no cliffhangers and of course a happily ever after! Read as part of this series or as a stand-alone book.

His Best Friend's Ex: A Forbidden Second Chance Romance (Thorne Legacy Book 3)

She is the *one* girl I can't have...

I had it easy around ladies, I mean around the ones I didn't really want to be with.

But the moment I met Mel, I knew we were meant to be together. She is all you could ask for, a beautiful, strong and independent woman taking over the business world.

There is only one problem... She is my best friend's girlfriend.

I know my best friend is a d*ck, a manipulative serial cheater who only thinks about himself.

But my dumb a$$ thought that he has changed for Mel and I left the two alone.

As destiny would have it, I meet Mel again after 5 years. She finally saw his true colors and called it off.

Years of frustration and sexual tension gets the best out of me we end up having most earth shattering s*x ever. Who could have thought, you could have tears in your eyes when you actually have the only thing you ever wanted.

Now her ex wants her back...

He wants to pull up his old sneaky tricks

I won't let him have her,

Not this time...

IF YOU LIKE FORBIDDEN ROMANCE WITH INDEPENDENT WOMEN AND CLASSY MEN WHO WOULD GO TO ANY LENGTH TO PROVE THEIR DEVOTION THEN READ THIS HOT ROMANCE FROM ALINA PARKER!

This book can be read independently or in series.

Or maybe binge read the entire boxset of the entire series!

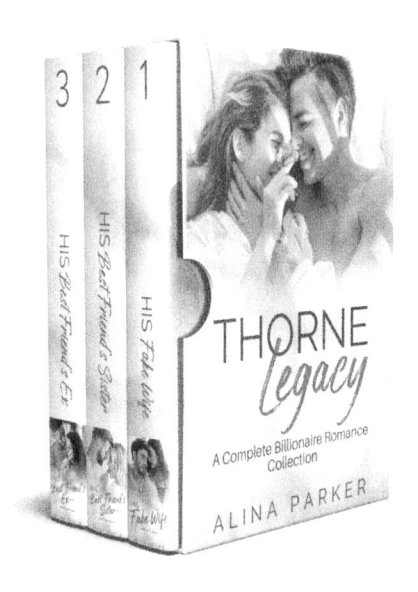

Thorne Legacy: A Complete Billionaire Romance Collection

Meet the Thornes, rich and drop-dead delicious!

If your want to read stories full of billionaires and the strong women they love then sit back and be prepared to go through a roller-coaster of emotions with the Thornes as they find and fight for their special someone.

Book 1

His Fake Wife: An Enemies to Lovers Billionaire Romance

Book 2

His Best Friend's Sister: A Billionaire Forbidden Romance

Book 3

His Best Friend's Ex: A Forbidden Second Chance Romance

All the books are independent reads with guaranteed Happily-Ever-After and a strict no-cheating policy.

Printed in Great Britain
by Amazon